PAUL FORSTER

The Last Bite

Deadweight Part II

First edition

Cover art by ebooklaunch

This book was professionally typeset on Reedsy.
Find out more at reedsy.com

Contents

Chapter 1

The Land Rover was barely over the horizon, and the major went straight back to work. "Resume your duties, men. When Kenny comes back, I don't want to have to bollock him for your falling standards!" The major tried to convey a calm and confidence that his men would believe everything was alright, but the hungry gnashing teeth at the fences betrayed his lies. The soldiers hurriedly got back to their patrols within the safety of the second gate, and the major retired to the main building and made his way to the lab.

The door was locked, as had become standard practice when the soldiers weren't able to keep a watchful eye. Those trapped inside hated the idea, they saw the danger outside not in. They were too scared to take any risks with the captive creature. Their fear was a major catastrophe outside of the lab, seeing all the soldiers fall and themselves trapped forever in their coffin of a workplace. The major unbolted it and entered.

"Dr Srnicek, may I have a word?"

"Why major, you can have as many as you like if you can see yourself to not locking that door every time one of your brave and bold boys leaves us alone."

The major offered a pained smile and invited Dr Srnicek to follow him out of the room. She followed and the major took a little pleasure in loudly locking her people in the lab behind them.

They made their way to the director's office the level above. The office was plush, borderline luxurious. Walls adorned with pictures of a well-dressed, older man with many a famous politician and personality. The director of the site hadn't gone down with his ship. With his powerful political connections, there was a good chance they had tipped him off about the building disaster with enough time to get to somewhere safe, if such a place existed. Dr Srnicek and the major were in charge now. With comms to the outside world no longer functioning, they had both agreed to downplay this information from their people. Hope was a precious commodity, one not to be pissed away in the name of being open and honest.

The major made himself comfortable in the expensive leather executive chair and said, "Kenny has gone, I'm not sure we'll see him again."

"Shame, he was a good one. Hard, but good. Where does this leave us?" Srnicek asked as she looked out of the window, observing the many feeders surrounding the fences.

"I'm half tempted to walk out that gate myself and join the hungry bastards. See how the other half live."

"Half? We should be so lucky, I'm pretty certain there are more of them than that. We've made progress in our lab, but we need months, not weeks."

"Weeks?" the major said and smiled. "We should be so lucky! We have days."

"Is there any chance some of those lovely choppers with the big propellers will come and rescue us?" she questioned. Her people wouldn't be any use dead, whether that was through the creature's hungry mouths or their own empty stomachs.

"We should be a priority, but who knows what's left. We can still get a few broadcasts on that old thing, but it's automated, although it has changed," the major offered. He signalled at the radio in the room's corner. "We will hang on, hope a Chinook will appear with either supplies and reinforcements or to get us out of here. If we have any more insurrections, though I'm of the mind to let them go. Kenny's mission should buy us a day or two before anyone suggests leaving again. After that, we need to protect the lab and its data."

"People are secondary?" the doctor asked. She had always believed, even before the world went to ruins, that people were valuable and a great asset.

"I don't think your computers will put a knife in my ear whilst I sleep to get out of here."

Dr Srnicek looked out of the window, seeing the hundreds of the dead at the fence line. If the world was all like this, then a cure was already too late. "Major, I wish I had answers, we will continue working until it's over. What else are we to do?"

The major stood up and joined Dr Srnicek by the window.

"Doctor, we have plenty of power, water is still running. If we just had half a dozen more men, a few thousand rounds of ammunition, and two month's supply of rations, we would be fine."

"No time left for ifs major. I'll return to the lab, please, can you think about not locking us inside? If we are truly damned, at least try to give our last few days on this Earth some dignity. None of us want to die in that fucking place."

It was the first time the major had heard her swear, not so much shocking as a relief. There was a certain calmness in damnation.

Chapter 2

The major sat on his own outside the main building. He had just accompanied a civilian on sentry duty for the last two hours, eager to give one of his tired men a rest.

Chris Stevens, a squaddie with a few years' experience in the army, gingerly approached, hobbling on his tired feet. "Sir, I want to help Kenny."

It had been three days since Kenneth had left. The men were expecting him back, if anyone could survive out there, it was him. "Stevens, he'll be back soon. Knowing that big bastard he's probably running ops with the SAS team. When they get back, there will be more interesting work coming our way, more worthy of your talents than keeping the eggheads safe."

Chris didn't seem satisfied with the answer but nodded in approval anyway before heading back to the barracks. Like his fellow soldiers, he'd spent more time walking the grounds of Wellworth and pushing metal rods into the feeders' skulls than he'd care to think about. But it hadn't stopped him from striking up a friendship with Tara, the tiny IT girl. They were roughly the same age, and both knew life would be short and painful. Tara was much more at ease with herself than Chris. She was confident and outgoing, whereas Chris was one of the quieter soldiers. On their second sentry patrol together flirting took over from their duties and ended with a quick fuck behind the barracks. It gave them both comfort and took their minds off the world, even as the dead watched their romp from a few feet away behind the relative safety of the fence. They had tried to stay discreet but had enjoyed each other several times since the first encounter.

He entered the barracks and was greeted by Gary sitting on the sofa where he'd been flicking through a well-thumbed adult magazine. Immediately, he placed the magazine down and stood up to greet Chris. "Hello lover boy, fancy a knee-trembler by the fence?"

Chris felt instant embarrassment and anger, Gary had mainly pulled sharpshooter duties in the observation post. He must have seen them either at it or shortly afterwards. "What the fuck are you talking about, Gary? Have you been having fantasies up there in the O.P with your boyfriend? Tell him I'm not interested in a threesome."

Gary moved closer to Chris and said, "Mate, you've got to get me a crack at that girl."

"Fuck off Gary, I don't know what you're talking about," Chris defended. The denial was weak.

"I know what you two have been up to, I want my turn," Gary spat. There was a menace in Gary's voice. It was less asking for permission to woo Tara, more a demand to let him know he was next.

"Leave her alone, I mean it," he seethed. Chris showed an uncharacteristically aggressive side, it surprised even Gary.

The soldiers squared up, going nose to nose before Gary pushed forward with a shit-eating grin before he broke off. "Chris, you need to learn to share. That's all I'm saying."

The men glared at each other as Chris backed his way to his bunk, and Gary resumed with his magazine.

Chapter 3

The scientists, when locked in the lab, found themselves at the very least, the freedom to speak freely, if not to leave. Their precautions with the beast had become more relaxed, it was always restrained and never looked close to escaping its bindings to lash out. Where most had worn PPE, they now ignored the gloves and masks. They left the creature out in the open whilst they went about their work, they just gave it a wide berth when passing close by.

Dr Srnicek had gathered the group for the day's briefing. "Good morning everyone, I hope we all managed as pleasant a sleep as possible. I know that many of you feel our work is of little value, I understand your concerns, but I disagree. Our communications have become patchy, but the data we're collecting is still valid."

"Jana, we seem to be going round in circles now. The test subject and samples we have really aren't telling us anything new," Robert spoke. Robert was one of Dr Srnicek's most experienced team members. His dissent wouldn't be unnoticed by their junior colleagues.

"Robert, we have a live subject. Well, as live as they get, it still has much to tell us. We continue, we document and when possible, we update our colleagues at other sites and they will update us. The major and I are in agreement that we should proceed as we have been until we cannot. His men are continuing their duties, even with some of our civilian colleagues assisting, and as you know, we're expecting the return of Kenneth, our own little ray of light."

A few of the younger colleagues smirked at the giant's mention.

"A new specimen would help. That one is old, it's not changing. We know how different that was from the early samples they sent us. Maybe if the soldiers can get us a new one from the gates, it could help," Robert suggested. The idea offered by Robert wasn't universally popular. The prospect of two of these things inside the fence wasn't warmly greeted.

"Agreed, I'll see what I can arrange. Thank you, everyone," said Dr Srnicek. The scientists got back to their tasks, their enthusiasm waned. Dr Srnicek looked on, unsure how much longer they could keep up the charade.

Chapter 4

The major hadn't been any keener on having another feeder inside the fence than anyone else. He saw it as an opportunity to display to his men, the ongoing importance of Wellworth's work and their job in keeping it safe. The men had groaned when he told them, and temporarily at least, he had to perform the role of tough major. He made sure they knew that they didn't have to agree. It was an order, and not up for debate.

The practicalities of how to get another live specimen would be more difficult this time. Hundreds were outside the fence compared to the dozens previously, and firearms were now a last resort, rather than the first choice. The major volunteered himself, and this act inspired one of his men to step forward. Chris hadn't been keen to step forward, but with Tara watching on with the other civilian sentries, he wanted to show her he wasn't afraid. She had been losing interest, and she was the only thing keeping him going. The other soldiers would happily remain within the fence, killing and distracting the hungry horde, or providing cover in case things didn't go to plan.

The major and Chris didn't want to waste any time, both wanted it over as soon as possible. The major set the civilian sentries to the fences far from either side of the gate, they were to make a noise from the safety of the inner fence. They would station a handful of soldiers to the outer ring of the fence, they would attract the feeders and thin out a few of their numbers. When the gates were clear, the major and Chris would spring out to grab the nearest one, secure it and drag it back through the gate. It was simple but laden with danger. A few rifles on the ground and Gary in the observation post with his L129A1 sharpshooter rifle would be their best protection if the situation turned bad.

The civilians and the soldiers got to work and the masses of gnashing teeth on the outside of the fence played their part as they started to move towards the teased meals. Chris placed his rifle on the ground, he wouldn't be using it and placed his trust in his fellow soldiers. The major unbuckled his holster, easing access to his pistol should he need to defend himself and his man. They sarcastically stretched and smiled at each other. Their nerves were getting the better of them, better to laugh than to show the fear that filled them. Chris picked up a piece of wood that he took a practice swing with, weighty enough to be useful, but easily discardable.

Most of the creatures had moved, only a few straggles hung back, not taking the obvious bait. The majority of the threat was slowly shuffling away from the gate, eager to find out what tasty treat was on offer further down the fence line.

"I'll bag its head, you crack it on the back of the knees and we'll drag it through the gate across the ground. Be careful, it'll thrash around, no scratches, no bites, we do this clean," the major ordered; he was ready. Chris nodded, and they signalled to a soldier who had been hanging back but now approached the gate, ready to open it but not wanting to attract the attention of the monsters on the other side.

The soldier quietly unbolted the gate and looked on for reassurance. The major gave the nod, and they all sprang into action. The gate was thrown open, and the major ran through first, bag in hand, and sprinted towards the closest beast, its back turned as it hobbled after its own kind to investigate the potential feed. Chris followed closely behind, ready to strike.

They caught their victim unaware. The bag was slammed down on its head, but the major and its legs swept out from underneath it by Chris and the piece of wood. Within seconds they were dragging it towards the gate, only fifteen feet, but it seemed like a mile. Neither man keen on getting touched by it, their attempts to drag it were clumsy. Dragging it under its arms, they stumbled as they closed the distance to the gate. They recovered as the first of the creatures turned to see a meal was closer than they originally thought. The men recovered, but their progress was slow, slower than the creatures. The first was within two feet when its head popped open and it slumped to the floor.

Gary looked through the rifle's scope at his handiwork before picking out his next target.

The next creature dropped to the floor as Chris and the major got to the gate, a third feeder was on them, Gary fired but missed with his first and second shot. The major let go of their captive and drew his Glock, firing at it, striking it in the throat then square in the nose. Chris had dragged their monster through the gate on his own as the major withdrew, firing twice more into the approaching mob. Chris let his attention wander from the danger he was holding to that bearing down on the major and he tripped, dragging the creature on top of him. It thrashed widely, anger, fear, or just hunger driving it to free itself. It whipped off the bag from its head and turned to Chris. His odour was intoxicating, it became more ferocious, desperate to taste his flesh. He was trapped underneath, helpless to fend it off, its broken teeth and stinking breath terrifyingly close to his face. With all of his might, he pushed it up.

Gary had the creature in his sights but had struggled for a clear shot until Chris lifted it above him. Gary took the shot. The round struck the base of the feeder's skull; the round smashed through bone and flesh, making it limp instantly. Chris pushed the creature off of him and crawled free. He looked to the observation post with a smile before giving Gary a thumbs up.

The major helped shut the gate and reset the lock as the soldiers lining the fence and the civilians in the second ring withdrew.

"For fuck's sake," the major exclaimed. The major stood over the creature and gave it a light kick. It didn't move, but it let out a low, quiet groan.

"Sorry sir, it got the better of me," Chris apologised. It had covered Chris in its blood, and he was still visibly shaking.

"It's alright private, the important thing is you're okay, and it's still alive. Mostly," the major said and looked at the creature. The hate in its eyes.

The creature was disabled, but definitely fulfilling its own definition of alive. The major hoped it would satisfy the scientists, but truth be told, he really didn't give a fuck. Neither he nor any of his men would repeat the feat again.

"Get yourself cleaned up, you've earned an extra break," the major told Chris as he helped him to his feet.

"Thank you, sir," He replied. Chris hobbled off, he wanted to be sick but needed to get to somewhere private first. He couldn't let Tara or any of his colleagues see how upset he was.

Inside the barracks, he stripped off, he threw the blood-soaked uniform in a heap on the floor, he'd offer it to the scientists to play with or burn it after he had cleaned up. He stopped himself from being sick; he had calmed as the adrenaline had left his bloodstream. He walked into the shower block and looked at himself in the mirror; he looked a state, he could only imagine how he'd looked before he'd stopped shaking. He noticed something on his shoulder, small but protruding. He gently touched it and flinched with pain. Carefully, he squeezed it between his fingers until it popped free, a little of his blood followed.

A small piece of bone, it could only have been a few millimetres long. He examined it in the light; it had a slight grey hue.

*

The scientists and soldiers all had their own areas, the remaining civilians had to make do with the space they were given. Two small converted offices served as sleeping quarters, the canteen was small, and as well as serving up the meagre meals, it served as a social space. The cleaners, canteen workers and office workers were bored. At first, they had dreaded their sentry duties with the soldiers, but after they realised it was relatively safe, they craved the excuse to get outside. The creatures on the other side of the fence were initially terrifying, but soon became just part of the background, their grotesque appearance and constant groans little more than an annoyance. Tara volunteered for all the extra duties she could. Fit and attractive, the squaddies all enjoyed her company. As the situation became bleaker, she began enjoying theirs too.

Chris had been her favourite, she had shagged him first, but he wasn't the last. Watching him drag that creature through the gate, wrestle with it on the ground, it was so brave, so exciting, and it only made her want him more. When he emerged from the barracks, she was waiting.

"Hey, want to hang out?" she asked. Tara had been waiting for nearly an hour for Chris to emerge. He still looked a little shaken, but managed a smile when he saw her.

"That's all I want," he replied. She led him by the hand behind the barracks. The feeders watched them, helpless to get to them to take a bite.

"That was incredible what you did," she complimented. Tara

unbuckled Chris' belt and dropped his trousers to the floor.

"It was nothing," he lied, he still felt uneasy, but this was why he did it, to impress Tara. Tara smiled and pulled his face to her level to kiss.

"You deserve a reward," she replied. Tara teased down her own oversized recently issued trousers, as Chris stood back to admire her pert body. She turned around and backed into him, grinding against his penis.

Chris reached into her t-shirt and moved to her breasts, as she became more vigorous, his erection grew until she guided him inside her. He rested against the side of the barracks as he allowed her to do all the work, not that she minded. Chris moved his hands down to her hips as he tried to slow her down.

"Not so fast."

"Don't worry, just cum, we can go again later," she said. If anything Tara picked up speed as Chris fought against his release until he couldn't hold it any longer.

He groaned in pleasure and hunched forward a little as Tara finished before turning to face Chris with a smile.

"You were amazing today, the bravest man here," Tara praised. She kissed him passionately again before pulling up her trousers and skipping off backwards into the main building, looking back to wink at Chris.

Chris felt amazing. He looked on at the creatures who had been watching them. Their interest followed Tara and they looked at him confused as he slowly buckled up his trousers. The canteen wouldn't be serving yet, but after his heroics, they would surely sort him out with something. He was hungrier than he'd been in a long time.

Chapter 5

The new specimen had proved ideal on many levels. The bullet had entered the base of its skull and severed its spinal cord. It should have been dead, instead, it was completely paralysed below the neck, not that the injury spared it from being tied down. The major had demanded it. The creature was far more vocal than the older one. It moaned and groaned with no provocation, its teeth gnashing at anyone in sight. The samples it provided were astounding. Dr Srnicek couldn't believe the difference. The tissue samples were definitely related, but much had evolved. Comparing this poor soul to the first they had studied and the samples from before society fell was like comparing a tadpole to a frog. Identifying the microbe and seeing its evolution laid out was fascinating. It didn't bring them any closer to finding a cure, but it gave the team purpose once again.

Chris had been granted the luxury of guard duty in the lab. The biscuits had long run out, but he'd helped himself to some food from the canteen to munch on, not that it did much good. He felt dreadful, and he knew why.

"She's quite the pistol. One moment we were talking, the next, she'd dragged me into a cleaners closest and had my dick in her mouth," a young lab assistant, Martin, boasted to his friend within earshot of Chris.

Chris' ears pricked up. It couldn't be, could it?

"She's the village bike, everyone's had a ride," the friend piped up.

"You haven't," Martin said. The pride in Martin's voice was irritating.

"Because I don't want my dick to fall off. I know three others who've slept with her. She's an attractive girl, but I'm not into that. If Tara comes near me, I'll politely decline, thank you very much," the lad lied, knowing he wasn't about to get that offer.

"It's the end of times, the apocalypse, shagging some tart takes your mind off it, believe me. If not her, hook up with someone else. In the last few days, it's all gone last days of Rome around here."

Chris couldn't believe his ears. He glared at the two men, wishing that they were lying, but he knew it was true. She had become all about the sex, and before his stupid act of bravery had lost interest. It had only been a few days, but she was already drifting away. No doubt to others. He had risked it all for her, and she didn't care about him. He stood up and pushed past the two gossiping lab techs to Dr Srnicek.

"Doctor, I need to leave for a few minutes, I'll be locking you in," his voice quivered.

"Of course you will, private. Are you okay?" she queried. She wasn't impressed but felt some concern for him.

"Yes ma'am, I just need to use the bathroom," Chris lied. He didn't stop to talk further, he left the room and locked them in as quickly as he could. He ran down the hallway to the bathroom and threw open the door. He barely made it through the stall door to the bowl before he was sick. He thought for a second it was because of the betrayal, but he knew he was infected.

He slowly rose to his feet. A shiver flowed through him as he tried to control his breathing. As he stumbled out of the stall, he looked around, pleased to see he was alone. He stood in front of the mirror looking at the pale, angry face looking back at him. It didn't matter how much water he threw on himself; he didn't look or feel any better. He carefully dried his face and straightened himself back up. He couldn't be gone too long, he couldn't risk attracting more attention. He needed time to think; he needed time to plan, but soon they would realise what he was.

Chapter 6

A few days had passed since they had captured the creature. The initial excitement had died down and the whole centre was at a low ebb. They had cut food rations, Kenneth hadn't returned, and after the initial flurry of data the feeder had provided, the old routine had returned. Chris had kept himself to himself for a few days, doing his duties and then stealing extra food where he could. It didn't seem to help. He knew what he wanted, and it was becoming harder to resist. He hid behind the barracks for privacy, sitting on the ground as he looked at his future, as the creatures stared back at him. They didn't look at him as food; they saw one of their own. There was no gnashing of teeth or snarls. If it were possible, they envied him. Inside those fences with all that meat.

A few of the creature's attention was taken away from staring at the lucky one. Something was approaching, but they weren't sure what. Chris straightened himself up and turned as Tara appeared. She looked worried but tried to smile.

"Hey, I've not seen you about," Tara said. She was nearly apologetic in her tone.

"I didn't think that'd bother you, plenty of other men here, as you well know," he sulked.

"What do you mean?" Tara asked. She knew, but thought she'd been discrete.

"How many have you fucked? Every bloke or just most of us?" Chris spat. He was angry, but he didn't care about her anymore. She was just someone he could throw his anger at.

"Three men, and one girl," she replied sternly.

"Was that including me?" Chris was eager for a confrontation.

"Four men, and one girl then," came a quick, firm correction. She wasn't about to apologise.

"Just fuck off, I don't even care anymore, fuck everyone, no-one, or just go and fuck yourself," he sneered. Chris was ready to rip her apart.

"I need to talk to you Chris, I think I'm not well," Tara said. She was scared, but not of him. He recognised the fear in her eyes and the anger. He had it himself.

"What do you want me to do about it? Go see one of those white coats, he'll get you some penicillin and that'll clear it all up," Chris spat. He couldn't forgive her, if she had left him alone he'd never have volunteered, been infected, and had his heart broken.

"I did, one of the guys I had… I was friends with. He's sick too. I think you're sick, aren't you Chris?" Tara replied. She looked at him trying to judge his reaction. "I think we have a problem and I'm scared."

Chris looked at her, he didn't feel any attraction to her. He didn't want her. The creatures had mostly lost interest, too.

"I've got to go to the lab, I'm on duty in ten," he said. Chris brushed past Tara, she wanted to cry but held herself together, he was being an arsehole, and she wouldn't give him the satisfaction.

*

Chris entered the lab and grunted at his colleague he was replacing before taking his place, looking over the lab and its staff. The white coats slowly went about their duties, their motivation had left them. Chris was hungry, he knew he wouldn't have long. He was changing far quicker than he'd imagined was possible. He looked at the people in the lab as they worked; it irritated him. He thought about shouldering his rifle and killing all of them. It would be no effort at all. A young female lab technician walked in front of him. He could smell her. She wasn't wearing any perfume, not even any deodorant, he could smell her. Her perspiration. Her skin. He leaned forward to hoover her scent in.

"Private, you can chase woman outside of my lab, never inside of it," she told him. Dr Srnicek herself was frustrated and happy to take it out on the squaddie.

Chris grunted at her.

"Excuse me, you need to show some respect to me and my staff in my laboratory," she sneered. Now she was angry.

Chris snarled and Dr Srnicek took a step back. She could see him now, see what he was. Chris leapt at her and pinned her to the ground. She didn't have time to scream before he clamped his teeth on her face. The rest of the lab froze, stunned by the sight in front of them. Chris stood up covered in blood and the lab panicked as Dr Srnicek crawled away, stunned and bleeding heavily.

Chris didn't have any words. He didn't need them; he ran at Robert, who tried to fend him off with a beaker. It smashed across Chris' face but didn't slow him down. Chris ripped a chunk of flesh from Robert's neck. Finally he felt satisfied, it was the only thing he felt. His rifle was still where he had been sat. A young lab technician grabbed it and snatched at the trigger but nothing happened, Chris had his next target. The lad was frozen as Chris moved closer before knocking the rifle from his hands and smashing his head repeatedly against the wall. He now stood at the door, ensuring no one could pass. They huddled together, all except Martin.

He knew he was infected too. The scent of the blood, filling his nose and sending his brain into a scramble. Chris wouldn't hurt him, they were the same. Martin stepped forward towards Chris.

"Don't be stupid, Martin!" his friend pleaded, but Martin looked back with a tear in his eye.

Robert lay in a pool of his own blood. He had stopped moving. Dr Srnicek was being held by a colleague. She was in shock, but still alive. The lad who had his head caved-in was perfectly still. Martin walked close to Chris, who looked through him. He carefully and slowly picked up the rifle, examined it briefly before flicking off the safety, and pulling back the bolt to load a round. Slowly he raised it and pointed at Chris, who didn't flinch. He pulled the trigger twice, two rounds struck Chris at point blank range in the chest and he flew back and onto the floor.

Martin wasn't finished.

He put another round into the lad on the floor, then walked to Robert and put two rounds in his torso, before standing over Dr Srnicek.

"Get back," he pleaded with the man helping her, who slowly obliged.

She raised her hand up to plead with him, unable to speak, but it was no use. Martin shot her in the chest and she slumped backwards. He lowered the rifle. He knew this was it for him too. He couldn't do it himself. Looking around the room, he didn't think anyone else could either.

"I'm changing too, you need to kill me, someone, please. I don't want to become one of those things," he pleaded. He approached the huddled scientists, but they edged away. "Someone needs to do this," he said as he held the rifle out, his friend stepped forward and took the rifle. Martin smiled at him and he half-smiled back. Martin closed his eyes and waited. A single gunshot struck him in the chest and he slumped down. He coughed and moved a few inches before his body gave up on him.

The rifle dropped to the floor, and there was a sense of relief in the lab. It was over; it was awful, but it was over. They comforted each other, some cried, others sat down with their heads in their hands.

Chris stood back up. Any hint of humanity gone. He charged the group to screams as his victims realised it wasn't over. Martin climbed to his feet. His eyes were glazed over, he wasn't Martin anymore and joined in the attack thrashing at anyone near with his teeth and hands.

The lab door swung open, the major entered with his pistol drawn. Another soldier ran in and moved ahead, rifle ready. In front of them a mass of white lab coats stained with blood, two attackers in a frenzy unwilling to stop.

"Private, stand down!" The major ordered. The major knew he was talking to a monster, not a man. He just hoped for an ounce of humanity to remain.

Both the creatures turned to the armed men, no fear, no recognition, blood covering their hands and faces, the injured white coats cowered in terror. The major didn't hesitate any further and fired once, striking Chris in his shoulder. It knocked him back, but not down. The soldier hesitated and Martin closed the distance on him in no time, pinning him to the ground, clawing at his face. The major edged back and assessed the room. There may have been two monsters, but almost all were now infected.

"For fuck's sake!" he screamed at everyone in the room. He hated them and pitied them all. He stepped back and slammed the doors closed, locking them.

The heavy doors dulled the screams, pleading for rescue, their route to escape blocked by the starving beasts. The major hastily removed his belt and secured the doors further before looking through the small wired window into the lab. His man had wrestled himself free and standing, unarmed and bleeding, with the scientists and lab technicians, slowly edging towards the only safe place left to them, the freezer.

The soldier fought off the creatures as the scientists quickly entered the large walk-in freezer. The major watched as the soldier slammed the freezer door shut, leaving the two feeders to enjoy the three bodies on the floor.

Two more soldiers ran to the major, ready to help.

"It's too late, they're all gone. Just the fucking dead in there now."

Chapter 7

The civilians and soldiers were packing up two cars and a van, the last of the vehicles onsite. There wasn't much to pack, a few scraps of clothes, and a few small boxes of food. Three of their number were gagged and bound, kneeling close to the fence line, the creatures on the other side showing them no interest.

A private approached the major. "Sir, come with us. There's nothing here," Liam said. Liam was a good soldier, he followed orders but kept himself to himself. He was thankful when the major ordered the evacuation.

The major felt relief that his responsibility for the centre was drawing to a close. Wellworth wasn't over, the world was. His men and the civilians were fleeing to nowhere, hoping for something better than this. It wasn't any more foolish than waiting for help that wouldn't come, surrounded by the hungry dead as you yourself starve to death. Soon it'd just be him and those condemned souls in the lab.

"Someone needs to stay here. Deal with those poor bastards and close the gate after you all fuck off," he said. Getting Kenneth out had been hard enough with a group of soldiers creating the distraction. On his own, it would be nearly impossible. A few petrol bombs were created, and the major kept a rifle and a single thirty-round magazine to give them the cover they'd need. It was important they got away safely. His future, and that of Wellworth, had already been decided. It was how it ended that was still up in the air. He'd rather the centre's integrity was maintained, in case one day reinforcements came looking for the research, but the lives of the survivors were his priority.

Several of the soldiers made their way to space between the two fences, the familiar pieces of rebar, and started clearing some creatures. Any creatures killed would help, but there were always more. Wellworth seemed to attract them, despite its location. The major wandered over to the three captives. Tara and two male civilians. Their skin was pale and greying, they were skin and bone bodies dusted with a mist of perspiration. The two men had a frightened look in their eyes, they weren't as far along. Tara was angry, she was barely human. They knew Chris had been infected first. His relationship with Tara was known by enough for her to be quarantined, and soon enough her other surviving partners were separated and secured. Nobody felt confident that these three were the only ones infected outside of the sealed lab. Now they would be more observant, they may survive together but they didn't trust one another.

"I'm sorry about what's going to happen, I don't expect you to like it. I don't. But there are too many of those things out there, I can't let another three into the world," said the major. The creatures on the other side of the fences could smell the major, his aroma teased them. Tara tried to speak, to force her gag away from her mouth, but she wasn't successful. "It's better that you don't talk, it won't change anything. It'll be quick and painless, and it won't be that existence for you," he continued. The major looked out to the feeders. They were monsters in every sense of the word. All desperate to taste his flesh, the desire driving them into a frenzy. Their appearance growing more grotesque by the day.

"Sir, we'll be shipping out shortly," Liam told him, he was embarrassed, but he needn't have been. He received a gentle pat on the back by the major.

"It's okay. We did everything we could. You might be the only healthy humans left in the country, look after yourselves. Get some supplies, get somewhere remote, and stay there," he said and allowed himself a smile. They had a tough road ahead, but there was a chance, which was more than they'd have here.

The soldiers thinning the numbers on the fence withdrew. Their work was brief and reasonably efficient. Every crumbled creature oozing grey blood from a head wound was one who would not be trying to force their way through the gates.

The major made his way to the vehicles as the last of the civilians entered. Several soldiers readied their rifles and looked to the major for one last order.

"Open fire!" he screamed it so loudly everyone flinched before they started firing.

They began clearing the creatures closest to the gate and working further away, concentrating on the left side of the gate. The major lit the first Molotov and tossed it to the left side of the gate. Several creatures almost screamed in pain as they burned. The major set light to the second and threw it in the same direction further down. More feeders stumbled in flames, unable to see or comprehend what was happening. The left side was looking clear for close to thirty-feet. He threw the last petrol bomb to the right side, creating a short tunnel of fire for the vehicles to escape through. The soldiers stopped firing and all but two jumped into the vehicles.

They opened the first gate and stood by the second. The major joined them, firing at the closest creatures on the right-hand side of the gate, walking close to the fence. He pulled his sleeve up and produced a knife before digging the blade in deeply and drawing down an inch as the thick red blood ran down. "Come and get it you gruesome fucks!"

The scent of the blood captured the attention of all of those creatures closest to him and several further back. They climbed over each other to keep up with him as he moved further away from the gate, flicking the monsters with his blood, increasing their lust for his flesh.

The outer gate was clear, the soldier threw it open, and the cars drove off at pace. The last one exited, the soldier closed the gate and quickly jumped in before a feeder could get close.

It was a successful evacuation.

The major held his wound and applied pressure and he slowly walked back towards the gate. It was shut, the slide engaged, but it wasn't locked. He didn't see the need to use the cumbersome lock. Those things couldn't use the simple slide bolt. If any of the living were still out there they were welcome to come in and enjoy the running water and electricity as they starved to death.

He closed the second gate and slid the bolt into place before approaching the captives. The scent of his blood was driving Tara crazy. She writhed on the floor, desperate to free herself so she might have a taste. The other two were interested but didn't appear as desperate as Tara.

He didn't say a word as he approached. In a single quick movement he shouldered the rifle, pulling the trigger three times, striking each of the bound infected in the head with a single shot each. The bodies were still; they were at peace.

The major looked down at his arm, he'd cut a little too deep in his eagerness to get the job done. If he had the time, it would have healed nicely, but he didn't. He had a few bits of admin to do before he could have his sit down. Tara didn't weigh much before she was infected. After a few days, her emaciated form was easy to drag one handed. He wasn't taking them far, just twenty feet further away.

The two men were more of a struggle, but he wasn't in a rush, taking a few minutes' break when he needed. With all three bodies stacked on each other, the major doused them with petrol from an unused Molotov and set the pile alight. He stepped back as the flesh sizzled as the fire took hold.

Chapter 8

The major looked out from the director's office to the grounds below. Overnight more of the dead had turned up to the fences, replacing their fallen comrades. His arm was sore, but he'd applied a dressing to stop the bleeding. He took a swig of whiskey and told himself it was for the pain, but he was numbing more than just a wound to his arm. Today was the day, he'd do a quick sweep of the grounds, check in on the lab and then take his seat. He picked up his rifle, checked his pistol and made his way out of the building.

When he emerged from the building, the creatures on the other side of the fence caught his scent and groaned. He didn't pay them any attention, there was no need. He checked on the charred corpses. They still smouldered in the early morning chill as he heaped a few shovelfuls of dirt on top of them. His sore arm felt every ounce of earth as he made sure it covered the bodies. He knew he had to show respect to these poor souls but looked on at the dead heaped around the outside of the fence and appreciated it was a hollow gesture. There was no longer enough living to bury the dead.

He didn't rush as he walked the perimeter, occasionally tempted to take a shot at the more gruesome creatures drooling in his direction. He knew it would be a waste, plenty more where they came from, and the few rounds he had in his rifle might find a better use one day. The fences looked good, they wouldn't be coming down anytime soon. At the gates, further charred bodies were on the floor, with more feeders, many sporting their own burns, standing over their fallen comrades. He gave the gates a quick check; they were secure, but he left them unlocked. Maybe the men would come back, maybe Kenneth would turn up with a hundred of Her Majesty's finest. If that was the case he wouldn't want them stuck outside with those stinking bastards.

Everything was in order, and the major smiled. He had failed, but Wellworth was at least secure. If nothing else, his men had thinned out a few hundred of the dead and attracted thousands more, every one of them clawing at the fence was one not attacking a survivor elsewhere. He entered the building. There was one last duty to undertake.

Two filing cabinets, an office desk and a myriad of random junk had been stacked against it the doors. A bicycle lock had been added to the belt securing the double doors shut. Nothing was getting out. He peered through the reinforced glass window. At some point, those who sought shelter in the freezer had let themselves out. As they changed they no longer feared the monsters in the main lab, they wanted out; they wanted to eat. Their humanity left them. They now either wandered aimlessly or stood still, looking through the window back at the major.

It was his failure. Wellworth stood, but it was a hollow victory. The victims entombed in the lab testified to that. The major made his way up to the office.

He set down the rifle and turned on the radio where a message played on a loop. He had heard it hundreds of times in the last few days. They were alone; they had been abandoned. Empty promises that were too late. He poured himself a whiskey and took an appreciative sip. The centre was in order. It was time to sit down.

The major scribbled a brief note and downed the remaining whiskey. He paused for a moment then pulled his Glock from his holster, chambered a round and without giving himself enough time to change his mind, he placed the tip of the barrel under his chin and pulled the trigger. The top of his head erupted covering ceiling, wall and window with brain, skull and blood spray.

The pistol dropped to the floor, and the major slumped in his chair.

Chapter 9

Peter held the Glock pistol as he stood over the major's body. He hadn't been dead more than a day. It was a tragedy that wasn't lost on Peter; he had nearly performed the same permanent act when he found himself alone without hope. He looked at the pistol; the idea washed over him; he wasn't that man anymore. He'd come too far and seen too much. He walked around the office, admired the whiskey, noted the pictures on the wall, but the rifle took his attention. It was just like Amy's. He had seen her handle her rifle, enough at least to check the ammunition, engage the safety and pull the trigger. With the few rounds it had left and the pistol, he felt empowered to explore the facility.

It felt even more like any other mundane building as he walked through the empty offices, meeting rooms and storage areas. For a secret lab, it lacked labs. Apart from the large main one he'd already seen secured with the dead inside, there wasn't anything of that level. He found three smaller labs, empty of equipment and personnel. They hadn't been in use for months. The canteen was a relief to discover.

It was small enough for maybe forty people to enjoy a basic lunch, but it was plenty big enough for him. The kitchen was appropriately sized, decked out with the latest in cooking equipment. The large refrigerators were empty, the freezer had a solitary bag of frozen peas and dozens of bags of ice. Something he could at least put with the whiskey.

The cupboards had a little more in them, tins of meat, tomatoes and more vegetables. Peter smiled to himself as he removed a tin of sweetcorn. *Of course.* He wasn't sure how long he could make the food last, even if he was careful.

He spent hours wandering the facility, forcing open lockers and drawers, eager to find anything that may be useful. He had always found digging through people's belongings a grubby activity and now was no different. Family photos and precious keepsakes reminded him of what the world had lost, but medication and the occasional chocolate bar or cup-a-soup made it a worthwhile endeavour. By the time he had jimmied open his last drawer, he had a good supply of paracetamol and high calorie treats, a few changes of clothes but little else.

He decided against looking at the outbuildings that day. It looked like he'd be here for a long time and had what he needed to get going. He made use of one of the emergency showers in an empty laboratory and discarded his bloodstained clothing. He made use of the clinically clean toilets and found a small office which he decided would be perfect to sleep in, a single sturdy door that could be reinforced with furniture allowing him to sleep with a degree of safety. With a little food, the weapons and a clean set of clothes he made himself at home, it was still light outside, but he was in little doubt he'd sleep through until morning. He lay on the hard floor and closed his eyes, falling asleep instantly.

Chapter 10

Amy looked back across the rundown room at Kenneth, before she lowered herself from the window. And then he was alone. Just the snarling beasts trying to reach him and the bloody corpse on the floor. He fired at the creatures, but within seconds they were in the house and making their way up the stairs. The door was barricaded but rotten wood wouldn't last long and he had only a few rounds left. The small stash of weapons in the corner were basic knives and bats; a large butcher's knife would be his best bet, razor sharp and a large twelve-inch blade. With only one hand, he didn't have the energy or coordination to fight off the monsters for long. A big sharp knife seemed his best bet to at least hurt a few of them.

They were angry. That bitch Natasha had really riled them up. They began clawing at the door, their nails digging away at the weak timber. Kenneth's time was running out. He fired the last few rounds at the feeders on the other side of the door, then his rifle clicked confirming it was empty. He stepped back, trying to give himself space from the imminent attack, but stopped as he nearly tripped over Gareth's corpse. He looked at the body, at his own dismembered hand on the floor and then the knife. Maybe it wasn't over.

He bent over and swung the blade down hard on Gareth's arm. The knife dug in deep, but he had to continue hacking at it before it popped off. Kenneth wasn't squeamish, he'd seen dismembered bodies, but he'd never butchered a one himself. It was a deeply unpleasant task, but he got on with it and started on the other limbs and then Gareth's head. In a few minutes he had created a pile of body parts. The first hand punched through a panel in the door, and then a second one competed with it, desperately grabbing at the air, hoping to catch hold of a handful of flesh. More thuds and scratches confirmed the number of creatures were continuing to grow.

They were close to breaking through. Kenneth dragged the torso to the window. The weight was surprising, but his weakness and only having one hand made it harder than it should have been. With all his might, he flopped the body out of the window. The thud and the blood attracted the closest creatures, others joined sensing a meal was available.

Those at the door didn't relent, the spilled blood from the pile of body parts did little to calm them. The creatures pulled apart a panel and Kenneth could see their furious faces, grey skin, chipped teeth and the red blood of their prey. He picked up his own dismembered hand and tossed it through the gap. The feeders on the other side greedily fought amongst themselves for it, with only one remaining at the door. It was easy pushing the large sharp blade into its skull. It slumped to the floor and Kenneth readied himself for the next customer, who was already clambering over the downed monster for its turn. Kenneth obliged.

They had stripped his severed hand of almost all of its flesh. The mob was already back at the door and again making quick work of the damaged wood. Kenneth couldn't hope to take them out one by one, feeding them morsels of Gareth. He had to make his move. He shoved Gareth's right leg through the door and again they fought each other to get the first taste. He didn't have much time. He checked the back window, Amy and Peter were already out of sight. A few stragglers were following, leaving the back of the house clear. Kenneth threw another arm through the door, then the remaining parts out of the front window. Any feeder not filling themselves with meat was jostling for position to do so.

He tossed the knife out of the back window; it landed blade first into the ground. He grabbed a bottle of water and dropped that from the window before following himself. He hit the ground with a crunch. He was sure he hadn't broken anything, but his ankle was stiff with a sharp pain. The water bottle shoved under one arm, he retrieved the knife and headed away from the house. Nothing pursued him, but he couldn't move fast enough to relax. He hoped to see a glimpse of Amy or Peter, but knew he'd bump into their pursuers long before he would catch up with them.

As the house became smaller in the distance, his head throbbed. He looked at his stump; the bandage was soaked through. He had to sit, just for a moment. Everything spun and he couldn't so much as sit up straight. He'd got out of the house, he had evaded the creatures, but now he was going to pass out in the middle of a field and he didn't know if he'd ever wake again. He couldn't sit up any longer. He fell onto his back and stared at the sky as it swirled uncontrollably and then everything went black.

Seconds, minutes or even hours could have passed, and Kenneth had no idea. His delirium interrupted by a muffled voice. Then another. He couldn't recognise them, he couldn't even think straight. He could feel himself being moved, being dragged across the uneven terrain. It didn't hurt, everything was becoming numb, his stump, his ankle. Then he didn't care anymore. The voices became a high-pitched whine as they merged into one sound. And then he was out cold.

Chapter 11

St. Joseph's primary school was in the small village of Nutwood, a village that was easily ignored by those who bypassed it or drove through on the way to somewhere larger. The village had been robbed of its post office and the local pub had barely stayed afloat. The school had been constantly under threat of closure, funding cuts and low pupil intake had increased the pressure, and if not for its links to the church, it would have gone long ago. Despite the financial help offered by the dioceses, had society not fallen, it would probably have closed before the next school year. It had educated the young from the village and the surrounding areas for over one-hundred years. They had supplemented its original stone structures over the years with additional, more modern buildings that ill-suited the look of the original building or the neighbouring church. The perimeter comprised of a formidable old stone wall and a modern, secure gate, a damning indictment of the path society had taken where the youngest and most vulnerable needed protecting from the outside world. When people started eating each other, that protection served a newer, more vital cause. The villagers supported each other, and the school became the perfect sanctuary to protect them. With their remote location and pooled resources, they had been relatively untouched by the chaos and destruction the more densely populated areas had experienced. Fifteen people had made the school their home, a few elderly, some children and everything in between. They had declined the invitation by the military to join them at one of the rescue camps, deciding instead to look after themselves, as the village had always tried to do.

Michael was in his mid-forties and had become the leader of this small community. He was a farmer, his late wife had been the head teacher at St. Joseph's before she succumbed to ovarian cancer a year before the plague. He was known and respected in the village for being brave with a level head. Michael had led many an expedition beyond the safety of the school, scavenging the abandoned homes, farms and cars for anything of use. As the weeks had gone on, the success had dwindled. As a farmer, he had already been thinking ahead. Ten chickens and three cows provided milk and eggs, animal feed was easy enough acquire, having been ignored by most looters. He had already planted a large vegetable garden, but that would take time to deliver a regular source of subsistence. Michael knew they'd have to move out further to get the supplies they needed to get them to the point of being self-sufficient. He also knew the risks. Like everywhere else, they had suffered losses. Those losses felt more personal to such a small village where everyone knew everyone else. They weren't just neighbours; they were friends. Some died at the hands of the infected outside of the village, others left with the military. All now were assumed lost. The thought of losing more friends kept Michael awake at night, failing to act now when they were fit and healthy would condemn them all further down the line. He had decided he would take Jake, one of his former farm workers and the son of the church's vicar, for his next foraging trip to a nearby village. Jake was in his early twenties and extremely capable. A crack shot with any rifle or shotgun, he was an asset protecting the group and providing wood pigeons, bunnies and squirrels for the pot.

They emptied the Range Rover, just the Ruger 10/22 rifle, a

hatchet, and the two men. They didn't intend on fighting and needed maximum room for whatever supplies they might find. A few concerned faces saw them out of the gates. The Range Rover didn't waste any time on heading out of the village, and the school gates were quickly secured behind it.

The next village was several miles away, the roads were narrow and unloved, some didn't even appear on any maps. Anyone unfamiliar with them would just as likely turn back looking for a major road as they would brave the unknown tracks that could lead anywhere. Michael and Jake didn't have those fears, they knew these roads well, but Jake still held the small rifle close in case a horde of feeders waited around the next corner.

The car pulled up outside of the village and both men left the safety of the vehicle and looked forward. They could see Thornhurst had fared worse than Nutwood. It was treble the size of their own village, but it was a wreck. They didn't need to enter to see the burned-out buildings, rotting fleshy skeletons on the streets and the creatures slowly shuffling or swaying on the spot.

"I can do it Mikey, there are only a dozen or so. I can ping them from fifty yards and we can move in," Jake urged. Jake was enthusiastic but impulsive. Michael wasn't open to taking such a risk, there was nothing but death and destruction in Thornhurst and he would not risk this kid's life here.

"For the dozen you can see, there are another dozen you can't. At best, you'll use fifty rounds of twenty-two before we have to withdraw, at worst they will overwhelm us. We're not going in. Not today. There's a series of houses on the London road heading out of Thornhurst, we'll head through Simmons' land. It'll be fine," Michael responded. Michael had scavenged enough houses to know that they would likely find a few tins of food, a defrosted freezer of rotten meat, and maybe some pasta and rice. It might get them another day, and every little helped.

Jake wasn't about to ignore Michael, he respected and trusted him. If he said no, it was a no. The men got back in the car and slowly reversed up the narrow track to the field's closed gate, and Jake hopped out and opened the gate as Michael edged into the overgrown grass. Jake had followed behind the Range Rover, rifle in hand, treading carefully through the field, wary of his footing. The hum of the diesel engine masked the groan ahead, Michael in the cabin couldn't see what was lurking in the long grass, Jake too was oblivious. Half way across the field, the car jolted as it drove over a bump, following closely behind Jake looked left and right, but failed to look down as it grabbed him. The Range Rover had crushed its ribcage, but its hands and teeth were still fully functional. Jake first thought was he snagged his foot on the pushed down grass, only when he heard it growl he knew he was being attacked. He looked down, and its face was angry, dried blood decorated its grey skin as it tried to pull Jake towards it. Panicking, he fired twice at its flattened torso, with zero effect. Michael barely heard to the pops of the rifle, but they were enough for him to check his mirror as he saw Jake fall to the floor. He slammed on the brakes and jumped out of the car with the hatchet in hand as he rushed to Jake. The creature was on top of Jake and he couldn't get the rifle back into action, instead using it to keep the feeders teeth from biting down on him. Michael slammed the hatchet into the back of its head, stopping its attack immediately. He wrestled the hatchet free and Jake threw the battered corpse to the side before Michael helped him back to his feet.

"Are you okay? Did it bite you?" Michael patted Jake down, checking him for a wound.

"No, I'm fine. I'm fine," he insisted. Jake wasn't sure himself, but didn't feel any pain as the adrenaline rushed through his veins.

"We won't tell your dad about this."

Jake nodded in agreement as the pair got back in the car, eager not to make that same mistake again. When they got to the edge of the field, Michael hopped out to open the gate. This field was much larger, and the first house on London road was just about visible in the distance. They both stayed in the car as they drove. This field wasn't overgrown, the grass was more mossy than tall. A few carcasses and bloodied clumps of wool were all that remained of the sheep who had grazed here. They were cautious. Despite his camouflaged green fatigues, they both spotted him. Lying on his back staring up at the sky he barely moved, he was bloodied and beaten; he was surely either a feeder or about to become one.

"What should we do?" Jake's instinct was to help this man, but he hadn't got over his encounter.

"Stay here with the rifle, I'll check it out."

Michael again left the safety of the car with the hatchet in his hand and slowly approached the man. Visibility was better, and he was certain he wouldn't be grabbed by an unseen, undead foe or jumped by a group of survivors desperate to steal supplies. The man was a soldier, even laying on the ground he looked like a giant, his eyes were closed and he shivered, his black skin wasn't tinted with grey. If he was infected, it was recent. One of his hands was missing, the stump covered in a bloody rag, Michael edged closer and gently tapped the man with his foot, ready to bring the hatchet into play if needed. Nothing. He gave a firmer, harder kick and nothing. He looked around to check and he could see figures ambling towards them around half a mile away. "Jake, bring her up," Michael said. He knew they couldn't hang around.

Jake shuffled across into the driver's seat and drove closer to the pair.

"He's alive, he's human. I'm not sure he'll make it, but we need to take him back to St. Joe's," Michael relayed. Michael was a decent man, he couldn't leave this poor soul to die in this field.

"We can't go back empty-handed, they're depending on us."

"This big lad is hardly empty handed. Who knows what he can tell us," he stated. Michael grabbed the man under his arms and signalled for Jake to help him, which he did. He was mostly muscle, a big lump he was hard to carry, but they got him into the car's large boot, dragging him across the ground with minimal bumps.

Chapter 12

Out of all the classrooms at St. Joseph's, this was the smallest and had received the least love. The paint on the walls, the carpet tiles and frosted single pane windows had remained the same for over thirty years. The room had in recent years been repurposed as a storage area, no longer seen fit to play a direct part in the children's education. Once the outbreak hit and the school became the haven for those who remained, it was cleared and made habitable in case they needed it. Until Michael and Jake had rescued Kenneth, the room had remained empty. Now, a simple bed, a few chairs and a table had been setup. It wasn't much, but it felt safe, safer than Kenneth had felt since he left Wellworth. He had enjoyed the prospect of getting out and doing some soldiering, now he was happy to be somewhere warm, dry and surrounded by people who had no interest in trying to eat him.

Jake watched over him, rifle in hand, ready to strike if the large soldier caused problems. They hadn't dealt with many outsiders and did not understand what to expect. Dr James Fredericks wrote on a notepad as he sat in a well-worn chair that had been liberated from the school's staff room. Like him, it had seen better days and in better times wouldn't be called into service. The doctor was nearly eighty years old; he had been retired in the village for twenty years after serving as its GP for another two decades. Known and loved by all, he couldn't leave when the army started evacuating civilians. He had enjoyed a good life and if just one person stayed in Nutwood, he would have stayed to help them. As the only medically trained person left in the village, his knowledge and experience was invaluable. Without him, Kenneth would have had a rougher road to recovery. Dr Fredericks had expertly cleaned the wound at the stump, tended to the sprained ankle, and applied an IV drip and antibiotics.

Kenneth had only been at St. Joseph's for a few days, but he was looking nearly like his old self. If it wasn't for the missing hand and limp, you would be hard pushed to guess what he'd been through. Still stiff and sore, his strength had returned, and the painkillers given to him had numbed much of the pain.

"Kenneth, I'm happy to clear you, but I'm sure you understand we need to assess you in non-medical ways," came the doctor's voice. The doctor was kind, but Kenneth knew he wasn't in charge, his fate was still to be decided. The young man with the rifle made that clear.

Michael entered the room and signalled for Jake to leave, but Dr Fredericks remained seated. He approached Kenneth and offered his hand to shake.

"Hi Kenneth, I'm sorry we've had to keep you here, like this. I'm sure you understand that trust is a hard commodity to give away freely these days, and we have people who depend upon us," Michael explained. Kenneth shook the hand and nodded. "James, the doc, has said you've made a good recovery, and he's happy that we can talk," he said and looked over at the doctor who gave a shrug and a weak nod. "I'm Michael, we brought you in. First, you're safe with us. I understand you've been through a lot out there and we're happy for you to call St. Joseph's home for as long as you need or want to," Michael smiled, he was welcome, but another mouth to feed wasn't ideal. Two further trips out had offered only a meagre selection of supplies. He hoped Kenneth might have information on where they should look, or perhaps even be able to offer the help of his military colleagues.

"Thank-you," Kenneth replied. And he was thankful, but he knew very little was free in this new world and trust was a two-way street. Only a few days ago, his trust in humanity cost him his hand and nearly his life.

"I'll cut to the chase. When we found you, we were scavenging for supplies. We have little knowledge of what has been going on beyond our own village since the outbreak. We know it's bad, but we have kept ourselves to ourselves, but that is increasingly not an option. We need your help, any information you may have. Our supplies won't last more than a few weeks," Michael informed him. He prayed this man might be able to help.

"Everyone's hungry, both the dead and the living are facing a dwindling supply of suitable food. We all need to eat, but you need to be careful. It isn't just them and us, there's something else, something that can't be trusted," Kenneth said and raised his stump. "I've seen three types of them, the stupid ones, the big bastards, and her. If you reach out and touch the world, eventually it'll touch you right back."

"I'm sure you're right, but we won't have to worry about the dead when we've run out of food," Michael was keeping on message. There was a lot he needed to know, but food had to be their priority. "We know the local area, but we don't know what's out there. For us to survive, we're going to need to reach out."

"You don't understand, they look like us. She was walking, talking, she even fucked a guy then ate him," he responded. His passion was to be expected after his ordeal.

"We understand, we need to be careful, but we need food. Can you help us?" Michael pleaded with Kenneth, they didn't need him to go out on patrol, they just needed some information.

"I can show you two locations I had gathered supplies, you can't have them all, but I can provide you with some as a thank you for your help. The rest I need to get back to my men. They're starving too and I've been gone far too long."

"Are they near?" he asked. Michael was interested. The military perhaps hadn't fallen as the broadcasts had suggested, but it was obviously weak.

"Lewes."

"That's not too far. Help us gather up those supplies and we'll get you a working car and you can go back to your men, stay with us or even bring your men here if you prefer," he replied. Michael was happy with all those scenarios, the idea of soldiers providing protection was enticing.

"Take me back to where you found me and I can lead you from there," Kenneth said. Kenneth was ready to leave at that very second.

"The day after tomorrow," the doctor stated. Dr Fredericks had been sitting quietly, listening, but he didn't need to get involved until he could hear his patient being coerced into leaving. He rose to his feet, but his eyes didn't leave his notes. He wasn't asking, he was telling. "He's not going anywhere until I say so, and I won't say so for two more days."

Michael looked at the doctor, then Kenneth who confirmed his intention. "I need to get back to Wellworth."

"Young man, you are no good to us or your friends if you pass out and become a feast for one of those damned fiends. You will continue to rest, then when you leave the safety of our home, you might not die," Dr Fredericks explained. He kept his authority even after all these years spent in retirement, tending to his garden. Kenneth nodded in reluctant acceptance.

"Kenneth, you're welcome to explore our home and we can answer any questions you may have. You can meet some of our people and see what we have to offer. Jake can show you around," he promised.

Michael opened the door and smiled, Kenneth wandered out and was met by Jake.

Michael closed the door behind them and stayed with the doctor. "You're happy that he's not infected?"

"I can't see any evidence of it. Apart from the minor injuries and the lack of a left hand, he seems healthy. I have little experience diagnosing the dead, but you should make sure Jake isn't too far from him, just in case. If he's fine in two days, I think it's safe to say he's clear."

Chapter 13

The house was set in the middle of two other similar looking ones, alone along a dirt track surrounded by fields and a scattering of small wooded areas. It was not particularly big, nor interesting, or of any note, but the buildings were remote from any habitable areas. The Range Rover pulled up out front and Jake hopped out of the back passenger seat and opened the gate, letting the car onto the driveway. With the gate closed, Jake jogged to the car as Kenneth and Michael climbed out. All three were armed, Jake with his rifle, Michael a shotgun, and they had given Kenneth a hatchet. Kenneth's British Army Land Rover was still abandoned at the side of the house, covered in dry gore and two flat tires. It had been lucky to make it this far before Kenneth had to leave it behind.

"That's got about a quarter of a tank of diesel if you've got something to siphon it with," Michael nodded as he stepped towards the front of the house. "The door isn't locked, a firm shove should do it," he said. Kenneth stepped aside and once again, Jake stepped up and obliged. It popped openly cleanly, with much less effort than Jake had expected, nearly sending him tumbling into the building. He regained his balance. The three men stepped back and paused for a moment. They listened intensely for a possibly lurking creature, but nothing.

Michael led the way, his shotgun ready to blast a hole in anything that may have sneaked into the house. Kenneth had already told them he'd stored everything in the back upstairs bedroom, and after a quick check of the downstairs, they cautiously made their way upstairs. The bedroom door was open, and Kenneth dreaded what they'd find.

"Fucking hell," he exclaimed. Kenneth hadn't been here for over a week, but someone had. The room had been looted. He'd scavenged dozens of ration packs, tins of food, slabs of chocolate, packets of soup, and bottled water. Now a slab of tinned sweetcorn, a few sachets of soup, and a half-empty bottle of sparkling water was all that remained. "There was more, much more than just some fucking sweetcorn."

"There are a lot of hungry, desperate people still roaming and surviving. Who-ever took it probably needed it as much as we do," Michael was pragmatic. Supply trips had become increasingly unrewarding. At least they had some tinned veg and maybe some diesel to show for this trip.

"I'm sorry. There wasn't as much at the next place, but it isn't too far," Kenneth said. He was sorry, these people had saved him, and he'd admired their small community they had created in Nutwood. He had desperately wanted to repay them and have enough to take back to Wellworth.

"Don't worry lad, what will be, will be," Michael smiled, no point worrying about things you can't change.

They scooped up the meagre finds and left the house. The twenty-four tins of sweetcorn and packets of soup looked lonely in the large boot of the car. Jake was already making quick work of siphoning the diesel from the Land Rover into a small red fuel can. Kenneth rummaged in the back of his former vehicle, but they had taken anything approaching useful. The hosepipe filling the fuel had stopped and Jake tapped Kenneth on the shoulder. "Time to go, fella," he said. The men all resumed their positions in the car.

"Take the left and go down about a mile, then go right, follow the road for about three miles. There's a farm," Kenneth directed as he closed his eyes, trying to remember the way. A lot had happened since he last had been at that farm.

Michael followed the instructions to the letter. The farm was right where Kenneth said it was. Michael vaguely knew the former occupants, a good family, hard workers who looked after their herd and their workers. The fields would have been filled with sheep during the day, but now a few dried out, bloodied carcasses were all that remained. They pulled up to the front of the house and repeated the previous routine.

This time the stash was unmolested. Hundreds of tins of meat and vegetables, bottled water, chocolate, bags of flour, sugar, UHT milk, and tea. Jake and Michael smiled, Kenneth did too out of relief he'd be able to repay his hosts with something.

"Jesus Kenny, how much did you have at the last place? Mikey, have you ever seen such a sight?" Jake asked, impressed.

"This is good, this is great." Michael beamed. "Let's get the car loaded up and get back to St. Joe's. There will be a lot of smiling faces when we get back."

"I do need to get back to Wellworth." Kenneth knew the supplies weren't enough to make a meaningful difference to both St. Joe's and Wellworth, but he couldn't stay away any longer.

"Don't worry, we'll get you back, I hope you don't mind driving a little Fiesta? It's got a few prangs, but it runs well enough and it's an automatic. We'll fill the boot for you too," Michael smiled at the idea of this giant squeezing into this old, compact car.

Chapter 14

Kenneth helped put the supplies into the storeroom. It was more a token gesture. His stump was still sore, but he could help in a small way. The stores also held the armoury. Two shotguns, a bolt action hunting rifle, and seven air rifles were stored in addition to what had been issued. Kenneth couldn't help himself and started examining the weapons. The double-barrelled shotguns were of a similar appearance, useful weapons against one or two creatures as close range. The rifle was a .17 HMR with a scope and five-round internal magazine. Good for a short to medium range, but not a big round to put on target. Head-shots would be kills, anything else would barely be an irritation to those things. The air rifles made him smile, "Fucking useless," he whispered to himself. A couple looked fancy, bottles of compressed air, fine walnut stocks, and large impressive scopes. The rest looked like the basic airguns of his childhood.

"See anything you like?" Michael had been watching the soldier admire their meagre selection of weapons.

"That rifle is neat." Kenneth picked up the seventeen HMR and shouldered it, it was light enough that his stump could steady it for him to aim, and then cycle the action. "The air rifles, why?"

"They're our most effective killer," Michael smiled.

"Bullshit," he called. Kenneth didn't believe the farmer.

"I'm serious. Rabbits, wood pigeons, and squirrels. Those pellet guns have put more food on the table than the firearms. A pellet won't do a lot to those hungry bastards, but a pellet in a rabbit means we have a bullet or some buckshot to put into their stinking flesh. You're welcome to take an airgun, might get you some fresh meat if you think you can handle it?" Michael said and picked up a rifle and handed it to Kenneth. "That's a break barrel, you should be able to handle it with your… little disadvantage."

Kenneth took the rifle, compared to his old service rifle, it felt like a toy. He handed it back to Michael. "Probably better you keep hold of it, if I can take this?" Kenneth held up the hatchet.

"Sure, but I'll be honest Kenneth, I think you should stay with us. You've been gone for weeks, they were already in bad shape so either they got help elsewhere or, well, they didn't and you don't want to see it."

"I'm a good soldier, I follow orders and I do my duty. As much as I'd love to stay, I can't," Kenneth shot the idea down quickly. He wasn't looking forward to returning with little to show for his absence, but he had to return.

The two men walked out of the storeroom and Michael reached into his pocket producing an old car key which he handed to Kenneth. Walking across the playground there it sat, the promised blue Ford Fiesta. It was an old model. It was beaten up, but Michael had assured him it ran well.

"Can I ask, why with all the cars in the world, did you take and store that thing?" he asked. Kenneth was grateful, but couldn't understand with all the abandoned vehicles around, the little Fiesta made the cut.

"The Blue Beaut? It was my wife's. If I had my way, we'd have a playground full of Land Rovers, but it was already here. The boot is full, as promised."

Kenneth was ready to go, Jake appeared with a map which he sprawled out on the bonnet in front of Kenneth. "This is us, that is Lewes, I couldn't see a Wellworth marked on there, but I guess you know where it is once you get there."

Kenneth nodded. He thought to himself Jake would have made a good soldier; he followed orders, showed initiative, was intelligent, in good shape, and if he was half as good with that rifle as everyone said, he was deadly. "If they've been reinforced, I can see about getting you some resources."

"That's a kind offer, but I think we're probably better off out of the way, unnoticed," he replied. Michael didn't think Kenneth would be successful, but didn't like the idea of their tiny village attracting any further attention. The initial interest in having military support had gone. They'd seen a little more of the world and heard a little more of what Kenneth had to say. Any armed forces still left, were as alone as they were.

Kenneth smiled back at Michael, and they shook hands.

"I hope to see you around," he said and Kenneth did. These were good people, and he was glad to see that with all the death and destruction, they had made it this far. He waved at a few people, patted Jake on the back then climbed into the car. No matter what he did to adjust the seat, he couldn't get comfortable. Much to Michael's amusement.

The gates were opened and Kenneth drove the little Fiesta out and through the empty village.

Chapter 15

Kenneth's frustration was growing. He'd been driving for nearly two hours but was a little over fifteen miles from Nutwood. Anywhere near a town was swarmed by the dead, the roads often impassable. He knew there must be a safe route through, there had to be. He just had to bloody find it.

He pulled up on a country road between an open field and a neglected wood. The hatchet in the driver's door compartment and the map folded over on the front passenger seat. Kenneth moved his finger around various routes, almost all paths he had marked as danger zones from his previous failed attempts. With two hands and a rifle, he may have been brave enough to attempt at least one of them, but he didn't enjoy either luxury any more. Before meeting that group, that evil fucking bitch who took his hand. Before that night, he had travelled this diseased land successfully. Even when he knew there was no hope out there, he hadn't given up. He had a purpose, to get supplies to his men, his friends. He was much more than a day late, and infinitely more than a dollar short, but he was determined to see them again.

The car had got their attention when it passed them a few hundred metres back; they didn't have a hope of catching it until it stopped and pulled over. Quietly with determination they moved through the undergrowth, closing the distance quickly.

Kenneth thought he had it. He traced the route carefully with his finger; it looked good, avoided by some distance the overrun areas, and could be as little as an hour away. He hadn't noticed them approach from the rear and surround his car. Then came the tap on the window. Kenneth froze, unsure of what to do next. He stared at the map, quickly thinking through his options. The hatchet was close, but to get it out of the door compartment would be awkward. The engine was still running, however the small car couldn't pull the skin off a rice pudding, but perhaps that was his only genuine option. Slowly Kenneth rose his head, bringing his hand and stump up into view. He looked round to the driver's window. A creature wouldn't be as polite as to knock. He first saw the rifle barrel pressed against the glass, he recognised it as that of an L85A3. Then he saw the face smiling back at him. Liam hadn't been close to Kenneth, but it was such a small team they knew each other well enough. Kenneth rolled down the window and smiled.

"Kenneth, you big bastard, where the fuck have you been?" he growled. There was a tone to his voice, easily missed as sarcasm, but Kenneth picked up on it.

"You know Liam, just chilling out. What are you guys doing here? Is Wellworth still standing?" Kenneth looked around and recognised the other faces peering into the car, interested in the occupant.

"Kenny, I guess we need a little talk. Not here, we were tracking a herd of those fuckers and we lost them half-a-mile back," Liam said. He was anxious, this was no time for a tearful reunion.

"You boys are slipping," Kenneth commented and smiled, relieved to see some of his friends again.

"Maybe so, but we have digs and they're better than this dogging spot. I'll hop in and we'll meet the boys back at the house," he replied. There were collective groans from the other men, wishing they'd volunteered their navigation skills for a free ride. Liam jumped into the front passenger seat. "Nice wheels, couldn't you find something older, shittier, or smaller?"

Kenneth manoeuvred. "Wellworth?"

"It got in, not straightaway, but it worked its way through enough of us that the lab was fucked. The major stayed, everyone else alive and not infected left," Liam said bluntly.

"I should have been there." Kenneth lamented. He was sad, embarrassed that he hadn't made it back to make a difference.

"Looks like you were busy, wanking accident?" Liam gestured to Kenneth's stump, trying to lighten the mood.

"It's not dull out here, is it? There are more than just the stupid ones we used to poke in the eye at the fence. How many got out?" Kenneth concentrated on the narrow country road, waiting for odd casual signal from Liam.

"We were a few men down when we left, only a few civilians made it out. We lost a few more of ours out here, but the civilians haven't done so well," Liam made it obvious that was all he was willing to say. "Just here mate, then follow the track."

It was only a few miles away. Had his former comrades not intercepted him, Kenneth would probably have driven past the vast house. It was large, luxurious, and surrounded by open land, only the near waist-high length of the grass providing any concealment on the approach.

"Pull up for a second." Liam said. Kenneth obliged the command, Liam got out of the car and signalled ahead to an unseen sentry. A loud whistle back confirmed it was safe to proceed. Back in the car, Liam tapped the dashboard. "Up to the house, park it next to one of the Bentleys."

Kenneth was intrigued as they neared the house. It was a grand stately home, worth tens of millions before the world had ended. Now a bunch of squaddies used it like a clubhouse. The Bentleys were nice, but the two Ferraris really caught Kenneth's attention, as did the Lamborghini. It made the Tesla next to it look boring. "I feel like I should park this in the river, not next to those things."

"They're useless, no space for loot, and you try finding a road you can go faster than forty on. They're his pride and joy though, he loves them more than anything," Liam criticised. He resented the cars, amongst other things.

The men got out of the car, Kenneth reached back for his hatchet.

"You won't need that, Kenny, leave it in the motor," Liam was telling, not asking.

Kenneth obliged as several soldiers and civilians watched them. Kenneth didn't recognise any of them. "Who are these guys?"

"We weren't the only soldiers aimlessly wandering the Great British countryside looking for a home. We have some engineers, two cabbage heads, and a few weekend warriors."

"And civvies?" Kenneth asked. He knew civilians had survived and was surprised to not have seen more of them with the soldiers.

"I don't know, maybe a dozen," Liam said, being purposefully vague.

Kenneth didn't like the sound of that maybe. The fancy digs were one thing, but where was the discipline? He looked around at the faces staring back at him from the numerous windows or standing in the courtyard. The soldiers he didn't know looked at him with distrust. They may have only had their little group for over a week, but they had faced much together. The civilians were harder to read, each face plain and lacking emotion. Then he noticed. The civilians were all women. Maybe there were men inside and out of view, but the numbers tied in with Liam's maybe.

"What are the current orders?" Kenneth questioned. He needed to know what exactly this was.

Liam led Kenneth into the main building. "We're going to need a chat with Charles."

Kenneth felt nervous. This wasn't a military outpost carrying on the fight, this was a group of armed men doing what they needed to survive. He was led through to the kitchen. Like the rest of the house, it was huge and opulent. The marble work surfaces alone cost as much as Kenneth's parents' house. They had stacked boxes of food and supplies at the far end. An armed soldier stood watch, and then there was Charles. In his thirties, he was in a mismatched military uniform, a non-standard issue handgun hung from his left hip, and a pump-action shotgun was slung across his back. If he was military, he had taken his own path.

"Charles, this is Lance Corporal Kenneth Addo. He was with us at Wellworth, he's a good soldier, an outstanding soldier."

Charles turned to face them, a beaming smile on his smooth, well cared for face. He cleared six-feet, with broad shoulders and a muscular physique. Had he played rugby, Kenneth imagined he'd have been a prop. He approached, left hand outstretched. Through habit, Kenneth stretched out his stump. An awkward exchange saw the hand and stump shake lightly. "Kenneth, will you be joining us?"

"What is us?" Kenneth asked. He didn't like this situation, it felt wrong.

"We're alone and we've got to fend for ourselves. You've probably heard the radio broadcasts, that fucking automated message chirping on about them coming back. Maybe they will, maybe they've found somewhere jollier than here and will never return. Either way, they are of no help to me now, or you, or anyone."

Kenneth looked Charles up and down as he spoke. He was posh, he could've been a commissioned officer, but he just didn't seem like a military man. His uniform didn't match and missed several key features. He was a civilian, playing soldier, playing commander.

"This is my house Kenneth, it's been in my family for many years. I have a lot of food, a great wine cellar, a small arsenal of shotguns, rifles, and some more exotic pieces, but I was alone. After the staff left or turned, it was just me. I couldn't keep this to myself, however much I wanted to," Charles said. *Charles definitely wasn't a sharer.* "I was doing okay, but between the looters and the feeders, I was under constant attack. Then a few abandoned soldiers found their way here, and we teamed up. We strategised and together, we found more supplies and your people. Now we have a unit of crack soldiers, a safe headquarters, and we're set. We perform missions on the very ground that the government is too gutless to tread. That's us. Want in?"

Wellworth was all but gone, but the major, maybe he should try to reach him. Nutwood was appealing, kind people who could use him. Charles? He was a rich boy who still thought he was wealthy. Why Liam and the other soldiers would take his shit was beyond him.

"Where are the male civilians?" Kenneth had to know, Liam quietly groaned and turned away.

"I provide the house and supplies. You soldiers supply the muscle. The women supply, themselves. We're not a damn charity and the men provide nothing," he replied. Charles was proud of his hard-nosed approach. "We can't patrol the neighbouring towns and villages protecting those few who survive for no payment. We accept food, guns and other things."

"So, the women, they're slaves?"

"No, they're free to leave at any time after they have repaid their debt." Charles said.

"Out into the hands of those hungry bastards? Liam, how can you be okay with this?" Kenneth asked shocked. He was exasperated, he wasn't close with Liam but he thought he knew him better than this.

"Kenny, your beloved army abandoned us. Left us to die. Your moral code is useless out here and you fucking know it. This is the good life, for us and for them," Liam was trying to convince himself as much as Kenneth. He still wore the uniform, but he wasn't a member of Her Majesty's armed forces any more.

"It's no better than rape," he spat. The judgement in Kenneth's voice cut through the room, the tension could be felt by all.

"It's better than starving to death or being torn apart. Kenny, stop thinking this is the old world. You've been out there, how much death have you seen? You lost a hand for fuck's sake," Liam had a touch of fear in his voice. This arrangement was simple and there was safety in numbers.

"Kenneth, you're not comfortable. That's fine, you can go. But don't you dare judge me for surviving," Charles said. He was calm, but it was obvious he was insulted. With money and power all his life, he wasn't used to being challenged. "So, feel free to take your monkey arse out of my fucking house?"

Kenneth was already disappointed in these people and what they had allowed themselves to become. Now this fuck, thinking he's in charge because he had twenty bedrooms, is a fucking racist. "Excuse me, would you care to rephrase that?"

"What? This is my house, I will speak however I damn well like! You will do well to get out of here now before I have your one-handed nigger arse shot." Charles puffed out his chest and placed a hand on his pistol, ready to draw it.

Kenneth looked to Liam, he was uncomfortable but was siding with Charles. He knew which side his bread was buttered.

"Kenny, just go mate, please," Liam said. The resignation was in Liam's voice, he didn't want to shoot Kenneth but knew he was moments away from doing so.

"I'm going," Kenneth replied. He marched himself out the way he came in. Charles signalled Liam to follow Kenneth.

"Kenny, life has changed. You've got to change with it. There isn't a good or a bad, we just have to do what we have to, to keep on going," he told him. Liam didn't believe the words himself, he was disgusted for even trying to justify what they did.

"Liam, tell yourself what you need to, but there is good and bad in this world, if you're not one you're the other. Look after yourself and try not to hurt too many people," he said in response. Kenneth got to his car, the boot was open, the food all gone. The fuckers. He didn't question it or protest. There was no point, they wouldn't deny it, they wouldn't need to. He felt like smashing up the fleet of super-cars but doubted that posh psychopath would let him leave if he did. They'd either beat the shit out of him or take him out back and shoot him. At least they'd left him the hatchet.

He got in the car and drove. His former comrades were marching up the driveway, he rolled down his window, "You're all better than this. All of you."

No one could look him in the eye. They knew he was right but couldn't bring themselves to admit it.

Chapter 16

Kenneth had to see for himself. He couldn't take Liam's word as the truth, not now. The lad had gone wrong and was obviously only interested in his own wellbeing. He knew how bad things were heading when he left Wellworth. Half a dozen lads deserting wouldn't have been unrealistic. The drive had been long and arduous. The car wasn't fit for going off-road, and sometimes that had been the only option. Every time he crossed a field or climbed a verge, he was certain he'd get hooked up on an unseen rock or an axle might snap. He hadn't attempted to engage any of the feeders he came across, there were too many to make a difference. The herds had been growing, their frequency increasing. He could only speculate with the fall of the rescue camps more concentrations of the dead existed and wandered together. They hadn't saved survivors with the camps; they recruited soldiers for the ranks of the monsters.

When he arrived at Wellworth, Kenneth had wished he hadn't. The mass of feeders at the fence line kept him back. As much as he concentrated and stared, there were no soldiers patrolling the grounds. The OP looked unoccupied, and there were no signs of movement in the main building. Two lights left on, but that was it. He thought maybe he saw a figure move, but he couldn't be sure. Liam was right. Maybe the major was still there, but even if he was, how would he get inside with so many feeders lining up for a meal? It was useless. He was useless.

After looking at all Wellworth, the death surrounding it, the knowledge of all of those innocents who died or were turned because he wasn't there, he decided he would head back to Nutwood. He should never have left the small, kind community of survivors. They were resourceful people, lucky to a point but hard workers who he could help. He turned the car around and started the drive back. It frustrated him, his blood boiled as he thought of those inside who had died. He knew he was to blame, these rotten fuckers would never had got inside on his watch. Then he saw his punchbag.

An old one hobbled towards his car. It was in terrible shape. It was male, had been shot several times in its torso, and its face and hair badly scorched. It had been in a fight. It was hard to tell if it had won, but the fact it was still standing confirmed it hadn't lost.

This stinking fucking cunt has no right to exist. It was death, not life, so it should bloody stay dead.

Kenneth stopped the car and got out, the hatchet grasped tightly in his hand. He ran towards it as he swung the hatchet striking it in the neck knocking it to the floor. He struck it again and again in the neck until the head dislodged and separated from the body. Still its teeth gnashed at him. Tossing the bloodstained hatchet to the floor, Kenneth started stomping on its head with his boot. Harder and harder he struck it until the skull cracked and popped open. Grey blood and gore leaked onto the road.

Moments passed before Kenneth composed himself. *Now it was proper fucking dead.*

Kenneth noticed the noise of feeders approaching. His grunting and exertion surely attracted them to the gruesome scene. He felt better and didn't give the corpse a second look as he grabbed the hatchet and jumped back into his car.

He was going back to Nutwood, he could still do his duty and protect the good, kind people of that village.

63

Chapter 17

Jake walked through the quiet village street, listening for any sign that he wasn't alone. The road was narrow, having originally been built to serve horse-drawn carts rather than modern motor vehicles. They had removed most vehicles, leaving only sporadic cars to provide cover and concealment in case they were caught out in the open during an attack. A dense woodland protected the entire village, with vast fields beyond that. It helped slow the stream of unwanted, hungry and murderous visitors. Stopping to listen every few feet, it was a relief when only the wind rustling through the leaves could be heard. Since they had set up camp in the old school, he had performed this patrol many times. Young, fit and able were his qualifying skills, his ability with the rifle a bonus. Rarely had he been presented with the need to put that sharpshooter skill to the test, but Michael had drilled into him the importance of not becoming complacent. They both knew the numbers the feeders roamed in; but even a single creature would be fatal if you let it get too close.

Movement up a few hundred yards ahead caught his eye and instinctively he dropped to his knee, .22 rifle pointed forwards. Stillness. Silence. But he'd definitely seen something, he was sure. Then he saw the figure stumbling down the road, pursued by two other creatures. Then a third. With the iron sights on the rifle, he couldn't make out more than the silhouettes of the targets at this range. He could wait. There were only four of them. He could drop them when they got to fifty yards and not have to reload. He tensed up and controlled his breathing as his heart pumped wildly, getting the better of him. One hundred and fifty yards, and a fifth appeared, giving its determined pursuit. One hundred yards, nearly there. They tempted him to take a quick shot, but he stuck to his plan and waited. Nearly there. He still couldn't clearly make out the feeders, but it didn't matter. With the first in his sights, he began to gently depress the trigger. Suddenly the creature swung at one of the following monsters with a hatchet, taking a slither of scalp clean off as they both tumbled to the floor. *What the fuck?* The first scrambled back to its feet. It was a big bastard. *Kenneth?* Jake turned his attention to the pursuing feeders, slowly sending the small .22 calibre bullets into his targets. As the small rounds struck their victims, the creatures dropped to the floor and ceased moving. He waited a moment for the last to reach his desired range and a single shot through the bridge of its nose knocked it to the floor.

Kenneth looked forward to Jake with a beaming smile, then back at the handiwork of his friend. He bent over, trying to catch his breath as Jake approached, loading a fresh ten round magazine into the rifle.

"For Gods' sake, Kenny. That car survived the end of the world, but it couldn't survive a Welshman. I can't believe you lost it."

"Lost?" Kenneth panted, slowly getting air back into his lungs. "I know exactly where that piece of shit broke down on me. It's about four miles that way, just follow the trail of those dead bastards laying on the floor," Kenneth gestured back up the road, still wheezing.

"You okay?"

"Bloody knackered."

Jake handed him a bottle of water, which Kenneth gulped down before handing back empty.

"Are there any more of those things following?"

"You put three down in addition to my one?" Kenneth's breath had returned, Jake nodded. "That should be all of them then."

Michael and Jake's father appeared, running towards the men, wielding shotguns. They slowed when they saw Kenneth, who gave them his big smile and a wave as they got closer.

"We heard the gunshots, are you two okay?" the vicar asked, to which Kenneth and Jake nodded.

"I wasn't sure we'd see you again. Glad you came back. I take it things weren't well?" Michael looked sympathetically at the tired man before him.

"No, it's all gone. Just the dead and thieves in that direction. Never go that way," he replied. His mood changed to a more sombre one, Michael knew not to press him.

"Mikey, I got three bastards, right in the fucking face!" Jake was excited to tell of his kills, then looked at his religious and disapproving father. "Sorry dad."

"Let's get you lads back in St. Joe's, looks like Kenneth needs to work off the debt of a lost mint condition 1997 Ford Fiesta."

As the men walked back, Michael followed, glancing back regularly up the road. He knew Kenneth wouldn't bring trouble to them, but he wanted to make sure no wandering corpses were making themselves at home in his village.

Chapter 18

The ship was enormous, but Jenny could feel every wave. Having lived on the HMS Reckoning for nearly two weeks after a spell on the much smaller HMS Belfast, she still hated being on the ocean. The HMS Reckoning was much like several of the ships in the fleet, liberated from countries that had fallen to the plague. Its new crew named the Reckoning after being taken from Naval Station Rota in Spain. Several teams of Special Boat Service soldiers and Naval personnel secured the Reckoning and several smaller vessels before joining with the main fleet in the English Channel. The Juan Carlos I had been the pride of Spanish Navy, but as mainland Europe descended into chaos, the Spanish government evacuated to the mountains and old cold war bunkers. The shipyards were abandoned. The interim prime minister and her advisors reached out to the Spanish Government, but contact was sporadic and didn't fill anyone with hope. The ships weren't being used, and the prime minister decided it was better to seek forgiveness than ask permission. The newly named HMS Reckoning was better than most ships in the British fleet, modern and plenty of room for the refugees and personnel who would call it home.

Jenny found it more comfortable than the HMS Belfast, the former World War II light cruiser had been decommissioned over fifty years ago and served as a tourist attraction on the Thames. It was small, cramped, but seaworthy. Decommissioned ships and those borrowed from neighbours made up nearly half of the military class ships at the British Government's disposal. They lacked the most basic of creature comforts, and safety was questionable, but all agreed it was better to be on an eighty-year-old vessel than stuck on the mainland with the feeders.

Before the plague, Jenny had worked as a project manager within a government department overseeing infrastructure upgrades. It had been boring work, endless meetings to decide the best company to buy concrete from or agreeing budgets for portable toilets. As she hit her thirties, she had hoped to have been doing more interesting things with her life. She had never expected the world to have taken such a turn. Her organisational skills were put to use by the interim government. Now she worked with a small team, ensuring those aboard the many ships in the armada didn't starve to death and received all the care they required to survive. Many personnel were families of those in service, high-ranking politicians or, like Jenny, had been lucky enough to be deemed useful. Most evacuated civilians that didn't fit into the friends and family box were put aboard a civilian vessel.

Much like the military ships, ferry, cargo and cruise ships had been rapidly pressed into service to save the civilians that hadn't succumbed. They kept this flotilla separate from the military and government vessels for security. Each of the civilian boats had rapidly become their own little, and sometimes large, communities. Each enjoyed a distinct personality, taking on the characteristics of the ship. Those on a luxury cruise liner felt a great sense of entitlement, compared to those in the bay of a cargo ship who were just grateful to be alive. Jenny often had to deal with the heads of each ship. Negotiating supplies, manpower or civilian transfer. These meetings would often become heated. There were not enough supplies, no manpower to spare, and nobody wanted more mouths to feed on their boat. Jenny was sure that if it wasn't for the naval vessels patrolling between the vessels, piracy would have taken hold and half of the ships would have sunk the other half.

To be called into a meeting to discuss the status of the civilian ships wasn't unusual, she had an insight through her dealings. It was unusual for the prime minister to be in attendance. Jenny was taken aback as she entered the briefing room. Despite the PM's attendance, only an army general and naval admiral were with her. Normally, a dozen faces from various logistics departments would be in attendance. If the PM had shown up, it was normally for a quick photo opportunity before she was whisked away. Normally a low-ranking representative of the navy would be in attendance if only to make sure they knew what was going on. Never had she seen the two highest ranking members of the remaining armed forces show up. General Stuart McKinley had been put in charge of the remaining army units, and the marines who would normally be under the direction of the navy. Admiral Grant Hollis oversaw his ships and those of the civilians that made up their armada. These two men were vastly different, with the general having been on the ground in various war zones, many times with his men under fire. Whereas the admiral, much like the PM, found himself over promoted through the death or disappearance of his colleagues.

"Jenny Fairbrass, please come in and take a seat," she called. The prime minister was in her late forties, she had a welcoming smile but was an experienced politician. Before the outbreak, she was going nowhere in a party that had no hope of ever taking power. She had overplayed her hand a few times too many against the various leaders of her party over the years and was pushed to the sidelines as a punishment for her failed power grabs. Margaret Norville was an MP before society collapsed. Now she was the prime minister she insisted that she addressed by her title, not her name. Now she controlled what was left of Great Britain and wanted everyone to remember that. Jenny accepted the PM's outstretched hand and shook it.

"As one of our logistics coordinators, I'm sure you're aware of the strain we find ourselves under?" she stated. The tone was firm and authoritative, Jenny nodded. "Which ship has been the most troublesome amongst the civilians?"

"Troublesome?" she repeated. They were all troublesome, scared, desperate people are.

"Who needs the most, provides the least and, in your opinion closest to breaking?" The admiral asked as he took over and the PM sat back.

"That would be the Angel of Vengeance," Jenny replied. She had dealt with them many times, often ending in a shouting match when she wasn't able to provide what they needed.

The admiral looked over a list of ships, running his finger up and down the A4 printed sheets, beginning to look confused.

"That's not the ship's official name, it's something Greek. But nobody uses it. It has three-hundred and seventy something civilians onboard," Jenny offered.

"The Carman Spyros?" The Admiral said. He was satisfied he had found it.

"That sounds right," Jenny nodded.

"We need to get a package onboard, we need a familiar face to get it on there," the general took over. He seemed resigned to this course of action, unlike the admiral who seemed happy, nearly excited.

"You understand how close we are to extinction. Law and order fell on the mainland, it's beginning to do the same out here. Food and fresh water are perilously close to running out. I need to do what's best for the many, even if it means hurting the few," the prime minister explained. She needed Jenny to see the situation as it was, sacrifices had to be made.

"I don't know what you mean," Jenny lied. She knew, of course she did.

"Cut the shit, Jenny. I don't like it, but we can't maintain our current situation. We need to reduce the demand on our limited resources and set an example. People are pissed off and complacent. They're not grateful to survive, they're angry because they want more. If we don't take action now, we risk losing all of the civilians, and then what is the point? The Angel of Vengeance, three-hundred, and seventy people?"

"Three hundred and seventy-nine civilians, ten military, and ten sailors. No high-value personnel or VIP's," The admiral stated. He had already seen the numbers.

"Under four hundred? Good. Not too many, but it will make a difference. Is the package ready?"

The general nodded.

"We're not going to abandon them, we can't," Jenny protested. She hadn't let herself believe the full extent of what they were actually implying.

"Jenny, you're here because you're intelligent, dependable, and pragmatic. Without this one ship, the rest of the fleet will have one less mouth to feed, but that's not enough. We're losing hearts and minds as we're seen as aloof and out of touch. They've forgotten how to be scared and subservient. We need to remind them so we can retain authority," she tried to explain to her. The welcoming smile had long since been replaced with a hard stare.

"We need you to use your normal channels to get the package on board. Our men will do the rest," The general said, as he started scribbling notes that he kept to himself.

They would not abandon these people, they were going to murder them. When the evacuations began, they had taken tough decisions. Jenny had seen many infected executed, towns bombed and survivors left to die. She had always told herself this was necessary; the group was more important than the individual. Is destroying this one ship any different from levelling a village? Is it morally less acceptable than leaving people to certain death? She knew there were people on the ship who didn't deserve to die, but how many were on other vessels that deserved the best chance of surviving? She didn't need to answer these questions of ethics; it wasn't her decision. And that's what she told herself. It was just a package; she didn't need to know what it was. They weren't telling her because they needed her to enact the plan; they needed her to make sure she kept her mouth shut afterwards in case questions were asked.

"You understand how important this and your discretion are?" The PM asked. She tried to force herself to smile but it appeared fake, more vile than Jenny had previously noticed.

Jenny nodded.

"You can wait outside whilst arrangements are made," she ordered. The three conspirators waited for Jenny to stand before they talked amongst themselves, finalising their deadly plans. As instructed, Jenny left the room in a daze. What had she agreed to do?

Chapter 19

The news of the bonus crate of supplies had been greatly received and spread quickly amongst the inhabitants of the Angel of Vengeance. Civilians and crewman alike lined the side of the unimpressive cargo ship as they carefully lifted the container into place. Women, children, young and old, all excited by the prospect of a little extra. Some hoped for clean clothes, maybe a chocolate bar or bottle of Whiskey to drink away their woes. Many a former smoker fantasised about that cigarette which could shortly be resting on their lips.

The sea was blissfully calm, but that didn't stop Jenny from vomiting over the side of the smaller boat as the load ascended into the sky by the skilled crew on the Angel. She wasn't sure if it was her motion sickness or the guilt of what she knew was going to happen. Jenny looked up at the smiling faces. A child waved at the boat and Jenny waved back. The crew wasn't one she had worked with before. Unusually, they were armed with pistols hidden beneath their coats, but not so well hidden their shape couldn't be seen up close, the impression bulging through their clothes. It wasn't a regular occurrence that she would accompany drop offs, but it happened often enough that her presence would help remove suspicion. Just seeing her face and dropping off crates to other ships on the same trip would remove doubt in most minds that the disaster to befall the Angel of Vengeance wasn't part of a government plot. She stood looking up at the eyes staring down at her, trying to force a reassuring smile and hold back the tears before a crew member emerged with a satellite phone and handed it to Jenny.

"Hello captain, we've got another two stops to make so hopefully your people will enjoy the extras. I'm afraid there isn't much food, a few confectionary items, and non-critical luxuries. Some cigarettes, alcohol - but not too much, and civilian clothing. Hopefully, they will give your people some comfort," Jenny offered, then stood and listened. The praise and gratitude on the other end of the phone added to her nausea. "You're welcome," Jenny added and handed the phone back to the nearest crew member. "Can we get moving now?"

"Don't look so worried, it's gone well, you've done your job. We'll head off in two minutes in two hours you'll be back on the Reckoning sipping warm cocoa," he assured her. He took the phone and disappeared back into steering house.

Jenny stared at the Vengeance as all eyes were on her little supply boat. Those eyes hadn't noticed in the fading light the four-man team of SBS soldiers as they pulled up next to the larger vessel in their two Klepper canoes. They had approached silently and were barely visible on the dark sea as those hopeful souls dreamed of the goodies in the pallet, not the nightmare that was about to occur. Two civilians, bought and paid for aboard the ship, had thrown four lines down for the SBS team to climb. Their canoes secured to the side of the ship, they began ascending the ropes. It should have been hard and tiring work for most, but these special forces soldiers were at peak fitness. They heaved themselves onboard and were readying their silenced MP5 submachine guns before the crate had touched down. They rewarded the two civilians for their treachery with a knife blade in the base of their skulls, before being thrown overboard. The splashes from their bodies hitting the unforgiving sea could have attracted attention if it wasn't for the excitement on the opposite side of the ship. There were to be no witnesses, no one to testify of this conspiracy to commit mass murder, perpetrated by the only authority these people had.

The four-man team expertly navigated the deck, staying out of sight of anyone who might raise the alarm at seeing four armed men dressed in black when they shouldn't have been there. The wheelhouse had just two crew members along with the captain, all other hands were eagerly awaiting the new bounty on the deck. The four-man team entered silently. The three seamen were laughing and joking, excited at the prospect of a few luxuries that their colleagues would secure for them. The three silenced 9mm rounds entered the men's heads with a crack; blood, bone and brain matter fizzed into the air. Before the bodies had hit the ground the four men in black began their true task, navigation and communication equipment was expertly sabotaged. The satellite phone was still in the Captain's hand as the soldier's boot smashed into it repeatedly until the mass of broken plastic was barely recognisable. The collection of panels were slowly, ripped from their spots, broken wires replaced the blinking lights. Within a minute the ship was effectively useless, with no way to talk to anyone else, steer or navigate. It would be dead in the water.

On the main deck, the large crate touched down to cheers from the gathered crowd. Several of the ship's crew stepped forward and unfastened the large supporting straps freeing the cargo from the ship's crane. Two men stepped forward with crowbars and began trying to free the front from the nails hastily driven into the large wooden box. Each successful shove of the crowbar opening the crate a little greeted with a cheer from the crowd as they continued to work themselves up in anticipation of what goodies they were about to receive.

The four-man team had exited the wheel house and quickly made their way back to their exit point. They all knew the drill and carried on their duty without so much as a word to each other. The lead soldier stopped and dropped to his knee, signalling the others to do likewise. Two soldiers lazily walked out in front of them, chatting aimlessly to each other. The poor souls not realising they were between a special forces team and their extraction. The lead SBS soldier raised his MP5SD submachine gun and fired four silenced rounds in quick succession, downing the two men. The small team paused, then quickly continued on their path.

The crate was nearly open as the gathered crowd edged closer, jostling for position. Whatever bounty was about to be unveiled, it would be in too short supply and every man, woman and child were determined to get something. The mood was jovial, excitement and smiles showed on every face.

The four SBS troops started descending their rope lines towards the water and the waiting canoes, displaying strength and athleticism they boarded their two-man crafts. Paddling to a holding position fifty metres from the Vengeance, several other small, darkly coloured craft waited, encircling the ship. Each Klepper or Rigid Hull Inflatable Boat was silent, the men on board armed with silenced weapons and marksman rifles, ready for action.

The crowd cheered and screamed in delight. Had they remained silent, they may have heard the scratching. The groaning. The slow thud of rotten grey flesh pounding the inch thick wooden wall that separated the occupants of the crate and their fleshy treat that was so close. The front popped open, those civilians and crew at the front surged forward, those at the back with no chance of claiming a share cheered on friends and relatives closer to the action. The confusion was instant. In the crate only waste, empty tins and bottles, they had lined the bottom with bricks. Those at the front fell silent, trying to comprehend what cruel joke had been played on them.

Then the first creature leapt forward. Screams replaced cheers as several more grey monsters sprung from the darkness of the crate. Angry chipped teeth, starved of flesh for too long, wasted no time in tasting the blood of the poor souls assembled. People began running in every direction as more of the dead spilled from the crate, chasing down those closest to the action, too shocked and scared to defend themselves. Two of the soldiers brought their rifles into action, firing towards the attackers, rounds at best, ineffectively striking the creature's torsos, at worst striking the innocent people closest to them. The two slowly moved back as they fired, determined to give themselves space as they desperately looked for answers, for help, for a plan. More sporadic gunfire could be heard above the panicking crowd.

"Fuck this, let's swim for it!" The soldier screamed as his colleague, he could see it was already hopeless. They'd not faced these creatures since the evacuation, and then they had been fortunate enough to engage through a barbed-wire fence. They were everywhere, at least a dozen, probably more. In less than a minute they had caused chaos, bloodied civilians and crew ran in every direction being chased down by these angry, starving bastards. Both soldiers had their backs against the rail, the black ocean calmly splashing against the ship below them.

The first soldier's head popped open, pieces of eye and cheek-bone flying forward as his body staggered a single step and slumped to the ground, his colleague instinctively crouched. He blindly fired towards the mass of feeders and people in front of him, no idea what was happening, just knowing he should do something.

One of the SBS soldiers on an inflatable raft looked through his scope for his second target. He had fired five times and missed with every bullet before the fifth shot. The sea was calm, but it was far from ideal on such a small boat, even for a skilled marksman. With the noise and confusion on the ship, those onboard did not understand the threat bobbing up and down in the water so close to them. The SBS soldiers were all looking for armed targets to take out of the fight and survivors jumping overboard. Several splashes at the ship's aft alerted a nearby Klepper canoe, and it's two troops. They paddled towards the site and three humans waved and pleaded for help. The response was swift and brutal as they were peppered with silenced 9mm bullets until they moved no more. The canoe casually paddled back out to the holding line and awaited their next piece of business.

Jenny was four hundred metres away as her boat continued pulling away. Each gunshot or scream of horror filled her with more guilt. She held her mouth before running to the side of the boat and vomiting into the sea as the crew members onboard watched the Vengeance as it descended into hell.

"You did well," a voice said. Jenny didn't see the man who was standing behind her in shadow, as if he had appeared from nowhere. She stared at the dark sea and didn't turn to talk, she didn't want to look at anyone.

"It's an awful thing, there must have been another way," she muttered as she fought back the tears, but a single one had escaped and rolled down her cheek and into the sea.

"I'm really sorry, but we all have our orders. You had yours, they had theirs, and I have mine," The man said. He raised a silenced pistol and pointed it at the back of Jenny's head. She froze, she couldn't see or hear the weapon, but suddenly she knew what was about to happen. They couldn't let her live, she knew too much, enough to break this so-called government, take down these remnants of humanity. She was a fool.

She never heard the shot, quick and to the back of her head, killing her instantly as brain and bone fragments splashed into the sea. The man put his pistol away and threw her body overboard before joining the others in watching the show.

Another crew member approached him. "Ready to make the call?" he asked. He was handed a radio and nodded.

"Mayday, mayday. This is a crew member on the Angel of Vengeance. We're under attack! Repeat, we are under attack! Several civilians have weapons and are attacking us. They have been protecting infected. We have many dead and injured, the infected are everywhere. Please help!" He nodded and one of his men fired two bursts from a rifle close to the radio. He handed the radio back. "That should be enough. Let's go, we don't have to watch this."

"Angel of Vengeance, this is the HMS Dasher, we are two miles off. Evacuate survivors, we're instructed to initiate the fleet safety protocol. Our Wildcats will engage within two minutes. Anyone onboard will be deemed hostile," came the response. The SOS call was answered nearly immediately by the nearby destroyer. The fleet safety protocol dictated any ship deemed infected was to be destroyed. They had shown a kindness by giving those on the Vengeance an opportunity to escape, one they wouldn't be allowed to take even if they had heard the broadcast.

The screams onboard the Angel of Vengeance had died down, those onboard either dead, injured, or hiding below deck. The surrounding craft and canoes had made quick work of the handful of those desperate enough to jump overboard, many withdrew slowly, only a few canoes covertly remained.

The first anti-ship missile struck the front of the ship's stern, the second the bow before another three missiles struck everything in between. The Sea Venom missiles were overkill against a civilian vessel, but the ship had to be destroyed as did those on board. The two Wildcat helicopters began peppering the deck of the ship with machine gun fire as flames rose from below. Those onboard were surely already dead, and the ship was sinking fast, but it was clear there would be no survivors.

The remaining Special Boat Service troops paddled away. An awful job well done.

Chapter 20

The prime minister's cabin had been nicknamed number ten. It was larger than most, enjoying a separate sleeping and living quarters, with an office and briefing area for her to perform her duties. The furniture was almost as basic as any other cabin on the ship. They had requisitioned a few luxuries, some art from the real number ten on Downing Street, a few bottles of expensive single malt scotch, a proper bed, and an extensive collection of books. Nothing outrageous, and not one person begrudged her these small things.

She sat on a hard metal chair at her desk in the office, sipping a glass of the single malt, reading the latest status reports when there was a knock on the door. "Enter," she called. She was used to interruptions at all hours, but she was expecting this one.

The general entered and sat down, pouring himself a large scotch and knocking it back. "It's done. Reports confirm no survivors. Public comms are already putting out the official story."

The PM smiled, not happy but satisfied. "We'll play on it for a week, start cracking down on any insurrection, and blame the Vengeance for lack of supplies. Empower the civilians to self-police, that should see a few of the silly buggers finish each other off. Hopefully that'll buy us some time before we can clear out the Isle of Wight. How is that going?"

"Slowly. Of the 40,000 or so who we believed remained, estimates put the feeders at around 10,000. So far it looks at least double in both counts," the general answered. He was glad to be discussing something less murderous and more militaristic.

"Can't you speed it along? What do you need?" she pressed. The PM was impatient.

"Besides carpet bombing the entire island, or launching a Trident nuke from one of the subs? We have 2000 soldiers, what armour we could muster and jet cover dropping ordnance at every cluster that is reported in. These damned things didn't take the world by being a pushover, they're difficult," the general replied and topped up his whisky.

"Of course they're fucking difficult. If it wasn't for them, being difficult I wouldn't be the damn prime minister and you wouldn't be here, telling me why you're failing."

"With all due respect, we can blow them up, but they keep on crawling. We can shoot them a dozen times, but unless you hit their brains, they keep on coming. They don't starve, they don't sleep, they just want to eat and they will keep going until you kill them or they kill you. And then there's the others. The smart, the strong, the big. They are a whole different problem that we're only just getting to grips with. I pray there isn't another incarnation waiting to bloody try to eat us."

"I'm aware of the challenges, but you told me it was doable. You and the rest of the so-called experts said it would be ours two weeks ago. How many more ships am I going to have to sink before we have solid land beneath our feet again?" she growled. She slammed down the report on the desk and stood up. "The teams on the mainland, any progress?"

The general looked glum. He didn't have any good news to offer. "We've got six teams across the South, nothing as yet. We've identified another two areas of interest. One near a research centre, Wellworth. Satellite images suggest it should be secure and we'll have a team onsite within 48 hours."

She said nothing to him, her angry stare was enough to make him aware it was time to leave. The experienced general didn't like being subservient to little more than a low rent MP, promoted through survival rather than skill, but he respected the chain of command. He finished his drink and let himself out.

Chapter 21

A month had passed and Peter had stretched his supplies as far as he could. He had lost as much weight as many of the creatures that stared at him with their lustful eyes. Peter had built up his sleeping quarters, scavenging bedding, clothes and even books. The world might have been over, but he didn't want boredom to claim his life. He sat out on the grass in front of the main building, pistol holstered and rifle within reach as he read. It was how he had been spending the good days. The creatures on the outside had grown in numbers, but not in threat. Peter was relaxed. He wasn't going back out the front door. In a week's time he may have to accept a last meal of a bullet, just like the major had.

He'd start and finish the day doing a circuit of the grounds, a slow walk checking that nothing had changed. That morning, for just a second, he thought he'd heard something, an engine. He even thought he had seen a plane way off on the horizon. He had forced it out of his mind. It wasn't a plane; it was a bird. It wasn't an engine; it was a group of the dead, groaning in near unison.

As he sat there, again a noise caught his attention. He placed his book down and climbed to his feet, looking beyond the fences. This wasn't a bird. This wasn't a group of feeders. It was a fucking helicopter. He could see it clearly as it approached, coming directly to Wellworth, to him. Like an idiot he started jumping around waving his arms.

No doubt the crew of the Chinook didn't see him, it wouldn't have mattered if they had, they had their orders. The cargo doors opened as it moved into position above the compound.

Peter shielded his eyes as he tried to watch, but the dust flying around from the downdraft made it impossible. He was being rescued. In minutes they would have landed and be whisking him off to safety.

But they weren't landing, that wasn't their mission. The crew in the aircraft's rear started moving into position. These men were clean shaven in military fatigues, their rifles strapped to their backs. Two pallets were left in the hold, a number of crates were bundled together on each pallet, secured and ready. The men didn't talk; they had done this several times over the last few days. They wheeled the crate to the doors and waited for their signal. Another soldier emerged from the cockpit and gave the thumbs up. With one good push, the pallet was out of the cargo door.

Peter didn't see it as it crashed to the ground twenty feet away. He fell to the ground and crawled away. Looking back just as the helicopter gained altitude and drift away.

"No!" Peter pleaded, why didn't they land and rescue him?

Within seconds it was picking up speed and moving away until he could barely see it. The bastards. Peter got back to his feet. It was cruel; he had become used to his life at Wellworth; he didn't need the hope. He looked over at what they had dumped out of the back of the helicopter, and suddenly he forgave them.

The pallet had spilled its load, several boxes and a crate spreading their contents across the grass. Food and ammunition. Enough to last him months, maybe even a year. He ran over and tore open one of the field ration packs; he pulled out the packets of food and found it. A Yorkie chocolate bar. It was out of its wrapper and a piece of chocolate in his mouth within seconds. It felt so good. The temptation was to gorge himself on this new bounty, but he wouldn't. His inner nerd took over. It looked like a lot of food, a lot of ammunition and extra equipment, but he had to plan.

Peter finished the chocolate and started separating his supplies into piles until he had one large of food, one medium of ammunition and a tiny pile of anything else. He was delighted with what was before him. Over one hundred twenty-four-hour ration packs, he knew he could make them last twice as long. The ammunition was mainly 5.56mm, as written on the side of his rifle, 9mm as on his pistol and 7.62mm that didn't appear compatible with anything he had. A box of 40mm grenades were equally useless but the hand grenades he could use, although the prospect scared him nearly as much as the teeth on the other side of the fence.

He started moving his new found wealth inside the building; it was heavy and would take most of the day, but he could reward himself with a meal larger than his shrunken belly could handle.

Chapter 22

It was less of a farm, more of a small village now. When Amy had arrived with the others, they were looking to stay a few nights before moving on. That was more than a month ago. Since then, more survivors had turned up looking for a haven, tents and camper vans put to good use. The original older group had been supplemented with younger, able-bodied men and woman. There were even children running and playing in the relative safety of the new walls and fences. Unlike the rescue camps, there was no fear of the authorities here. People shared the limited resources and were eager to contribute rather than just take. Any troublemakers were brought into line or invited to leave.

Bo had made a bench in the garden his own spot, he had spent many hours sitting there watching. Watching people, the boundary, the surrounding fields and even the skies. His small shotgun rarely left his grip. Babs would spend time with him, but he often remained unusually quiet. Bo was a strong man, but he was becoming tired. Every extra person arriving at the farm added to his burden. He saw every smiling human face as his personal responsibility, even if his responsibilities had lessened. Babs was worried, but she knew her husband. She knew he couldn't be consoled and his bubbly personality was showing itself less and less each day.

"Bo, I think you should have a rest, you've been up longer than the sun," she nearly whispered, afraid of upsetting him.

"Don't be daft, I've been sitting all day, these fellas are doing the work, I'm just an old man sitting on a bench in a garden. It's just like the retirement we'd always promised ourselves," Bo countered. He didn't so much as look at Babs, but she found hearing his voice a relief. It was as many words as he had spoken to her in nearly a week.

"Cuppa?"

Bo nodded, and Babs made her way to the farmhouse. He continued to observe. He knew all the faces, even if the names were more often than not a blur. The farm continued to evolve, and he had stepped back from the early days. The last month seemed like a year. Amy had been relying less upon him and more on the younger community members. Bo understood, but it didn't stop it bothering him. He almost hoped a feeder would approach the farm so he could show the youngsters he was still capable. He caught sight of Amy as she headed off with Jack. Bo knew Jack's name. He was hardworking, brave, smart, handsome, and useful. Bo hated him. His youth and his importance in the camp contrasted harshly against his own age and place in the community. In a world that had gone to shit, Bo was sulking like a toddler.

Amy and Jack had grown close, their relationship had become physical in the last week but they were still uncomfortable with the prospect of their relationship becoming public despite spending nights together. Amy was the leader of the group. She saw a personal relationship as a weakness, but she was still a person in a lonely world and Jack was a good man. The attraction had been instant; they had done well to keep it professional for so long.

"Are you okay?" Jack was nervous, he didn't want to upset Amy. She was the one bright spot at the end of the world.

"Let's do the loop, then we'll find a spot," she replied. The loop had become the regular patrol, it could take an hour, but it gave the community a sense of protection, even if its utility was highly questionable. Since Amy and Jack had hooked up, the patrol gave them an opportunity to be together far from prying eyes.

"We don't have to have sex, we can just talk. If you like," Jack said. He hoped that she wanted to do more than just talk, but things were moving fast and he didn't want to be seen as taking advantage. He needn't have worried.

"Jack, I don't know how many more times I have to tell you it's okay, I want to fuck you too. You're not making me do anything I don't want to do, you couldn't," she said and smiled.

"Couldn't?" he asked. It sounded like a challenge to Jack.

Without warning, Amy swept his legs, rolled with him to the ground, and brought herself on top of him, a knife to his throat.

"I can kick your ass all day," Amy boasted. She was confident, but she was right. They both smiled and Amy rubbed herself against him before a quick kiss and then she jumped to her feet. "Let's keep moving."

Jack slowly got to his feet. The takedown, whilst playful, was also effective. Amy carried on ahead as she slid her knife back into its sheath. She missed carrying the rifle, but it now remained firmly at the farm. It was too valuable to lose, too powerful not to be protecting the camp. The firearm count had risen to slightly, with a few shotguns, bolt action rifles, and service rifle. Each too important to the farms' security to risk losing. But that didn't mean Amy and Jack were defenceless. Each carried a knife and another weapon, Amy favoured a machete and Jack a mallet. They were all weapons of defence. If a group attacked them, their best bet would be to run. The big bastards were slow, the regular ones were easily outrun too. The creatures could perform a light jog and they could jump onto their victims if they got into range, but they had no speed. The thinkers, like Natasha, were a different proposition, but Amy had seen none since that bitch.

No other survivors at the farm had seen one and weren't entirely sure Amy hadn't made an error. They trusted her enough to know she wasn't lying, but she couldn't be right, she must have been mistaken. When she wasn't in earshot, they speculated her path had crossed with a psycho, someone so scarred by the dead walking the earth and attacking people, that they joined them. The survivors had all seen enough of the feeders to know that of the many things they were, intelligent wasn't one of them.

The pair reached a small road, the wall and fence that lined it were sufficiently high to stop most threats from wandering into their fields. They followed the boundary on their side of the road towards the far corner. It was the furthest point from the farm and sheltered from view by a dip, anyone nosey enough to care what they were getting up to would have to be within metres to know for sure. Both stopped and looked around, listened for a groan or rustle that might signify they weren't alone. Nothing. They were clear. Amy was already removing her top as they walked down the gentle slope to the spot.

Amy kissed Jack as she unbuckled his belt and forced his trousers to his ankles. She pushed her hand down the front of his boxer shorts and gently began rubbing his penis. Jack tried to reciprocate, but Amy pushed his hand away before pushing him down to the floor. His erection was growing and Amy moved down his body and teased him, a gentle kiss on the end of his dick before placing it in her mouth and withdrawing it before making a solid contact. He was ready and Amy finally obliged, stroking his cock and sucking it for a few seconds before taking off her own trousers and lying next to Jack, legs spread open. Jack rolled on top of her and entered her.

"No, not yet. Kiss me," she commanded. Amy knew what she wanted, and she was very much in charge. Jack kissed her on the lips and Amy pushed him back. "No, kiss me," Amy whispered. She pushed him down her body and finally Jack got the message. She closed her eyes as Jack went to work. He wasn't the best of lovers, he tried hard but lacked confidence. It had always surprised Amy that for a man as handsome and smart as he was, he wasn't more outgoing. Despite the mutual attraction, she had done most of the pursuing.

As he gently carried on, Amy clenched the back of his head and encouraged him.

It had seen nothing worth chasing in days, so it just walked. Its instinct drove it to wander for a chance to find something. This one wasn't fat or thin, it was toned. Skin didn't hang off bones or wasn't stretched to bursting by an enormous frame growing beyond what the body could cope with. It was barely dressed, a pair of tattered trousers were held up by a belt on its tightest notch, a blood-stained oversized t-shirt was torn wide open and loose. No shoes, the remnants of a pair of socks clung to the ankle even if the grey feet were no longer covered. Underneath the shirt a six-pack was clear, the forearms flexed impressively and beneath the trousers powerful legs were evident.

Amy was close. She moved Jack back onto the ground and climbed on top of him. Slowly at first, she rode him, building up speed then slowing down again. Jack was loving every minute of this, and Amy controlled him.

The feeder stopped. It could hear or smell something. It wasn't sure, but it tried to track it down.

Amy was really going for it. She came but didn't stop, Jack was close she knew he'd be done in seconds.

The sound of a grunt, heavy breathing. It knew food was close. The road didn't offer great visibility, but its ears and nose were primed for any signal of a feed. It looked around then locked on; the noise was coming from the other side of a wall a little over one-hundred metres down the road at a junction. The wall was five feet tall, but that wouldn't matter to this thing. It began walking, then broke into a jog, then a full-on sprint.

Jack grabbed Amy's breasts as he came and she slowed down her pace, both out of breath and satisfied.

"I think I love you," Jack confessed. Maybe he meant it, but Amy learned long ago most men will tell you they love you seconds after they fucked you, it's when you ask them to pick up your dry-cleaning you know if it's true or not.

"We should finish the loop and get back, " was all she said. Amy slipped her top back on as she made her way to the wall before squatting and peeing, Jack looked away.

It didn't hesitate as it strode forward and leapt into the air, clearing the five-foot wall with ease, but the landing was less impressive. It slammed into the ground with a crunch and rolled to a stop. Amy slowly rose to her feet, urine dripping down her leg, her trousers, and weapons next to Jack who was trying to get his trousers past his ankles. The creature turned and snarled at Jack, who reached for his mallet as it leapt at him, swinging the large metal hammer he connected with its jaw. The lower jaw smashed to one side, barely hanging on, its teeth gone, a disgusting grey tongue left flapping in the large open chasm flicking angrily at its prey. It didn't slow down. Now on its feet between Jack and Amy, it switched its target to her. It sprinted at Amy. She dived to the side as it smashed straight into the stone wall behind. As it tried to get itself back to its feet Amy dashed back to Jack and scrambled for a weapon.

"Get behind me." Amy said, putting one foot in front of Jack, but he stepped beside her, eager to be her equal. Both were still half-dressed, but now armed, Jack's gore covered mallet and Amy held her machete.

It charged again, unsure who to lash out at first, instead, clawing in both their directions. It received a second blow to the face with the mallet caving in an eye socket and a slash across its neck with the machete releasing its thick grey blood. Confusion replaced its anger. It had never been attacked before. This wasn't its natural order. Its vision impaired, it began sniffing to make up the loss in sight; it stumbled forward, its speed had slowed, now little faster than a regular feeder. Its threat was greatly diminished and Jack brought down the mallet a final time on its skull. A loud crunch and it was over.

Jack and Amy looked at each other and the creature.

"Is that one of the thinkers?" Jack enquired, still unsure of what had just happened.

"Fuck no, that's something different. It looked similar to other feeders, but that wall, its speed. I've never seen one like that before. Look at it, it's pure muscle, its legs are like tree trunks," she explained. Amy gave it a gentle kick, and it barely moved. "It might be a one-off, a freak. Maybe Natasha was unique too," she added. Amy didn't believe it, thoughts turned over in her mind about how many types were out there and how vulnerable they still were.

"We should get dressed, toss that thing back over the wall and head back," he said. Jack wasn't eager to hang around and quickly finished getting his clothes back on.

"Don't tell anyone about this, please," she begged. Amy was getting dressed but constantly looking around, unsure that the threat was over. "People are just starting to think they understand the world, I'm not sure they will understand this."

"We need to prepare, there might be more," Jack replied. He hadn't survived to this point by taking his chances. He tried to stack the odds in his favour and being prepared did that.

"Our defences will not get better, we won't have more guns or bullets, we can't triple the height of our walls just because these things may exist," she said. Now dressed, Amy continued to exam the feeder.

"We should at least tell Bo and some of the others," he suggested. Jack positioned himself at the creature's head and gave Amy a nod, prompting her to hold its legs as he took its arms.

"Careful," she cautioned. Amy didn't need to tell Jack, neither relished touching it, but better that than leaving it where it was. "I'll deal with the others when we get back," Amy said. The feeder was heavy, but they hoisted it over the wall. The thud confirmed it hit the floor on the other side. They took a moment to check themselves and their weapons, wiping the grey blood off onto the grass, and continued with a little more speed, a bit more wariness. The world had found a way to become even more dangerous and unpredictable.

*

"You've got to be fucking kidding?" Bo exclaimed. he was sat at his bench, watching over the farm. Amy sat beside him, with Jack standing a few feet in front of them.

"Bo, this thing was different. Its muscle mass was amazing. It cleared the wall as if it wasn't there."

"It was a real tough bastard too," Jack felt the need to chip in.

"But you took the bugger down and you're okay?" Bo replied unmoved.

"If Jack hadn't landed that first hit, if it hadn't had to jump that wall, I think that would have been us done."

"And if my auntie had bollocks, she'd be my uncle," Bo said; he was unimpressed.

Amy got to her feet and stood next to Jack. "Bo, what the hell is wrong with you? All you do is sit on this fucking bench watching the world. This world doesn't need you watching it! It needs you to get involved and help fix it!"

"New dead thing wants to kill us. That's not news. And you want me to fix this nonsense? Then why the hell have you been cutting me out of everything? I might as well be the pot washer for the respect

I'm shown," Bo hissed as he got to his feet, his knuckles white as he gripped his shotgun ever tighter. "Amy love, bollocks to you," Bo cursed and stormed off into the farmhouse.

Amy sat on the bench, and Jack joined her, placing his arm around her.

"We can increase patrols, up the numbers to teams of three. Get some more tin can lines on the west side," Jack suggested. He had been thinking about what they could do to mitigate against the new threat.

"I agree. We've never seen one before, we'll probably never see one again, but let's be safe," she replied. Amy knew they'd see another one, there would be another Natasha and who knows what else. She also knew it changed nothing. They had what they had.

Chapter 23

Being a small island, the people of the Isle of Wight believed they wouldn't be afflicted by the plague destroying the mainland. It didn't take more than a few days to prove how wrong they were. Ferries full of refugees fleeing the infected had arrived at Fishbourne, the authorities unable to cope with their numbers. The amount of small private vessels was vast, touching down wherever they could along the coast. Thousands of people looking for safety. Hundreds already infected and bringing death with them. By the time those on the island realised what was happening, the mainland had completely fallen, and they relied upon a few Territorial Army soldiers based on the island. They put up a good fight, but within a week they had run out of ammunition and down to a handful of men. Against a traditional foe, they would have surrendered, but the dead didn't take prisoners. Within the next month, the dead had hunted down and devoured the last few survivors who didn't have the means to flee the island. Not a single living soul remained on the Isle of Wight. Barely a patch of the island was free of blood or carcasses.

When the two remaining companies of 42 Commando Royal Marines touched down on the southern part of the island to establish an operating base, they were nearly overrun within an hour. Airstrikes and the sheer determination of the boots on the ground stopped the landing craft pulling out with just a handful of survivors. More

Marines and soldiers would reinforce the position, but they could not push out. Dinner had been served and every feeder on the island was hungry. The manpower needed to maintain a square kilometre of the island was more than could comfortably be afforded. The men tired. The dead didn't. After a week, suicide became the biggest killer amongst those present. The constant fighting with an enemy who didn't stop was too much. A thousand of the dead lay incapacitated, but more came. They always came.

The generals and the makeshift government were ready to abandon the plan, try again at one of the Channel Islands. Sark or perhaps even Guernsey were far less ambitious than the Isle of Wight and had been favoured by many. Sark was tiny, but they could have taken it in an afternoon and would easily accommodate many civilians and military personnel. It had little to sustain them, but neither did the ships. They would have had a safe base of operations on solid land, but instead they had expended thousands of pounds of munitions and lost hundreds of men. Morale being down the toilet concerned the generals more than the politicians. The last hope was to send a second landing party to the north of the island. Reconnaissance had confirmed large hordes had made their way from all over the island to the first landing zone. The explosions and gunfire too tempting for the starving feeders.

They spared just 50 men, several small vessels acting as landing craft for them. They didn't go big; they went quiet at the dead of night under a full moon. The boats glided the last 30 metres to the shore, and the men disembarked so quietly, a sleeping baby wouldn't have woken. They headed inland. A farm half a kilometre away was their rendezvous point.

As the soldiers moved, they didn't make a sound. Any feeder encountered was silently dispatched with a Fairbairn-Sykes fighting knife. The full moon and clear skies allowed the men optimum visibility to move at speed.

It had smelled them before their boots hit the water. It watched them under the moonlight as they finished off the unthinking beasts. He slipped in behind them at a safe distance as they walked further from the shore. He had nearly gone insane through hunger, but now a meal was close.

Mason had been clever, but never academic. An overweight barman before he began taking FatBGone. He was eager to lose weight to get the attention of his childhood crush, who had never paid him attention. The more weight he lost, the less he cared about impressing her, and instead enjoyed a hedonistic life he'd never dreamed of. Sleeping with tourists and locals, he enjoyed himself. When the hunger came, the mainland was already in trouble. He kept his head down and picked off those poor souls foolish enough to trust this pale-skinned man. Once the feeders outnumbered the living, he indulged himself. He never stopped to think about what would happen when the food ran out.

He was weak, but still dangerous. He knew the island better as a feeder than he ever had as a normal person. He had armed himself with a double-barrelled shotgun shortly after society fell. It had proven useful in slowing down his prey. He was outnumbered and outgunned, but he knew what to do. These soldiers were avoiding trouble. He'd bring it to them.

Mason didn't dare get too close, but he didn't need to. He caught sight of a soldier 50 feet ahead and raised the shotgun. He took a quick look to check that no other soldiers were close and squeezed the trigger.

The soldier's scream of pain was nearly as loud as the shotgun blast. His colleagues immediately took defensive positions, ready to be attacked. Two marines rushed to their fallen colleague as he sat up, not as hurt as he initially thought.

"I thought one got me!" he stated. His adrenaline was pumping, he touched his face, several small wounds littered his cheek, ear, and just below his eye. He gingerly touched his arm and winced.

"Shut the fuck up, do you want them to get us all?" a harsh whisper reminded the injured soldier of their situation. But it was too late. The gunshot, the scream, and the following movement had alerted the handful of creatures nearby that hadn't succumbed to a blade, and many further out started moving towards the brief ruckus. He examined the small wounds, "It's birdshot. You'll live."

Mason watched, careful not to move and risk being spotted. He could smell the fresh blood and everything in him wanted to run towards the soldier and eat. He had to wait his turn.

Another marine screamed out as it attacked him, a single feeder leaping on him and pinning him to the floor as it bit down on his face. The knives were hastily placed in their scabbards and rifles brought into play. Soldiers started popping off rounds into the darkness. "Pull back to the beach," they all knew how the last landing had deteriorated and none wanted to be part of a repeat action. A Minimi light machine gun burst into life, its tracer rounds shooting in all directions as its user provided cover for the retreat.

Shit. Mason hadn't expected them to give up so easy. He ducked down, eager to avoid detection, but a marine stumbled over him in the darkness and fell to the floor. The soldier turned to see Mason and paused before bringing his rifle to his shoulder. Mason fired the second barrel of his gun at the soldier's face. It didn't kill him. The birdshot had decimated his features, his eyes punctured and face a mass of smashed meat. He was in too much shock to pull his own trigger, and the rifle dropped to the floor. Mason couldn't stop himself and launched at the soldier ripping out his throat. He barely chewed as he wolfed down large chunks of flesh. It was the first good feed he'd had in a long time. Two marines fired behind them as they carried on their retreat. They saw their colleague; they saw Mason covered in his blood, a piece of skin hanging from his teeth.

Mason closed his eyes. Time to die.

The roar was deafening. The huge feeder appeared from nowhere and picked one marine up by his helmet and batted the other away 20 feet with a single powerful swing of its enormous fists. The soldier fired as he flew through the air before he hit a tree, stopping him. Mason was saved by this huge feeder, maybe 10 feet tall. Everything about it was oversized, but its head seemed disproportionately big. He'd seen this huge one previously and given it a wide berth. Even monsters feared bigger monsters. It gave a sharp twist of the soldier's head and ripped it from its torso. The lifeless body fell to the floor in a crumpled heap as it began chewing on the face.

The new combatant hadn't gone unnoticed, and it started drawing fire from several of the fleeing soldiers. Bullets harmlessly entered its body or glanced off its skull. Angrily it launched the decapitated head at a cluster of soldiers knocking one on his arse and the others in shock at the sight of their friend's head in front of them.

Mason smiled at his new ally and continued gorging himself on his own kill. Seconds had passed, and he didn't know what was happening, the pain in his back, and the sensation of movement as it launched him through the air. His new friendship hadn't lasted long as he landed on a marine, he realised the big fucker had picked him up and thrown him at the soldiers.

The soldier panicked, unable to move under Mason, "Kill it, kill it!" he screamed to his nearby comrades.

Mason was as confused as the man he was lying on top. "No, don't!" he blurted out.

"It's one of the smart ones, grab it!" a marine screamed. They dragged Mason off their friend, then smashed down on his head with the rifle butts until he was unconscious.

The huge feeder started moving towards the soldiers and Mason. Rifle fire did little to dissuade it from continuing its attack. It was nearly upon them when another marine further back lined the monster up in the sights of his LAW-80 rocket launcher. He panicked as it was nearly on top of his fellow soldiers. He fired off the rocket, and it struck the creature's stomach, detonating with a large enough explosion to knock those nearby to the ground. It had blown a hole the size of a football in its ribcage. Broken ribs and bile spilled from the gaping wound as it staggered in disbelief. The creature wasn't dead, but it was out of the fight. It hobbled away as fast as it could, even it knew its chance of recovery was slim. The men grabbed their prisoner and beat a hasty retreat.

Air support from an attack helicopter started lighting up the land behind them with rockets aiding their retreat. Only 20 marines made it back to the shore, boarding the small vessels that were waiting for them. Maybe a hundred feeders pursued them onto the beach. They had come from nowhere, this place truly was infested.

They dragged Mason aboard a small boat, his arms hastily bound as they pulled away from that damned bloody island as fast as the diesel engine would allow.

The odd scream or panicked plea for help from comrades who didn't make it back could be heard above the engines. A few rifle shots, then silence. None of the marines could look at each other as the boats made their slow retreat to the fleet. They had failed miserably, but this smart feeder was a consolation prize. The white coats would be very interested in dissecting it.

Chapter 24

With his extra ammunition, Peter had decided it would be a good time to teach himself how to shoot. Some cartridges were preloaded into magazines, others were in small packets. He made his way to the top of the building to the small fortified observation post. The empty cartridges showed this must have been a good place for shooting and felt safer than being on the ground if he was going to piss off his ravenous neighbours. This was his third practice session, he limited himself to two magazines a session, wary his supply of ammo was healthy, but not infinite.

He lined up a target in his sight and gently squeezed the trigger. The creature's lower jaw exploded, and it stumbled back, confused, but not down.

"Fucking hell," he groaned. He was frustrated it wasn't a kill shot, but for a self-taught marksmen he'd made tremendous leaps in ability. He lined the disfigured creature up for a second shot, this time finding its cranium.

Then he heard it again; the helicopter. He looked around frantically, trying to see where the sound was coming from, and from nowhere two smaller helicopters appeared flying only ten metres from the ground. Both did a circuit of the site and Peter started jumping up and down waving his arms.

The two Westland Lynx helicopters had been taken out of service years ago, but as society fell many, including these two, were brought out of storage and put to use. The evacuation had needed every piece of equipment that could be scrounged together. A utility helicopter like the Lynx was a valuable addition to the effort against the dead. Whether ferrying equipment, soldiers, or civilians, it was a reliable aircraft that didn't stop. The evacuation had been over for a month. These two choppers had a different mission.

The door gunners started spraying the feeders at the fence line with their machine guns. The heavier 7.62mm rounds did more damage than Peter's rifle. Their fire wasn't massively effective, but those that weren't struck in the head and permanently taken out of action were damaged. A snapped femur here, damaged spine there all helped. The men firing seemed better for letting off some steam.

One helicopter broke off and hovered one hundred meters away from the fence as the other stopped its assault and positioned itself over the centre and began to lower.

This was it, Peter was being rescued. He was saved. As soon as he was onboard, he'd direct them to the farm, to the others. He hoped Amy had made it back, but he had a responsibility to those that had remained to help them if they were still there.

The Lynx touched down for a mere second as four heavily armed men hopped out and took a position covering each other as the helicopter joined the other one and both circled Wellworth once again, ready to engage if their men came under attack.

"Clear!" Sgt. Spencer Matthews was facing the main building and moved towards it. His three men followed, providing 360 degrees of cover. Spencer had been with the SAS for ten years, spending most of that time with Boat Troop, his experience had put him back on dry land for the mission.

"Sarge, where's our shit? They said they dropped it off," he enquired. Billy Clegg was the least experienced of the men. He'd found himself assigned to the SAS after society fell because they needed numbers for the operations they would be running. Billy was a good soldier, a serving Royal Marine before his transfer. He had failed SAS selection once, but not by much. In normal times, a fail is a fail, but the SAS had needs and near enough had become good enough, much to the disgust of those who made it to into the regiment the old-fashioned way.

"I'm guessing that bellend on the roof and his mates have been tucking in," Mike said. Mike Stelling was old school SAS, he'd killed men on most continents, but never in his own country. He was gruff and looked too old to be running around playing soldiers, but at forty-two years old, had the world not ended, his SAS career would have. Now he'd probably die on active duty, and that pleased him, he lived for the regiment, he would rather die for it than be forced to leave it.

"It's not as if the cunts could nip over to Sainsburys and pick up snacks. Well fucking played for digging in for this long," Gary said. Gary Waddle had been with the SAS for three years after ten with the paras. He was a calm man, even for the regiment he had ice running through his veins when bullets started flying.

"Shut the fuck up, heads on," Spencer ordered. He didn't know if those who remained at Wellworth were friendly or not. He knew that the dumb fucks in logistics had delivered food, ammunition, and explosives to a potentially hostile force and then the head sheds had dropped him and his men in the middle of it all.

Peter had run down through the building. It didn't occur to him that these armed men might not be friendly. He reached the ground floor and headed through the lobby. Outside he could see silhouettes of armed soldiers. He slowed down, unsure of himself, the rifle in his arms he didn't know whether to lower it to show he wasn't a threat or bring it to his shoulder to show he wasn't to be fucked with. The barrel of the L119A2 carbine pushed against the base of his skull stopped him in his tracks.

"How many others?" Spencer pushed his carbine's barrel harder into Peter to drive home his point.

"None. No one, just me," Peter answered. He was nervous, unsure if this man would accept his response.

"Just you, no one else?" he asked again. Spencer didn't feel Peter was a threat, despite him having both a pistol and rifle.

"The main lab, there are feeders, but they can't get out."

Spencer signalled for his men to join him. "You're with me, Billy, watch this one," he commanded. Gary and Mike formed up and Billy led Peter to the side.

"Set them down mate, easy does it." Peter was told. Billy was ready to empty a magazine into Peter if he so much as hesitated, but he didn't. Peter carefully put down the rifle on the floor and pulled the pistol from his holster with his thumb and index finger before placing it next to the rifle.

"Is this a rescue?" Peter queried. It embarrassed Peter to ask, was it obvious?

"You ain't going anywhere for a while, anyway. And neither are we," was the response. Billy walked around Peter trying to see what this man was. One who had survived on the mainland surrounded by these monsters. That alone proved he shouldn't be underestimated, but Jesus, he looked like a nerd.

"How many survivors are there?" Peter hated an awkward silence, and he had questions.

"You'll get a debrief if we decide not to feed you to those ugly bastards. Until then, we ask the questions," Billy asserted. He didn't stop moving for a moment, he was nervous. The clinical and mundane office building was more uncomfortable for him than any desert or jungle. He'd rather have been clearing the building with the others, but he respected Spencer and would do whatever he ordered him to do.

Within a few minutes, the others returned and seemed more relaxed, satisfied the main building was clear.

"Billy, join these two and clear the remaining outbuildings. I'll stay here with this one," Spencer ordered. His men departed, and Spencer stood in front of Peter. "I imagine you have questions, so do I. As I'm the man with the helicopter and special forces team, I'm going to go first. Who are you and what happened to everyone else?"

"I'm Peter, my group met a soldier from here and we came looking for help."

"We? There were others?"

"Me, Gareth and Amy. We met up with a thing, Natasha, one of them but smart and passing as one of us. She killed Gareth and the soldier. Nearly killed me."

"So where is Amy and this Natasha, did they make it in?"

"This was about a month ago, Natasha nearly killed me and I was out cold. When I woke up, her body was on me, I was in the field and Amy had gone. I assume Natasha is still rotting out there somewhere, I hope Amy made it back to the farm."

"On your own, injured, you made it past all those hungry fuckers? With no help?" he asked stunned. Spencer couldn't believe it, armed or not that was an impossible task for a man like this.

"I was caked in her blood, I guess it masked me from them. They didn't give me a second glance. And there weren't half as many as there are now."

Spencer pulled out a small kit, no bigger than an old tobacco tin, and tossed it to Peter before raising his rifle at him.

"What's this?"

"You don't look like one of them, but you've been exposed. That's a basic test kit, use the syringe, take a small sample of blood, two-mil should do, and then empty the sample onto one of the white slides."

Peter opened the kit, two small syringes, four white ceramic slides, alcohol swabs, cotton wool, and a small vile of a white liquid. He hated needles; he hated the idea of sticking one in himself even more, but he was under no illusions it was a needle in his arm or a bullet in his head. His hands shook as he removed the needle, Spencer was unmoved, Peter inserted it into his forearm and pulled back on the plunger, he winced as the chamber filled with blood. He couldn't look at it, so fearful of the needle, he pulled full five-millilitres of blood out. It didn't seem like much, but it felt like it.

"That's enough, you'll need some left. On a slide."

Peter withdrew the needle and looked at his blood. It wasn't grey, that was a good start. He fumbled for a slide and squirted the red liquid onto it, emptying the whole syringe. It was a mess, but he had followed his orders.

"Take out the white bottle, remove the cap and pump twice at your sample from six-inches away."

Peter did as he was told. The white spray finely covered the blood, but nothing else happened. Spencer motioned for Peter to step back so he could get a closer look. The corner of his mouth broke into a subtle smile.

"Is it okay?" Peter grew nervous with the wait.

"Bad news Peter."

Peter looked at the door. Could he make it? Even if he did, there were three other heavily armed men and then a thousand pissed off and hungry feeders.

"You're going to have to suffer this shitty life for a bit longer. You're clean. Good news is you have four members of the SAS, a pilot, two crew, and a helicopter joining you in your big fancy digs."

"How many more of you are there?"

"Thousands, military, politicians, VIPs, and civilians. When the camps became unviable, we evacuated to the sea. It was quite the operation. Cruise ships, ferries were pressed into service alongside frigates and aircraft carriers. There were some issues, a few outbreaks before they perfected the testing, but since then, it's been safe. Some other countries have done likewise."

"So you're here for the research?" he questioned. Of course they were. He wasn't important.

"Not really, we'll pick it up, but the Americans were ahead of us. They traced the source, some fucking weight loss drug, and you should see the dossier on these things. They say there are five confirmed variants, including the smart one like you came up against, I've not seen them myself. We're not here for data, we're looking for a man."

"Five variants? I've only seen three, I think," he said. Peter guessed anything was possible.

"It's a big dead world out there, mate. When our mission is up, we'll bring you back to the fleet."

One helicopter landed, Spencer and Peter walked to the front of the building. Billy, Mike, and Gary approached it, welcoming the crew who hopped out as the pilot shut down the Lynx's engine and the rotors slowed. The two crew members, Andy and Kyle, were slight men, not soldiers but obviously handy with the door machine guns of the helicopter.

"Andy, Kyle, this is Peter. He'll be assisting you. Get the kit in, and the chopper secured. I want one of those gimpy's dismounted and on the roof set up with a bipod. Take three boxes of ammo, Peter will show you to the supplies, take the ammunition from there," Spencer said. He would not waste any time getting settled in. He wished the roof would have been able to take the weight of the helicopter, but without guarantees, it was safer to leave it in the grounds, any sizeable breach would cut them off from it, so they had to make sure there would be no unwelcome guests. "Billy and Mike, check of the fence line, any weak points or damage report back, don't engage the fuckers unless there's an imminent threat." he continued. The men set off to their task, rifles in hand.

The pilot left the cockpit. An odd little man in his sixties, Seb McKenna had never served in any of the branches of the armed forces, but he had been a pilot since his twenties. Helicopters had been his passion and his career. When he pitched up in the English Channel flying a small Robinson R22 helicopter and asked for permission to land on the back of a Duke class frigate in choppy waters, it impressed even the most experienced naval pilot. When he successfully touched down and produced six cases of Bushmills single malt, he became an instant hero to those onboard. His R22 was promptly dumped off of the side of the frigate to make room for its designated Merlin helicopter, but his ability made him stick out, as did his personality. He wasn't phased by the dead at the fences. The SAS soldiers were hardened and well-armed, so their calm demeanour seemed appropriate. Seb would struggle to outrun even the most damaged of feeders. He was armed, though. He had demanded a pistol so had been issued an old Smith & Wesson .38 which he wore proudly from his belt like a cowboy in an old western.

"I told them not to shoot you." Seb said. He was all too happy to tell Peter how close he'd come to death.

"I could swear it was you screaming that we should shoot the cunt on the roof," Spencer replied, equally happy to correct him.

"Well, it all worked out, didn't it? Where am I sleeping?" Seb asked. He was already walking towards the main building, a small bag under his arm.

"You'll get used to Seb. He's probably as experienced a pilot as there is left without grey skin. He's the most important person here. None of us can fly that thing, so don't be in any doubt that any one of us would put a bullet in you to save him. Now make yourself useful and show Seb to the canteen, then you're with Andy and Kyle," he assured him. Spencer turned his back on Peter and approached the helicopter.

"Do I get my guns back?" Peter asked. He felt foolish for asking. He now had elite soldiers with him, but he had grown used to the safety and bravery the firearms gave him.

"No," Spencer replied. He didn't even turn to look at Peter as he gave him his reply. In time, he may give this man a weapon, but he didn't need to trust him now, he had his men, and they were enough.

Chapter 25

In its previous life as an aircraft carrier in the Spanish Navy, the HMS Reckoning stored a dozen F-35 Lightning aircraft and nearly the same again in Chinook and Seahawk helicopters. When the British naval forces borrowed the vessel, the helicopters were gone, as were all but one inoperable Lightning aircraft. These had no doubt been pressed into vital service, fighting off the dead in their own homeland. Their absence allowed a few of the British choppers to have an appropriate home, far better than sitting on the deck of a cargo ship. The rest of the space allowed for the civilian population to have an open, but covered area to live in. If you were a civilian and you had made it to the HMS Reckoning, you were someone, knew someone, or were close to someone in those two categories. Here the civilians were trusted, and each given a job. Whether that was cleaning or cooking, analysing data or assisting in the labs. Each had something to do that helped keep them from the hell that most of the civilian ships had become. Those that didn't pull their weight were transferred no matter who you were or knew.

Two soldiers stood at the door. It was unusual, but what wasn't unusual aboard a repurposed Spanish aircraft carrier housing the last remnants of humanity in the fight against the dead? Paul couldn't help it any longer, "I heard it's one of them, a smart one."

"Don't be retarded. They don't exist. You've been talking to those knobs in the armoury again, haven't you? They see shit all and they know even less," Trevor said, he was older, wiser, and didn't have time for conspiracy theories.

"Shall we have a look?" Paul asked. He was eager to find out what they were guarding, if the rumours were true.

"If you want to be clearing out the crappers for the next month, be my guest. I'm staying right here, making sure no one enters," he maintained. Trevor was pissed his fellow soldier was even thinking of disobeying orders.

Paul was wrestling with the idea. He turned to face the closed door. Sure he could grab a quick peek before anyone disturbed him. An elbow in the ribs straightened him up as Trevor coughed to clear his throat.

The prime minister was flanked by her entourage, the general, admiral, a man in a suit, and a group of the special boat service soldiers. The two sentries stood aside to allow the party to enter the sickbay.

A single doctor stood over Mason, who was bound to a table, unable to move.

"Is everything okay, doctor?" the prime minister asked, she felt she was disturbing something.

"This is the most vile creature I have ever met. He's disgusting, a damn liar," the doctor replied. He had been with Mason for only an hour, but he had got under his skin. Probing the physician constantly, hoping for a slither of information, something that may help him.

"Good. He wouldn't be here if he just used that filthy mouth to consume," she said. The PM's aide hurriedly found her a chair and slid it behind her at a respectful distance from the feeder in front of them. "So, you're one of the smart ones?"

Mason smiled. "I guess I am."

"Well, not smart enough to avoid being captured. You caused the death of a lot of our men, that's going to be hard for you. You didn't have any friends for what you are, for what you did even less," she scolded. The PM was observing the prisoner, trying to get a reaction, see an ounce of remorse, hoping for a chance of redemption.

"Look miss, I don't know who you are and frankly I don't care. You're going to kill me, experiment, and all that shit. Just do it. I don't need a moral lecture from some ropey old hag. I don't fucking care," he replied annoyed. They were going to do whatever they were going to do, and he was at their mercy.

"Kill you? No, you misunderstand. I want to recruit you. Your name is Mason, right?" she asked. He nodded. "You didn't choose this abomination, you're a victim as much as anyone who is devoured by those things, or who became one. I want to help you, but I need your help."

Mason was taken aback. He assumed he was about to be experimented on, killed, and thrown overboard. "I don't know what you want me to tell you. Trying to take the island, you need more, more tanks and more planes. It's more overrun than the mainland, I bet. So many people fled to us in the early days of the fall. If you want a guide, I'll tell you now it's pointless."

"Yes, yes. We've come to that same conclusion. We've already pulled out our forces from that godforsaken rock. A waste. No, we have many problems, and not taking the island has hastened them. We need time, sacrifices need to be made. Lose 100, to save 1000."

All but the black-clad soldiers looked uncomfortable at how the conversation was moving. She was talking to this thing like it was a person and not a monster. It was becoming harder to tell who was the cold-hearted killer.

"You've lost me. What do you want?" Mason enquired. Confused but intrigued, Mason wasn't sure of his role that the prime minister was alluding to.

"We need an outbreak on a ship or two. Thin out the numbers so that our supplies last long enough for our next move before we all starve to death. I want you to be you. A team will take you to a ship and you can infect as many as you can. We'll then pick you up, bring you back here where you'll be watched, but cared for until your next mission."

Was this woman serious? He hadn't even considered this could have happened. "How am I supposed to infect them? A bite is a little obvious."

"Mason, our scientists say you're a super spreader. You probably infected half of the Isle of Wight. And your potency has only increased. Kiss, screw, spit in the water tanks. I'm sure you'll figure it out," she said. The PM couldn't care less how he did the deed, as long as it was done.

This was a winning lottery ticket. "And you won't kill me?"

"Not if you play by our rules and do what we say. You'll be fed and protected, and you'll be quiet," she replied. She knew he'd say yes, a full stomach and a purpose, or a metal rod inserted into his skull.

"I guess I'm your monster," he agreed. If he had trusted them, it would have been a good deal, but his choices were limited. He could wait for his opportunity.

"Yes, you are," she stressed. The PM was thrilled with her new recruit.

Chapter 26

Night time always felt so quiet at the farm. Apart from those on sentry duty, no one dared to venture out of their shelter. No fires, no lights and no noise. It was the safest way, and so far, it had worked. Half of their defence was down to their basic early warning traps that were composed of tin cans and washing lines. No matter how well things felt like they were going, none of the community ever felt completely safe. They'd all fallen for that horrible trick before at least once. Whether in an army camp or barricaded in their homes. They all knew that if you let your guard down, you'd regret it. Everyone was armed with something and never ventured far away from their weapons.

Amy should have been fast asleep, but she couldn't get that damn thing out of her head. It was so strong and fast. The fat bastards were a challenge, but so slow that with practice, a small group could take one out without suffering casualties. These new ones were different. She was still unsure how they'd survived the encounter without injury. She looked at Jack, who was fast asleep next to her in the farmhouses' box room. It was a tight squeeze, but she thought it more cosy than claustrophobic. He didn't have a care in the world. These people didn't look to him for their survival, he wasn't responsible for their lives. That honour had fallen upon her.

Amy quietly got to her feet and got dressed, careful not to wake

Jack. She picked up her machete and looked at it disappointedly. The small amount of guns they had to protect the group wasn't enough. Ammunition for them just as pitiful. Knives, bats and improvised weapons would not work against the new threat unless they were lucky again. She already had concerns of what would happen if a large horde descended upon them. What if more of those new things got close? What if more Natashas emerged and staged an armed assault? Amy hated what ifs, but they filled her mind. She couldn't just sit and wait.

Amy crept downstairs. The house was less crowded these days, most preferring the space an outside shelter provided. No one slept in hallways anymore. They didn't believe they were safe from attack, they just had faith in their community to do its job and raise the alarms or defend them.

Amy poured a large glass of water in the kitchen's darkness and looked out of the window. Silence and stillness. Good. She had already decided what she needed to do. She was going to return to the camp. That horrible fucking place. She had heard from a few later arrivals at the community that it fell a day or so after they had escaped. Weakened by the riot, they had lost authority. They airlifted those of importance to safety, with as much of the military force as possible, as the dead closed in. With the protection of the soldiers gone, the civilians were easy pickings. Only a few escaped, those that weren't brutally devoured were turned. More hungry mouths looking for a feed. She knew it was dangerous, foolish even. But the camp would be good for two things, supplies and weapons. Surely if the stories were true that the evacuation of those in control was by helicopter, there would still be food, medical supplies, and weapons that had been left behind.

Amy hadn't noticed Bo sitting in the corner of the room. It was nearly 5 am, and his prostate made sure he'd not stayed asleep. "I'm sorry about earlier. I'm just feeling my age."

Amy walked over and sat next to Bo. "You're alright. We need you, we wouldn't be here without you."

"Nah, you don't. I've outlived my usefulness. In the camp I was a bit of a fixer, I had been a lot of my life. I could get most things for most people. Now I can't even get a good night's sleep. I'm just an old man with a fucking gun."

"You're still my number two. The brains to my…"

"Beauty?" Bo interrupted with a smile.

"I was going to say inexperience. I'm not a commander, I'm not a leader."

"Of course you are. You lead from the front, you don't hide at the back. You've led us here where we're as safe and happy as it's possible to be with those stinking things," he replied. Bo admired Amy. From the moment he saved her from being assaulted, she showed strength.

"You see everything that goes on here. Food is depleting faster than we're restocking it. Weapons are woefully basic, even the guns have little ammunition. Anyone has anything worse than a splinter or headache has to suffer."

"We can't exactly pop out to Boots, can we love?"

"That's kind of my point. We've cleared out every house, shop, or veterinary practice within five miles and we weren't the first. There's nothing out there that's easy to get. If we've not taken it, someone else already has."

"We're still getting the odd rabbit, the veggie patch is coming in and starting to produce."

"I'm going back to Chipstead," she bluntly announced.

"That's that inexperience you were talking about showing through. There's nothing there but the death. That's all what was ever there."

"They had medical facilities, guns, and thousands of ration packs. It's going to be hard, and that's why there might still be something left that's worth taking the risk for."

"Amy love, no. It's not worth it."

"You're my number two, Bo. That means you can advise and guide, but ultimately I have to make the hard decisions. You'll be in charge whilst I'm gone, I'll take Jack and we'll at least scout it out. If it's impossible, we'll come straight back here. I promise."

"Sounds like a waste of diesel to me, but you're the boss. If you take any stupid risks, I swear to God, Babs will be pissed with you," Bo warned. He knew there was no point pushing her, stubborn as she was brave. Just more for him to admire.

Chapter 27

The ship's brig was clean and bright; a modern prison for a modern warship. A stainless steel toilet and sink, a bed with clean linen, white-tiled floors and bright LED lights illuminating the space. It was basic, but luxurious compared to what some survivors on other ships called home. Mason had requested and been granted a few basic items. A change of clothes, a portable DVD player with a handful of films and some books. He'd lived as a monster for so long, he wanted to feel a little human, if only for a short while. He was relaxed as he laid on the bed and read through an autobiography of a TV reality star that he hadn't been familiar with or cared about. The selection of films and books illustrated the disdain they had for him, but he didn't care. He'd watch the shitty 70s Italian B-Movie with a smile. He read about that plastic celebrity as if she was the most important human to ever have graced the earth. He didn't give a fuck or want to give them the satisfaction. As long as they didn't kill him and fed him the precious meat, they could taunt him all they wanted.

A single soldier guarded Mason, sitting on the opposite side from Mason's cell, sitting on a metal chair, a submachine gun in his hands. "You know you're fucking dead, right? I don't mean dead like those cunts out there. I mean, you'll be proper fucking dead once you're off this ship."

"Didn't you hear, I'm the star man on this tub. You best watch how you speak to me."

The soldier rose to his feet and approached the cell. Mason rested his book on his chest and stared at the soldier. The soldier snorted, then spat in Mason's face before resuming his seat and guard duties. "There you go, star man, fuck off and shut up."

"And you call me a monster?" Mason said and wiped the spit from his face.

The prime minister entered with her usual group. The soldier stood up before he was relieved and invited to wait outside.

"Mason, we have an assignment for you," the PM proudly announced.

"I can't wait to start," Mason said. He was intrigued by his new arrangement and was ready to have some fun.

"Good. General, do you want to tell our operative what he's to do?" she asked. She looked at the general. His mouth stayed firmly shut, and he looked away from her. "I thought not. We'll get you aboard The Hope 2 amongst another small group of survivors. You'll be given a cover story, some belongings, and you're to do what you do. Bite, fuck, whatever it takes. I want that ship to be infected within three days. Got it?"

"Two questions; the Hope 2? What happened to the first hope?" Mason questioned. He thought he was being clever. "And what happens to me when that ship is full of the mindless fuckers, are you going to nuke me too?"

"There are four ships named The Hope, our survivors lack originality, they should all die just for that. Can you swim?" The prime minister had noticed herself the repetition of ship names when the plebs were put in charge over the minor details.

"I lived on an island all my life, I can fucking swim," he angrily replied. Even when he had been fat, he had been a decent swimmer.

"Good. When you get the signal, you'll jump overboard and we'll recover you," she made it sound so easy. As if jumping off the side of a large cargo vessel, that was turning into hell, and into the English Channel was as easy as popping to the shops for a pint of milk.

"That sounds lovely, but am I supposed to take your word for it you won't just leave me floating in the Channel?" Mason asked. He kind of wished they would. He was sure with a full belly he could swim for as long as he needed to and would find himself on land, eventually.

"You'll have two minders with you, they'll make sure you don't get lost and that you stick to your objective. They will have your food and you are to do what they say. Is that clear?" the general stepped in. He hated the mission, but he respected the chain of command and wanted Mason to do the same.

"Yes, sir," Mason joked. He stood and gave a mocking salute.

"You leave in three hours," the general replied. He cared less about this moronic monster than he did the horrific job at hand.

The delegation left the brig, their job done. As they walked back to number 10, the general stopped the PM, grabbed her shoulders, and looked straight into her eyes. "You can't do this, not again."

"Let go of me. Now," she ordered, calm, but authoritative. This politician was in control and the general complied.

"When does it stop? I've lost lord knows how many men, you've murdered one ship full of civilians and about to do the same again. You can't get away with this, I won't let you," the general insisted. He had been in the British Army nearly all his adult life, he'd never wilfully been involved with such a murderous human being as this cow.

"Don't threaten me general. You are complicit, so don't you dare attempt to take the high ground. You will pay for any treachery, I'll make sure of it," she spat and meant every word, growing increasingly angry at his challenge. "You're relieved of duty and confined to your quarters. Take him away," she ordered. One soldier complied whilst the other soldier followed the PM in the opposite direction.

"You don't have to do this," the general screamed at her as she walked away, continuing to ignore him.

Chapter 28

They were perfectly happy together. In the month since William found Natasha and brought her to his home, they had at first become the ideal, self-sufficient couple. They had topped up their supply of victims in the basement, enjoying walks together and happening across poor desperate souls unaware of all the threats that existed. Natasha had made a full recovery and could see her future. William had treated her with love, and she had more than repaid him. Natasha lay naked in bed alone, William walked in with a bowl of flesh and a smile. "You must be hungry after last night. I know I was. Some Gillian?"

Natasha happily took the food and ate it carefully. Gillian had been one of William's original captives, he didn't learn their names anymore. They would rarely tell him and he just didn't care.

"Unfortunately Gillian will need to be replaced, she had grown too weak. I've recovered what I can from her, but we'll need to drop her off later," he spoke so matter-of-factly it as if they'd merely run out of milk.

"That's a shame, she was sweet," she said. Natasha carried on eating, taking care that no blood dripped onto the bedding.

William had let Natasha into his life, but he didn't share everything. His bed, food, and home were one thing, but William had always been greedy and ambitious. He was a fool to have taken FatBGone when he himself was covering up results, but he had been overweight all his life and it had been the answer. He wasn't sure if his new existence was a curse or a blessing. Had he not taken the drug, he'd surely have been dead. He wouldn't have survived this world. Having taken it, he led a damned life but relatively safe life, preying on others but not bothered by the dead. Natasha had brought meaning to the new world, a partner in survival. It wasn't about making it to the next day; he could now enjoy himself. However good life felt, he knew he still had work to do.

"I need to head out to my lab, I'll be back in a few hours then we can go for a walk," he told her. He was already planning the time he had available in his head, samples to test and results to analyse.

"I love you," maybe she did.

"I love you too," maybe he did too.

*

The house was isolated, it had been William's parents' home. When he was a child, the fields would have been full of crops, he'd always found rapeseed his favourite. The bright yellow flowers lit up the countryside. Now no such colours shone through, a few wild flowers peppered the overgrown grass in the unloved fields. In the years since his parents passed, William maintained the house and would visit it infrequently. The property enjoyed a good amount of land, even more before William had started selling it off as he needed to. The old barn had a brief life as a holiday property before William's parents died. After years of lying vacant, it now found a new life. William's laboratory.

The equipment wasn't state-of-the art. It didn't all work, but it's what he had. He had looted hospitals, high schools, veterinarian surgeries, and local chemists. It didn't look professional; he didn't care, it just about suited his needs. Three large cages, courtesy of the vets, were covered in blankets. William pulled them off, one by one. Each cage housed a feeder. A young boy, a middle-aged man and a woman in her twenties. All appeared to have turned at roughly the same time, their clothes tattered, splashed with grey and red blood stains. Their hands and feet bound. They barely reacted to William. He wasn't food, so he wasn't worth bothering with.

William looked up at the clock, he couldn't get lost in his work again. Natasha knew he was working on some kind of cure, so they would never face starvation again. Natasha's arrival had delayed his work, but it had been worth it. He had an advantage the authorities didn't; he knew the full development history of the drug. They would have spent weeks trying to find the cause. He already knew. They would have spent as much time finding out how it worked. He had been there as it was created, when it was tweaked.

Weeks before society fell, he knew what was happening to him and he started working, preparing. His parent's house had been his priority. The cellar didn't become a dungeon overnight; it took work. Only after the evacuations was William able to fill his lab. The food supplies for his cattle, he started collecting before the fall and then scavenged more from makeshift camps and boarded-up shops. All his preparation didn't change the fact that he was racing against the clock. At some point, his food supply would dry up. Gillian wasn't the first to be used up. His freezer had the last butchered remnants of several of his captives. Finding fresh guests was getting harder and harder. He didn't want to cure himself. He liked his new form, his new place in the world. He wanted to cure the rest of the infected. They were a near infinite food supply. If he could turn them back to human, they would be edible. Their grey flesh was disgusting and he couldn't keep it down. As humans, he speculated they would be severely mentally scarred. It would be unlikely that they would enjoy any ounce of humanity, they would truly be cattle.

William loved the idea of repurposing the farm with his own herd of humans roaming the fields, but that was more a joke in his head than a reality he expected. A potentially cured feeder likely could not walk, talk, or feed itself. He knew the best-case scenario would see him with a large collection of cured feeders in a vegetative state being fed through tubes. It wasn't the dream he had, but it would be better than starving to death or going feral.

William approached the young boy feeder and opened its cage. Even with freedom in its sight, it didn't move or acknowledge him. William produced a scalpel and used it to cut off a small strip of the grey flesh, only a centimetre wide and three centimetres long. He held it to the light. It would do for his test. William locked the cage and took the sample to the repurposed kitchen table and sliced it into three equal chunks. He placed each into a separate Petri dish and placed a different beaker behind each. Each beaker contained a small amount of liquid, all a various shade of pink. Carefully William used a pipette to place a single drop of the first liquid on to the first sample. It rested on the surface of the flesh, slowly absorbing into the grey meat. The colour turned from grey to brown, a change but not the one he was looking for. He sniffed the Petri dish and was disgusted by the odour. A swing and a miss. A fresh pipette placed a drop of the second liquid onto the second sample. It bubbled and fizzed, hissing quietly. After a minute it died down and the meat looked red. It was promising. A quick sniff and it didn't turn his stomach. William was satisfied this had potential. The third sample had its turn. The flesh instantly turned black and dried out, an impressive if useless reaction. There was little need to examine this sample further.

The second liquid was a clear winner but testing on a slice of flesh was one thing. He was eager to test it more thoroughly. One of the good things about the feeders was their pure abundance, so many he normally had to actively keep them away. The boy would continue his usefulness, success or failure of the second solution would still be progress. William produced a large syringe, normally for use on livestock, it would never be used on a human, but the feeder didn't count as one, yet. The boy wouldn't be scared by its size, squirm as the large needle passed through his skin. The syringe was filled to its 50ml capacity with the pink solution, and William approached the boy.

He was unsure where best to start. One injection might not be enough, so he overwhelmed the body with the solution, injecting each limb, the heart, the lower spine and base of the skull. Each site was treated to a full syringe, nearly the whole of this test batch, but William was confident he'd be able to replicate it quickly. The boy became increasingly agitated with every injection. The flesh gained a little colour. The last injection into the skull set the boy off into a frenzy. Pain or fear were not traits these creatures usually displayed, but it was easy to believe that this boy was hurting and scared. William quickly shut the cage with the boy inside writhing in pain, thrashing at the wire trapping him inside. William wasn't sure if it was working or if he would need to pick up a new test subject and start again. The grey colour faded from its skin and the boy stopped moving, staying motionless on the floor of the cage as some colour returned to him. Blotches of pink and red spread across its body from the injection sites.

William smiled. In four weeks he had made tremendous progress, with the most basic of equipment and various old batches of FatBGone. If this worked, he and Natasha would never run out of food. They could enjoy a long and peaceful life avoiding the living, eating the cured dead. In a few hours, he would know how close he was to his dream.

Chapter 29

They had been at Wellworth for two days. Spencer and his men had checked, and double checked the perimeter. The double fence line had held up well, and the dead had done little to test it. The primary concern had been to build up the defences. The OP on the roof of the main building offered excellent views of the surrounding countryside, but little opportunities to engage anything that made it inside the compound. The helicopter was their lifeline. If the monsters got inside, they'd need the helicopter to affect their evacuation. Sebastian had again suggested putting it on the roof, he was sure he could land it there but Spencer wasn't sure the roof would take the load. He had more confidence in the fences holding under the weight of the feeders than the roof under the weight of a Lynx. The courtyard was their only option. To make up for this they had placed a line of Claymore mines at regular intervals from the main building and the barracks to the helicopter. If anything got it, it would wish it hadn't.

Peter had assisted in digging a series of foxholes. It had been hard, back-breaking work of the kind he wasn't used to. Spencer hadn't shied away from getting his hands dirty. A foxhole had saved his life on many occasions. If a localised armed force fancied their chances and tried to take Wellworth, small defensive positions within the courtyard might be the only cover they had. The soldiers had warmed to Peter quickly. He was timid, but he didn't want to disappoint. He may not have been particularly capable but set him a task and he'd give it his best shot.

Spencer had seen some action on the mainland after society fell. He had spent weeks extracting VIPs from infested areas. He'd lost more men rescuing former politicians than he had ever done in war. He resented that they'd died so that a man in his eighties might live a few more years, or a popular media darling or pop starlet might once again bring a smile to the nation. He didn't mind getting his hands dirty, but saving an old fart or young tart was hardly going to benefit humanity. Still, it had been better, more honest work than they had ordered him to undertake whilst at sea. He would rather be tasked with slotting as many of these things as possible. One less feeder was one less threat. At least now he felt like they might make a difference. A scientist who could find the cure to the creatures? It was too fantastical to believe that such a man existed and survived. The very idea that a geek in a lab had continued unmolested by these hungry bastards was preposterous. He'd seen experienced soldiers outmanoeuvred and overpowered by a handful of creatures, he couldn't think how a man of science could survive in this world without help.

"It's a load of bollocks, isn't it?" Mike asked, he had his doubts too. "Just more PR bullshit for the unwashed on the boats."

"If they sent us out here looking for Father Christmas, we'd do it with a smile and ask if they want the reindeer too," Spencer said as he checked his rifle and kit.

The other soldiers were loading the helicopter, Spencer and his men weren't sent to babysit a science lab. They had a mission to recover an asset who may hold the key to this damn plague, that's all they told Peter. It filled him with hope. Those in charge hadn't given up.

"Pete, fall in," Spencer bellowed his order at the confused figure. Peter jogged forward, ready to be given another order. "We will be back in six hours, you're in charge," he continued. Spencer handed Peter a pistol. Peter recognised it as the one he'd worn for so long on his hip, the one he'd cleaned the blood from when he found it. "Stay out of trouble, and for fuck's sake don't shoot yourself in the foot."

Peter took the handgun. The helicopter blades had already reached full speed as Spencer hopped onboard, joining his men. The door gunners cocked their machine guns and Sebastian smiled, offering a single-digit salute as he made the Lynx climb above Wellworth. At a height of around fifty-metres, it tilted forward and moved off. Peter stared at it until it was well out of sight. Some of the dead gave a slow pursuit of the chopper, they'd give up and return. They always came back with a few friends.

Peter looked around, alone again. He noticed it nearly immediately. The groan of the creatures. It had never gone away, but with the others at Wellworth he had zoned it out. Looking at the fences, a thousand angry, hungry faces stared back. He gripped the Glock a little tighter, for all the good it would do.

Chapter 30

The sea was rougher than it had been for a few days. The two minders were both well versed with operating in rough seas. Mason hadn't ever been one to get seasick, and since he changed, his body was even more resilient. The other five civilians transferring with them weren't so lucky, covering much of the exposed deck with vomit before the sea water washed it away. The small boat chugged along slowly, riding the waves that seemed to knock the vessel back at a faster rate than it could crawl forward.

The Hope 2 was stationary, the engine only used to maintain position if it strayed too far from its allotted space. It was expecting the new arrivals, a fair trade for ten of their own. A structural engineer and his family, along with a plumber and a carpenter with their families. Useful skills, but not best utilised on the small cargo ship. The captain was only sorry to see the plumber leave; the ship was never meant to service the waste needs of so many people. The toilets were a constant problem despite most of the inhabitants being forced to use buckets; the contents flung from the side into the sea after every bowel movement or emptied bladder. But the chance to reduce his headcount by two was just too good to turn down. He didn't care who was coming aboard, all he cared about was fewer mouths to feed and a modicum more space onboard.

The small vessel pulled alongside the Hope 2, and the unpleasant and clumsy act of transferring the passengers began. Both vessels bobbed up and down at different intervals, the smaller boat far more affected by the sea. Suddenly a six-foot drop became nothing, and the reverse was true. A broken ankle wasn't a rare occurrence when such transfers took place in anything other than calm seas. The two plain clothed soldiers took control, the first ascended the cargo netting with ease. Mason was prompted to climb next. He surprised himself with just how quickly he made it to the top. He'd forgotten how strong and agile he was with a full belly. The men were held on the deck by two armed crew members. They wouldn't be allowed to simply merge with the rest of the civilians without a few basic checks. No soldiers had been stationed to the Hope 2. Instead, a few civilian shotguns along with a small supply of cartridges had been supplied for the ship's crew to police itself.

The ten passengers waiting to climb down were dirty and apprehensive. Mason stared at them. They didn't know how lucky they were. This ship was marked for death and they had been saved to make his arrival possible. He hadn't turned anyone in a while, but he knew the time it took had become less and less. They had called him a super-spreader. From his briefing, they seemed to believe someone he infected could turn into a mindless feeder within 48 hours. He thought they were probably being optimistic, but it didn't matter. It would take as long as it would take.

After 40 minutes on the deck, the last of the departing passengers had boarded the small boat with only one sprained ankle suffered. The boat made its way back to the Reckoning.

Each of those who boarded, handed over their papers and test results to the crew of the ship. A quick glance and check of ID was enough. Anyone coming from the Reckoning would have been tested regularly. They were clean, their clothes fresh. They had come from paradise compared to the Hope 2. Here people lived on top of each other, fresh water was a commodity and food was in short supply. They led the group through the ship to a long, but wide, corridor. A row of triple height bunk beds flanked one side. As they followed down the corridor, the faces looking back at them from each bunk were tired and worn. The rigours of life were nearly too much for them. They had spent too long-surviving on too little, and despite the name of their home, they were devoid of any hope.

"Jesus, they're already dead," Mason whispered to one of his minders.

"What do you care?" the soldier asked. He resented having to talk with the monster.

"There's not much meat on the bones. It's not the feast I had in mind," Mason replied and realised his expectations of a plump child to devour were unrealistic.

"Just do your job and be grateful you weren't fucking slotted," he snapped. He was willing to cut the creature's head off there and then, he just wanted an excuse.

Mason had been taking everything in since they had boarded. Escaping his friends was possible, but to what end? They would find him on the ship, but even if they didn't, it had been condemned. Any freedom would be short-lived. He made his way to the crewman leading them. "Is there anywhere a guy can get, some company?"

The sailor looked him up and down with suspicion. "Nothing is free on this ship. Whether it's a girl, boy, or information. Everything costs."

Mason reached into his pocket and pulled out a bundle of three cigarettes wrapped in clingfilm and handed them to the sailor. "Where?"

"Next level down, starboard. It will cost you more than three fags when you get there though," the sailor replied. He pocketed them quickly, keen to keep them to himself.

Mason nodded and smiled. If he wasn't allowed to go nuts and eat everyone, he'd at least satisfy his carnal needs to get the job done. They had supplied him with cigarettes, chocolate, and a few small bottles of vodka. It had been deemed this would be enough to buy him access to whatever he needed on the ship.

They reached their bunks. Some hastily assembled frames with sheets of strong blue tarpaulin forming the bed. Not at all comfortable, but better than the damp, cold metal floor. Mason was given the middle bunk, sandwiched between his two personal soldiers.

"You can leave your shit here, but it won't be there when you come back. Don't report it to us, we don't care. Meals are served in the main cargo bay at 8 am and 8 pm. Bring your ID. If you don't bring your ID or are late, that's your problem," he said. The sailor left the new arrivals to get settled.

"I'm going for a look around," Mason stated and started walking off before a firm hand on his shoulder stopped him.

"I'll come too," the soldier said and gave him a shit-eating grin.

The men made their way down to the next level. It was like a medieval bazaar. Stalls trading whatever people had left of value. Food and drink, books, home-made blades, and clean clothes. The knives caught Mason's attention. He didn't trust any of these living fuckers. Knowing his two friends had enjoyed the comfort of carrying a 9mm handgun, each would make him an easy target once he'd outlived his usefulness. Maybe he paused a little too long, staring at the weapons, but he was soon moved on.

"Come on cunt, are you working or what?"

Mason nodded and headed to starboard. The small partitions were given the privacy of a dirty sheet to hide the depravity that could take place within. A dirty man in an ill-fitting designer suit stood in front, waiting for someone like Mason.

"What are you after?" he asked. Business had been increasingly slow, fresh blood on the ship was always worth exploiting.

"What have you got?" Mason enquired as he tried to peer behind the man, but the women were all hidden away.

"Sixteen years old, tight girl, a bit of a crier if you like that. If you want experience, I've got a 37-year-old with massive tits and a big arse. And two skinny girls in their twenties."

"Who's the most popular?" he asked. He thought he'd start at the top and work his way down over the next day or so.

"That'd be Cassie, the one with the big tits," the pimp proudly proclaimed.

"How much?" Mason asked and felt his currency in his pockets, uncertain how far it would get him.

"You're new? We have a special welcome offer, half a litre of spirits gets you half an hour of whatever you want. A pack of cigarettes for a blowjob, a hand job will cost you half a pack of fags or any good confectionery. Of course, we're open to offers if you have anything interesting?" The welcome offer, just like the repeat customer offer, the end of week offer, and any other offer the man could think of.

Mason produced a sealed pack of cigarettes.

"Cassie gives great head, you're in for a treat," the man bragged as he grabbed the cigarettes and shoved them into his suit's inside pocket as he led Mason to a partition. He opened his jacket to flash a large Bowie knife in its sheath suspended by a cord from his shoulder. "Don't do anything silly, we police ourselves here and no one will help you."

Maybe someone would help me, Mason thought to himself. "Don't wait up," he smirked at his shadow, who had no interest in getting any closer to the makeshift brothel.

The curtain opened, and Mason entered. Cassie wasn't any younger than 45 years old. Her much vaunted breasts were saggy and mediocre. She looked okay for her age, but hardly appealing. Mason thought maybe he should have opted for the 16-year-old. She would probably be in her twenties if the same math was applied.

"A blowie Cassie, okay?" the grubby man said. He waited until she nodded in acceptance, then he closed the curtain and left.

If Mason had been capable of it anymore, he'd have felt bad for her. But he wasn't, so he didn't. He pulled down his trousers and sat on the edge of the bed. She produced a condom and went to remove it from its wrapper.

"No condoms, please," he said. This was more business than pleasure, he'd hardly be doing his job if he allowed her to put a condom on him.

"Are you joking?" Cassie asked and looked at him as if he was crazy.

"Look, I understand, but look at me. I'm healthy, I've just come from the Reckoning, the big ship. I'm the cleanest thing on this tub and I've been tested regularly, I'm the safest thing you'll put in your mouth all week," Mason replied. The poor lighting below deck helped shield his pale complexion. She wasn't impressed. "Here, will this help?" he said then produced a 200g bar of chocolate and handed it to her. She looked around and pocketed the bar before getting to work on Mason. "Good girl, make it quick, I have things to do," he said. Mason sat back and relaxed. It wasn't the worst job in the world.

Chapter 31

They had been aboard the Hope 2 for less than two days, but Mason had undertaken his work with aplomb. Cassie had been the first, but not the last prostitute he'd visited. When he'd run out of luxury items to trade for unprotected sex, he began tainting the water supply. A surreptitious sneeze into a vat of drinking water, a lick of a door handle or an over enthusiastic greeting. He took amusement from each of them and everywhere he looked; he saw the fruits of his labour.

The unsatisfied look of hunger, the short tempers and outbreaks of violence. It brought back so many memories of the outbreak. The chaos had been a good time for Mason. With the panic and confusion, he ate well on the island. He knew the window this time around would be short. He had to shake his shadows, but they had only ever let him out of sight when he was with one of the ship's whores. He doubted that he'd make it back to the Reckoning once his mission was complete. Even if they didn't shoot him in the back of the head at the earliest opportunity, he'd be a prisoner who knew too much and was a risk. *Fuck that.*

Mason was lying in his bunk, looking up at the bulge above as the soldier rolled over. "Going to do my rounds lads, don't worry, I won't be long," he announced and hopped off his bed, triggering the legs from the bunk below to swing out.

"I need to stretch my legs too," the soldier said then rolled out of the lower bunk and stood next to Mason, checking his pistol under his jacket.

"I'm okay thanks, I won't be long," Mason let out. It was worth a try, however unlikely.

"We've got the food, you stay close to us," the menace in the soldier's voice was clear.

You are the food.

Mason led his keeper to the market. It was even more of a panic than usual. Those on board knew what was going on, they had seen it before on the mainland. History was repeating itself, but this time they would have nowhere to run. Those showing signs of infection either hid or were thrown overboard. It might have worked if the microbe hadn't spread so quickly. The prostitutes Mason infected passed it on to their many punters, who passed it on to their partners and families. The tainted water was used to wash with and drink. He found it amusing that they were killing each other, even though by now they were nearly all infected.

Most of the traders had shut up shop. No one was interested in buying chocolate or books, so only those with food or basic weapons to sell remained. The futility of it all. They just didn't understand how none of it mattered. A blade wouldn't do them any good, they were already dead. But to him it could be his key to freedom. If only that arsehole would give him some space. A crowd jostled for position in front of the only merchant with any halfway useful weapons left to sell. Pieces of the ship's pipes had been removed and repurposed. They wouldn't do. An array of shivs were still available, but were now being auctioned off, their value increasing with every sale. Most looked small, he wasn't sure how he could take two armed soldiers with little more than a sharpened potato peeler. Options and time were against him. Looking around, he saw his answer.

The pimp was still selling his girls, but business was understandably slow. A quick glance at the soldier and Mason approached the familiar face.

"If it's not my best customer! What can I do for you today?" he asked. The pimp was pale and agitated, he'd definitely been indulging in his own infected product.

"What are you doing?" asked the soldier who wasn't impressed. "You've done your job stop fucking around."

"Until we're off this tub, I'm still on the job. Be good and wait here, unless you want a fuck, my treat?"

"Hurry. We're expecting the call," he ordered. The soldier stood back, allowing Mason to carry on.

"Sorry about that. I was thinking maybe I'd try that young one out. Is she available?"

"Of course," the pimp piped up. The man led Mason to the partition through the curtain. The girl was young, too young. The minor cuts and bruises on her face and arms suggested her choices had been forced upon her. She sat still on the bed facing the wall. She was drugged or just too traumatised by the life they had forced her into to care anymore. Mason took off his jacket and t-shirt. His skin was pale and scarred, but the pimp either didn't notice or just didn't care. "The usual service, usual payment?" he smiled, this might be his last customer.

"I was thinking of something else," Mason motioned the man to come closer so he could whisper to him. Cupping his hand, he gently spoke into his ear. "I was thinking I would kill you and do whatever the fuck I want."

The pimp's eyes widened and Mason grabbed his face, forcing his mouth shut as he bit down on his neck. Mason's face contorted as he swallowed. The man was maybe only a day away from turning, and the meat was only just about edible. The girl didn't so much as flinch as the pimp's body went limp and Mason set him down on the bed beside her. Opening up the suit jacket, there it was, the large Bowie knife. It was nearly ridiculously big. Better than the sharpened toothbrushes being fought over in the market. He quickly removed the jacket off the dead man and slid the cord holding the sheath in place down the limp arm before he removed the blade. He gently touched the blade's edge with his fingertip, careful to not cut himself whilst still judging the sharpness. *Perfect.*

He looked at the girl. She was harmless, probably as riddled with the infection as the rest of the ship. Feasting on the bloody corpse didn't interest him in. It wasn't good meat, the soldiers would be better. A large bowl of discoloured water and some dirty towels were afforded to the girls to clean themselves up after a client. It would get most of the blood off him.

Dressed, and the knife now hanging under his own jacket, he was done. He'd worked quickly and only been a few minutes. Exiting the partition, he closed the curtain behind him and shouted back. "I wanted a woman, not a fucking man in drag, you swindling prick!"

"Did someone surprise you for a change?" the soldier asked, amused by what he had heard.

"Something like that. When are we getting off this shit hole?" Mason asked. He walked ahead of his shadow, a devious smile spreading across his face.

Chapter 32

Natasha was sitting on a picnic blanket reading in the small walled off garden to the side of the old house. Since society fell and she no longer needed to hunt for her dinner, there was remarkably little to do. William had provided everything for her she could need, but when he took himself away to his lab, she was bored and lonely. He didn't have many rules, but he told her not to enter the laboratory, it was so close she often thought about sneaking a peek, seeing if one of the old barn's blinds had been left open so she could see what was happening. All William had told her was he was working for the future, their future, and his important work was close to its objective. Natasha had come close to breaking this rule frequently, but never saw that it was worth the risk, so she continued on her own whilst he worked. It was a good life, but a dull one. Natasha had spent many years not leaving her flat, watching TV and wasting time on social media. There was no internet anymore. They had a TV and DVD player but watching the same seven films again seemed a waste of fuel for the generator. The collection of books at the house had mainly belonged to William's mother, nothing had been published within the last thirty years, and were romance or fantasy books. Not at all to Natasha's taste.

She thought about going for a walk on her own, beyond the boundary that William insisted they respected. The local village was only a few miles away. She surely could find a few magazines, some newer books and perhaps a couple of DVDs. She stood up and looked around, weighing up her options.

"Fuck it," she muttered to herself, almost in anger. He would be gone for hours, even if he popped his head out of his lab, she'd claim she'd just gone for a walk. William was so wrapped up in his work and her body, that he wouldn't notice a few new films or books.

*

Thornhurst would have been a pretty village before the outbreak. It was a good size, with tea rooms and antique shops dotted between the village store and the local pub. Now it was a wreck, bodies on the streets, stripped of flesh, buildings burned out or partially demolished, cars on their roofs and the feeders. A handful dead on the floor and several slowly wandering or standing still, waiting for a meal to present itself. Natasha entered the village without a care in the world. The dead didn't acknowledge her as she walked past them towards the village store.

The store had been the first to have been pillaged, food and medicines ripped from the shelves, but she wasn't looking for tins of beans or paracetamol. A feeder stood between her and the magazine rack, not wanting to get its blood or gore on her, she walked around it carefully. No one had stopped to pick up their lifestyle magazines as they fled the oncoming disaster. Natasha picked a copy up of each magazine from the limited selection. She'd rather read about gardening techniques than revisit the farmhouse's collection of fiction again. The film shelf comprising two DVDs, one they already had, and a big budget action film from a few years ago. It was better than nothing. The only book was one on the local history of Thornhurst, not a big book, but some new words to read at least. She had hoped for more, but for her first solo trip out, this was a success. She helped herself to a strong bag from behind the counter to carry her spoils and exited back out onto the high street.

She walked down the high street, stepping over rubble and bodies, looking for anything that might take her interest. It had been a month since she had freely walked the battered landscapes of the new dead world. This time she wasn't hungry, she wasn't hunting for flesh. She saw the world differently. Before William, before the fresh supply of meat, the death and destruction she witnessed was just the cost of doing business for being a creature who fed on the living. Now it was different, she felt something she didn't think she was capable of feeling anymore, she almost felt regret. This tiny village had probably been here in some form for hundreds of years, some of its population no doubt descendants of the earliest villagers. And now it was a wreck. The villagers, either dead in the street, evacuated or wandering it with less colour in their cheeks than they used to enjoy. It was just as well they didn't see their home in its current state.

The village pub, the Plough, had fared better than most buildings, it was an old-looking pub with plenty of charm and character. Natasha hadn't touched a drop of alcohol since society fell. It didn't do much for her anymore, but what better way to end her visit than a quick drink in the local? The door was stiff, but a good shove made it pop open.

Like the village store, the Plough had been thoroughly looted. Furniture knocked over, broken glass across the floor, a fruit machine had been toppled over on its side, its contents of pound coins spilled out across the floor. Hope of a drink was looking remote. The fridges behind the bar were empty, but Natasha hoped maybe a bottle of wine might have survived. She'd have settled for a warm can of cider.

Natasha hadn't seen the two men, but they had seen her when she first walked into the village. They couldn't understand why the dead that had stalked them didn't pay her any attention. Maybe she had been cured or immune to this damned plague. Kevin and Jules were in their twenties, they weren't originally from Thornhurst but found themselves in the small village after fleeing London. They had rarely left the confines of the big smoke before the dead starting attacking the living. They had briefly been guests at a small rescue camp before it fell and they had escaped. At that point they decided they'd stick together and away from the authorities. When they reached Thornhurst, they looted what they could before sealing themselves in the pub. The idea had been to only stay a few days then move on, but neither could face it. The longer they left it, the more they believed the number of feeders had increased, even if the number had remained near constant. It was far easier to wait another day than make a dash for it. They were trapped and their food perilously low, the small amount of stashed alcohol they had discovered gone leaving them with nothing to numb their fear.

They hoped this woman would visit the pub and help them. They had unbolted the door in anticipation and hid more through habit than having a plan. Kevin and Jules crouched behind the bar, slowly becoming aware that they were about to surprise a woman who may well be armed.

Natasha was about to hop over the bar when she caught their scent. It had felt like a long time since she smelled a free human. "Can I help you guys or are you going to continue hiding?" she asked. There was an awkward silence before Kevin stood up slowly, hands raised. Jules hesitated, but a nudge with Kevin's foot prompted him to stand. "What are two handsome chaps like you doing in a shit hole like this?"

"How did you get here, past them?" Kevin squeaked.

"We saw you, they didn't pay any attention to you, did they?" Jules added.

"Hi, my name is Natasha. It's kind of hard to explain how I can get past them, but you have to trust me," she replied. They didn't have any idea what she was, and she would not tell them.

"Jules, that's Kevin. Can you show us?" he nodded his head as he introduced them.

"No. But I can help you," she said. She could help them, there was plenty of food back at the farm, she didn't need to kill them for their meat. She quickly decided to help them leave the village. If they succeeded she'd decide on whether to eat them. "What do you have in the way of weapons?" she queried. Jules produced a small hatchet and Kevin picked up his homemade spear and held up a small knife. "No guns?"

"Just these," Jules confirmed.

Good, if she desired, they'd be easy enough to take down.

"You ready to go? Better to head off now so you're not stuck in the middle of nowhere in the dark if we do make it out," Natasha said, she was interested in this distraction, but didn't want to push her luck with William. As much as she'd liked to have stuck around to play, she didn't want to spend too much time away from home on her first trip out.

"Can't we come with you?" Kevin asked, assuming they would travel together back to her camp.

"Maybe, maybe not. I guess we'll see how you behave," she smiled devilishly.

The two men looked at each other. If she got them out, they'd behave however they damn well pleased. "Let's get moving," Jules chimed in. He was sick of that stinking old pub, sooner they were gone the better.

"Wait here and I'll be back in a few," Natasha said. She took the small blade from Kevin with a smile and left the pub.

"What do you reckon?" Kevin breathed a slight sigh of relief that finally, they may escape. It lasted a mere second before the prospect of walking down the street with the dead dawned on him.

"First woman I've seen in weeks, and she seems up for it. I was considering fucking you," Jules smiled.

"Mate, she's into me, you can go second," Kevin played along.

"Let's get out of here first, then we can decide on the order," Jules said and tried to look out onto the street, but was careful not to draw attention to them.

The pair sat down and waited for Natasha to return. They had nothing left worth taking with them besides the clothes on their backs and the weapons in their hands.

She was gone less than two minutes when the door swung open and a feeder strolled in. It instantly caught sight of its prey and lunged towards them. Kevin and Jules fell back as they tried to scurry away. It didn't get close before it dropped to the floor, the small blade embedded in the side of its head. Natasha closed the door and stood over her kill, the grey flood dripping onto the floor.

"There's your knife if you still want it."

"What the fuck was that about?" Jules was angry, was she trying to kill them or was she just messing around?

"You want to walk out of here in one piece?" Natasha snapped back. Both Kevin and Jules nodded.

"Start slavering that grey crap on you, avoid eyes, mouth and broken skin," Natasha advised. She kicked the corpse as if to assure them it was still dead. "It's not perfect, they can tell the difference if you get too close for too long but we won't linger."

"How come you're not covered in their blood?" Kevin asked, sceptical, and not very keen on getting the thick grey blood on him.

"I have a different method, but we don't have time for that," she revealed. Natasha was eager to avoid questions.

Jules didn't have the same reservations. A quick pause to slam the blade further into its head to confirm it wouldn't suddenly attack and he got to work. He flipped the body over and cut into its clothing, revealing more of this pale grey skin. The flesh separated easier than he thought it would, the internal organs either black or darker shades of grey. This creature was old, and not a lot of flesh remained on the bones. Jules began rubbing blood onto his clothes and exposed skin.

"This without a doubt is one of my worst ever experiences. Ever," he complained. A little of the blood went even further than he had hoped. "Come on Kev, can you do my back?" he asked. Kevin nervously complied then started on himself.

After a few minutes they were done, the blood smeared so thinly it was barely visible. Natasha inspected the two men, subtly given them a sniff, trying to detect their humanity. It was definitely still there, but it was much weaker than before. The plan should work.

"Let's go then," Natasha ordered and took the lead, Jules was suddenly less confident this silly blood idea would work and Kevin didn't trust Natasha or the plan. The absence of a better idea forced the two to follow Natasha through the pub door back out into the village.

Kevin and Jules kept with Natashas relaxed pace, the creatures paying them little attention. It was working. They had to fight every instinct they had not to run, break into a sprint and get the hell out of this godforsaken village. As they passed the decomposed corpses laying on the street and the greying one's shuffling about it was nearly too much. After what seemed like hours they were free, the five-minute slow wander from the village saw them now at the top of the main road looking down on that place. Both men were relieved, they'd made it, but now what?

"So can we come with you?" Kevin was back on his most pressing point, somewhere safe to stay.

"You're nice lads, but you don't want to come with me. My boyfriend, William really wouldn't like it. Head down this road and you're bound to find a farmhouse or barn before dark that you can rest up in," she said. Natasha had done her good deed, redeemed a small amount of her humanity, but she was done. It was time to head back home.

"You can't just leave us here!" Jules grabbed Natasha. She was obviously doing well, and he wanted what she had. He didn't want to scurry between abandoned villages and towns, hiding from those fucking creatures and struggling to survive. She didn't have much meat on the bones, but this girl was healthy and happy, a rare combination.

Natasha looked down at his hand gripping her wrist. *The ungrateful little shit.* "Let go of me, now!" she commanded. Jules didn't budge. She was holding out on them. He would not let her run to her cushy life whilst they struggled to survive. Natasha pulled her arm away, but Jules pulled her back. They both stopped their tug of war and she looked him in the eye and smiled. "Let go, I won't ask again."

Jules smiled back. "Take us with you or I'll break your fucking legs and leave you to those things."

Natasha had finally had enough. She had tried to be good, tried to be kind, and help these poor stranded boys. Redeem a little of herself for all these wrongs. But this fucking prick, it wasn't enough for him. He wanted it all. She relaxed her arm in his grip, moved closer to Jules, and whispered in his ear. "I know what you want," she teased. She kissed him on the mouth, then his cheek, and down to his neck. Jules winked at Kevin with a smile. Then the smile turned to shock.

Jules tried to push Natasha away, but her teeth were firmly clamped on his jugular, her arms hugging him tightly, her strength greater than he expected. The best he could manage was to topple both of them to the floor, with Natasha on top of him. "Kev get her off me!" he begged. His words were already failing. Jules reached his hand out and tried to speak again, but only a spluttering of blood passed his lips.

Kevin stepped forward, his spear nervously raised, not ready to do what was needed. Natasha turned around quickly, her face soaked in blood. "I was going to let you both live. This is your fault. Not mine!" Natasha spoke. She licked her lips. "Run or die."

Kevin didn't need telling twice, he ran as fast as he could, glancing back frequently to make sure he wasn't being pursued. Natasha wasn't wasting her kill. It had been the first in a long time. As much as she enjoyed the good life at the farm, getting her hands and teeth dirty on warm flesh straight off the bone felt good. William would be pissed if he found out, but she'd deal with that later. Right now, she'd gorge herself on this moron and enjoy every bite she could manage.

Chapter 33

He wasn't sure if they'd already been advised of their impending evacuation or whether they too might be sacrificed alongside him. Screams and shouts had become more prevalent in the last few hours, with the odd gunshot thrown into the mix. The three men were in their bunks, each keeping quiet but ready to spring into action if trouble came to them. The soldiers both gripped their loaded pistols, safety off, ready to defend themselves. Mason too had his weapon to hand. The tip of the blade rested on the bulging mass above him as he tried to decide on the place to thrust it. Starting at what must be the soldier's lower back, he slid the blade up until he reached what he believed would be the soldier's neck.

He hesitated. Once he plunged the blade through the tarp, he'd have milliseconds to strike again if his first blow wasn't effective and then deal with the soldier in the lower bunk before he could retaliate. Placing one hand on the base of the handle and aiming with the other, he plunged the large blade up and into its target. The body above convulsed and the trail of blood gushing down the blade confirmed he'd found his spot. If the bastard hadn't flung his pistol off of the top bunk as he bled out, it wouldn't have happened.

Mason heard the shots before he felt them. Two rounds passed through his own piece of tarp, the first striking his buttocks, the second grazing his rib cage. He didn't give himself time to feel the effects of the wounds. Instinctively he rolled off the bed, landing on the metallic floor with a thud. He could see the pistol being pointed towards him and he didn't think twice. The large blade swung towards the outstretched pistol and struck the wrist with force. The hand was nearly severed, only skin and tendon kept it from falling to the floor. The impact turned the hand nearly 180 degrees back, momentarily pointing the pistol at the shocked soldier before it dropped to the floor.

Anyone else near who hadn't already run away, made it their business to get away from this conflict as fast as possible leaving the men alone.

Mason sat up. But now he could feel the bullet. It was uncomfortable, but he didn't feel pain in the same way anymore. "When are they coming?" he asked. The smell of the blood filled his nostrils.

"Fuck you," he sneered. Fear and shock weren't enough to dull his hatred and defiance.

Mason grabbed the hand and twisted it off as the soldier rived in pain. The injured man pulled back his stump and held tightly as it bled profusely. Mason could not help himself as he stuck a finger into his mouth and stripped it of its flesh. *That's the stuff, fresh, healthy, and warm.* A few chews and he swallowed the delicious meat. "When are they coming?"

"Fuck you, monster!" he cursed. The soldier produced his own knife, and he threw himself towards Mason. The seven-inch blade was big, but was dwarfed by the fat 11 inches one on the Bowie. Again the soldier came off second best as the larger blade flashed across, this time taking the second hand off completely. The soldier slumped to the floor, balled up, holding his wounds close to his body.

"I will take your feet, your nose, your ears, and your cock. Tell me, are they coming?" he threatened. His mouth was watering at this partially butchered slab of breathing meat.

"Yes. They're fucking coming! They won't take you, that bitch wants you, but you're going to die here," he answered. He was in pain and dying, but he was determined to have the satisfaction of letting Mason know he too would be dead soon.

"Of course I'm supposed to die," Mason replied. He picked up the pistols, shoving one in his belt and the other his jacket, checking the soldier for the spare magazine. "What are my options? How do I get off this fucking tub?"

"You don't," he said. The soldier coughed as the words left his lips.

Mason struck down with the knife at the midpoint of the soldier's foot. He yelped in pain, the blade only going halfway through. Mason pushed down hard, slowly forcing the knife all the way through. "How is this supposed to go down?"

"We were to jump overboard at 21:00 hours. Swim 200 metres out and be picked up by a boat team. You're fucked, they'll shoot you in the face before you hit the water," he said and started laughing as he accepted his own fate.

The anger brewed up in Mason. This wasn't how he was going to die, on a floating hell of his own making. The frenzied attack lasted less than a minute. The soldier was dead within the first ten seconds as Mason repeatedly struck him with the large blade. Pieces of flesh had flown off in multiple directions as the blood-drenched him. He turned his attention back to his first victim and pulled him off the top bunk, landing on top of his colleague. His aim had been true. The puncture wound went through the back of the neck and out of the front. He lifted the limp wrist up and looked at the time, 19:00. A few short hours to go, *may as well grab a bite to eat.*

The knife made quick work of the bodies, and his greed quickly polished off several chunks of flesh. He had nearly forgotten how amazing fresh, warm and bloody meat was. Not the tainted stuff, not that cold hard rubbery slab of meat he'd been given on the Reckoning.

Warm and straight off the bone.

He'd been allowed ten glorious minutes to feed before the first of the civilians came investigating.

"He's one of them! Get it!" the shout was clear, as were the thundering footsteps towards him from the small, poorly armed mob. Mason lazily lifted a pistol and fired off several shots. A scream of pain and a hasty retreat. He knew his meal was over. Time to leave. He sheathed the knife and grasped both pistols in his hands. His only hope was to get overboard now and hope the welcoming party wouldn't be waiting. He was a powerful swimmer, not that he knew where he would swim to. But away from the soon to be scuppered ship was a good start.

As he walked down the poorly lit corridor he passed the mob member he'd injured and put a round into his chest. The rest of the mob hadn't stuck around to help their fallen comrade. The ship was chaotic with plenty of fights to pick. He hoped for a moment they'd wisely left him alone in order to bravely throw an infected OAP or child overboard instead. The sharpened tooth brush stabbed into the back of his neck confirmed that wasn't the case. These people were so far gone he couldn't smell them anymore, they smelled like the dead, like him. It was too hard to distinguish them. There could be fifty of them or just him. Mason reached behind him and shot the man in the gut before turning his attention in front as the fire-axe wielding maniac took a swing at him, missing by an inch. Both handguns discharged at his torso, felling him.

"Just piss off, all of you!" he expressed. He fired shots into the darkness ahead as he edged forward. More footsteps approached from behind, and Mason fired until the guns ran dry. He dropped one to the floor as he hastily reloaded the other. "I can go all day!"

He saw the hatch 20 metres ahead and picked up his pace. Anything that appeared to move, he'd fire at. Climbing through to the stairs, the pipe struck his head, tearing his ear and opening up his cheek. Two more shots instantly punished the attacker.

Bodies of feeders and the living littered the deck. The recently turned fought with the soon to be turned as the armed crew shot anyone who tried to get too close as they protected the wheelhouse. Something pushed him forward from behind. He could see the tip of the blade pushing out through his chest. *Motherfuckers!*

Mason tried to reach behind him to remove the object, but it was no good. The mob was maybe ten strong. Armed with the most basic of weapons, but each ready to die. Mason fired off every round he had until the pistol was empty, he'd killed or wounded half of his attackers but it wasn't good enough. He tried to get the Bowie knife into play, but it was big, heavy and cumbersome, and it was just clear from its sheath as they knocked him to the ground. A collection of box cutters, potato peelers and pipes being brought into action against him. His own weapon wrestled from him as he was slashed and stabbed repeatedly.

That Bowie knife really was quite the sight as they brought it down onto his neck. It took three or four powerful strikes to remove his head.

They didn't dwell on their victory. There were plenty more beasts that needed dispatching, and the number of uninfected were decreasing with every confrontation. First the head and then the body were tossed overboard. The mob gathered itself for a moment before moving on to their next target, a freshly turned feeder devouring what remained of a middle-aged man. They would spend what little time they had left, fighting to survive, unaware the feeders weren't their only enemy.

Chapter 34

The countryside still kept its beauty despite the chaos of the world. The speed and height the Lynx flew at obscured most of the monsters that roamed the ground below. Occasionally, a large herd would be spotted, sometimes standing still waiting, other times slowly moving, following a scent or glimpse of a potential meal. Some even tried to follow the helicopter once they saw it.

The intelligence, for want of a better term, suggested that William Johnson owned a farmhouse somewhere in the countryside, possibly near a series of villages. That was it. Land registry records were no longer available without accessing the physical servers in Plymouth. The site itself was out of town and easily accessible. That's why two rescue camps had been set up within half a mile of it. When they fell thousands were added to the ranks of the dead. It would take an army to take the unsecured offices, and those in charge deemed it too risky. Far better have a series of small teams exploring the various likely areas than risk the manpower that was needed elsewhere. Johnson was a punt. He may be dead, he might not have the answers they needed. This was a job for specialists.

Spencer had marked the day's targets from satellite images on a map that each man had a copy of. It was hard enough telling apart the dead from the living from the helicopter, how they managed it from space was miraculous. Hundreds of small communities had been identified and contact initiated where possible. So far none had seen or heard of a William Johnson, but each offered some information on their area. Spencer had used this with the satellite imagery to prioritise his targets. Today's properties had all been identified as being occupied by the living by the satellite images and backed up by those on the ground. In over four hours they had visited three of the four properties.

The first they hadn't even bothered to land. A dozen dead wandered the grounds and the doors to the house and the small cottage open.

The second property they landed and searched. An emaciated couple was in bed together, perfectly still, holding hands. They'd been dead for at least a week.

At farm number three, they were greeted with ineffective gunfire. The firefight had been one-sided. The door gunners earning their keep, ripping to shreds those foolish few armed with shotguns and small calibre rifles. Spencer and his team disembarked the helicopter half a kilometre from the farm building and hurried on foot to the site under cover from the chopper. Two survivors wept over the bodies of their fallen and swore at the soldiers as they continued to clear the buildings. Another bust. It had taken time to secure the farm and the two survivors were not cooperative.

Mackland's Farm was the last property, a dairy farm a few miles from the village of Thornhurst. The helicopter landed in an empty field, a fair distance from the farm. The soldiers spread out and advanced forward. The helicopter sprung back into the air and continued to keep moving, able to answer any call for help that may be made.

The field was open; it provided awful cover and only minimal concealment with the long grass. The four men moved quickly until they reached a stone wall that bordered the farmyard. The wall was easy to climb over and the four soldiers separated into two-man teams, each clearing outbuildings. The cowshed had fifty bodies piled up, all grey skin and dry grey blood.

"Can I help you?" a young male voice enquired.

Billy may have been green, but Mike wasn't. The fact this young man had got so close to them was impressive. Both raised their rifles. "Who the fuck are you?" he asked. Mike was angry with himself, this lad could have ended them both.

"Mark, this is my home. Who the hell are you?" the young man replied. Mark Mackland was in his early twenties, he looked tired and worn down. The price you pay for living in the middle of the apocalypse.

"This your handiwork?" Billy gestured to the dead feeders.

"Me and my dad," Mark said. He didn't know what to make of these soldiers, why there were here now.

"Tidy work," Billy complimented, impressed.

"We stopped burning and burying them a few weeks ago, couldn't spare the calories." Mark was too tired to be afraid of the soldiers.

"Your dad, is he close?" Mike questioned. He was keeping one eye on this kid, and the other darting around looking for others. He caught Spencer's attention and signalled him.

"He's in the house," Mark replied as he looked at his home.

"Alone?"

"Kind of," Mark answered. He was sheepish, even evasive.

"On your knees, mate, hands on head," Billy ordered, and stepped forward with a cable tie and bound Mark's hands behind his back.

An older man emerged from the farmhouse, a shotgun resting casually in his arms, Gary raised his rifle to cover the man but Spencer directed him to lower it.

"You okay, Mark?" his father asked. John Mackland was in his fifties. He walked with a slight limp and a plain expression on his face. He was a beaten man, hanging on to this life for his family.

"Yes dad, they're army."

Spencer stepped forward from his position and walked towards John, lowering his rifle.

"We're looking for a William Johnson," Spencer stated. He produced the picture and showed it to John. "We need to find him."

John looked at the picture closely but crossed his head. "I don't recognise him. If he was from around here, I'd probably know him. Johnson?" he responded. A flicker of recognition in John's eyes.

"Yes, William Johnson. He's a scientist," Spencer said, he hoped this worn down survivor may have something to tell them.

"We don't have a need for too many scientists here. But there was a Johnson family that had a farm out beyond Thornhurst. It was probably a good few years ago," John offered. He was trying to recall the details, but even if he had known them, in his current state he would have been unable to relay them.

Spencer produced a map and showed it to John. "Can you point to it?" he asked. John looked carefully, but it was all a blur. He crossed his head and walked back. "Anyone else in there?"

"Just my wife, Annie," John answered and looked back to the house.

"Dad, no," his son chimed in. Mark turned away, he couldn't look. Embarrassment and shame washed over him. He had tried to put an end to the nonsense weeks ago.

"Sir, can you bring her out please?" Spencer told him, he was respectful but wary. They were obviously hiding something, but hadn't been hostile. John obliged and slowly wandered into the house.

"You've got to understand, this farm and his family, they were his life. When we slaughtered the cattle, it chipped a piece of him away. When mum went to the rescue camp, he thought it was for the best. When we found her. It broke him," Mark revealed, he was desperate for them to understand.

John appeared from the house, Annie behind him. Her mouth was bound with a rag stained with her own grey blood. Her right arm missing below the elbow, the stump had healed over with scarred grey tissue. Her other arm and what remained of the damaged one were tightly wrapped to her body with bungee cord. She had obviously turned weeks ago; she wasn't a wife or mother anymore; she was just another bloody monster.

Spencer kept his game face on, the world was fucked. He wasn't about to make this man suffer any more than he had to. "Thanks, sir, I think we have everything we need," Spencer said and signalled his men to withdraw. John stood bemused as the soldiers moved away from the farm. Mark put his hand on his father's back, the creature behind looking at the pair. It gazed at them with hate. It had long become used to being unable to satisfy its hunger. It could wait for its chance, the desire would always be there, its instinct told it to wait.

"That was fucked up." Billy had barely waited until they were out of earshot from the farmers before he spoke.

"Have you not been paying attention? This is all fucked up." Mike said, but the other two thought it.

"Time to head back, get the mad bastard on the blower to take us home." Spencer was done for the day. Half a lead was all they'd achieved, but that was better than nothing.

Chapter 35

It had been good to stretch her legs. The unpleasantness had at the very least provided a fresh meal for Natasha, even if the prospect of explaining it to William wasn't one she relished. With any luck, he'd still be busy in his lab and she could shower and change before he even noticed that she'd left. Everything was as she had left it. She undressed in the garden, aware that a careless smudge of blood from her clothing would give her visit away. Cautiously, she entered the front door and listened for William. Not a sound.

She ran to the kitchen, dropping her bag of goodies off en route before throwing the blood-soaked clothes into the washing machine. She knew blood was a tough stain to get out, but she had to try it. The cycle began, and she rushed up to the bathroom and hopped into the shower. She might have got away with it. The water ran red. She had made quite the mess. She had wanted to do something good and had it had gone bad. She didn't blame herself; she wasn't even sure she cared, but she knew it was an act of kindness she wouldn't be repeating soon.

*

The boy was conscious but strapped to the table in the lab. Its skin colour was nearly normal, but it still acted like one of the creatures.

There was less anger, more agitation as it was poked and prodded. It couldn't speak, William hadn't expected it to. Its groans were little different than before. The week after the first injections, it was time for him to look inside. With the scalpel in hand, he sliced a strip of flesh off the boy's forearm. Little more than two inches long and half an inch wide, the sample came away cleanly. The flesh looked healthier than any feeder William had seen, but it didn't look like that of a normal human being. He held it up to a light. It was red rather than grey, but it was too dark. Under a microscope the problems were obvious. The scarring was easily visible, but how close did he need to get? The microbe was gone, only the damage it caused remained.

William took two more slices and laid them next to the first. The appearance was consistent. The truth was in the tasting. Would another creature go for the small slither of meat? They hadn't reacted to the boy since he had been experimented on. Not a great sign of success. William had hypothesised that they may sense the boy was food rather than one of their own, but they hadn't. William picked the slightly thicker strip of meat. It was a little more bloody, and he hoped that would appeal to them. He produced a metal rod from a selection of instruments, two feet in length it would be sufficient to pass through the meat into the cage. The female feeder was his preferred subject for this task.

He jammed the meat through the bars. But she showed no interest. He may as well have given her a copy of his thesis on obesity in domestic cats for the interest she showed. He put it in front of her eyes, hoping to get her attention, but nothing. She was all but in a trance. They all had been staring forward, occasionally treating themselves to a light sway. This is how a lot of the feeders acted outside. Some would roam continuously hunting for food, others would stop and wait for food to come to them. Why didn't she react? The meat was right under her nose. If she was outside and a human so much as passed wind within fifty metres, she would have sprung into life.

This was a failure, surely. William drew it back and sniffed. It smelled like uncooked pork, but it was a faint smell. His nose was nearly as good as hers, and neither the boy nor the meat appealed to him by smell alone. So why was he surprised it did nothing for her? In frustration, he pushed the rod back into the cage to the feeder's mouth. "Just fucking try it!" he growled. His anger had grown, he was so close and yet if they wouldn't eat it, he probably wouldn't be able to either. The rod knocked out two teeth of the creature as he forced the meat inside its mouth. And then it happened. Her eyes kicked into life and she instantly began chewing the flesh. It was barely a mouthful, finished in just a few chews and a swallow. It began clawing at the bars. This was the most active it had been since William had captured it.

He pushed through the other two slices, which were gratefully devoured. He looked to the boy, then to the feeder. It wanted more. Why not give it more? His instruments were varied, some would grace any laboratory in the world, others more at home in an abattoir. He produced a large cleaver and quickly approached the boy, then slammed it down. He struck just below the elbow, high on the forearm. He had expected to go clean through the bone, but he had rushed his blow. The cleaver had passed mostly through the flesh and bone, but it needed him to push down on the embedded blade until the crunch confirmed it was through. The boy reacted little differently than he had when the smaller samples had been taken.

The lower arm was quickly passed through to the feeder, who couldn't help itself. The meat had passed the taste test. Now the really big question, would it cure the feeder? FatBGone had an unexpected consequence of not leaving the body and thriving until the person became a monster like these poor bastards, slowly taking over their behaviour. Making the victim a slave to its desire to feed and spread.

William believed his cure would leave the system. It targeted the microbe, devouring it before it would effectively eat itself. His tests with the solution on blood samples had been promising, and from what he could see from the boy, it worked as planned. That's not to say he had any intention of risking it on himself until he was sure. He would no more eat the cured flesh than he would inject the solution into his arm. He didn't want to be human again; he had no intention of risking that outcome. He had a basement full of fresh meat. He had months before this long-term solution would be needed and a world full of test subjects.

*

Natasha had a small bowl of meat that she was picking at like popcorn, as she watched her big budget action film in the small living room. It was late and William hadn't shown his face all day. It was unusual even for him, but over the last week he had become increasingly distant. When he wasn't in his lab, he might as well have been for all the interest he showed in her. He entered and sat himself next to Natasha. He smelled of the lab. And something else, something equally artificial but not familiar.

"Good day, dear?" Natasha was more than a little sarcastic.

"Same as usual, darling. Just chipping away. How did you get on?" he asked, caring little for a response.

"The same, just stayed in the garden and did some reading.

William looked hard at the TV. They'd both watched every DVD multiple times, and he'd not seen this one. "New film?"

"I don't think so, dear. I found it behind the TV, it must have slipped back there," she replied. It was a weak lie, but it hardly deserved a bigger one.

William sat back and zoned out as a series of explosions rocked the screen. Both were oblivious of what the other had done that day. Not that they wanted or felt a need to share, they were content. It had been a good day for very different reasons.

Chapter 36

The prime minister waited in number 10 for news of the mission. She had expected word from the team over an hour ago and was growing increasingly impatient. The whiskey had been poured twice, and she was about to help herself to a third wee dram when there was a knock on the door. "Enter," she barked out the order.

In entered her most trusted advisor, who she had recently promoted to an official liaison role. He wasn't a military man, in an expensive tailored suit rather than an officer's uniform. Appearances were important to Gerard, he knew how to play to a crowd; he knew how to kiss an arse. He didn't get to where he was by being the best; he was there because he made others feel like they were. He had often lurked in the periphery, unnoticed by most. Since she had been promoted to the position of prime minister, he had been by her side, making himself invaluable to her. He observed and reported back in private. His information and manoeuvring were one of her most important assets. He ruled the shadows and wasn't comfortable with his new, more public position, but turning it down would have pushed him away, where he wouldn't have been able to apply his influence. "It's down. The S.O.S was received from the Hope 2. Four minutes later the first missiles struck. She sank in less than two minutes. The boys in black took care of any survivors."

"And our creature, was it recovered?" she asked. The PM stared at Gerard, ready to pounce on any bad news.

"Lost, as were the two men with it," he reported. He had hoped the good news of an otherwise successful mission would have been acceptable. The PM increased the intensity of her stare. He could sense the anger growing.

"Where the fuck am I supposed to get another one of those damned things? It was valuable, worth over 500 marines, worth more to me than a thousand pricks like you!" she lurched forward as she raised her voice.

"I know, I've already told those who ran the operation it's a damned disgrace that they failed to secure our asset and its safe return. I am demanding answers, believe me, I will make sure we have a head on the block before the end of the day for this dereliction of duty. Admiral Hollis is passing this off as a victory, the fool," Gerard said. He tried to mirror the PM's anger, an impossible task.

"Start drawing up replacements for Hollis, he and McKinley have got us in this bloody state. Incompetence and a distinct lack of balls are not traits that will see our survival," the prime minister spat. She was ready to burst a blood vessel.

"Prime minister, may I be so bold as to suggest we don't need to replace them? You have a firm grasp on what the people want, what they need. Hollis is a buffoon, McKinley is better off under house arrest where his softness can't permeate to the men. You can oversee those roles, your vision is what will save us. Dress Hollis down, but keep him in position, at least publicly, to appease the sailors. You serve the people, and they love you, let the military have their false idol whilst you call the shots," he proposed to her. Gerard was happy with his brown nosing, but unsure if the PM would be receptive.

"Don't you think I have enough to contend with?" she snapped. She liked power, and more of it wasn't a bad thing, but she was already working 20-hour days, sometimes longer.

"It would be short-term, it would give you that Winston Churchill image. It would play fantastically to the civilians. Delegate the mundane but be seen taking the decisions that will lead us, Great Britain, back from the brink," he added. It was working, he knew it.

"I will deal with Hollis in due course," the prime minister stated. She calmed, picturing in her mind the statue they may one day build of her.

"Very good," Gerard replied. He gave a quiet sigh of relief. He made his way out, happy to have survived the encounter with his job. He thought he'd get a pat on the back but underestimated the prime minister and her expectations. He walked through the narrow corridor and bumped into a marine coming from the opposite direction with a colleague. The marine glared at him, but not nearly as efficiently as the PM had done. "Watch where you're going cabbage head! Do you know how much this suit cost?" he roared. It was an uncharacteristic act. Had he not just endured a tense meeting with the PM, he would no doubt have just murmured an apology and carried on walking.

The marine stepped forward, ready to deal with Gerard, but he was dissuaded by his colleague. "Not now, not like this," he said. The pair carried on, leaving Gerard to straighten himself up.

The two marines walked in silence, angry and determined. The winding corridors all looked the same, with very little to distinguish one from another. One of their colleagues stood, rifle in his arms, outside of a door, marking it from the others. He acknowledged the two men and stood aside, letting them enter.

Inside the room, a dozen marines, a few naval officers, and General McKinley. They had been meeting for a few hours and the mood was light, even relieved. A growing number of those serving had been increasingly unhappy with the prime minister. Whispers of callous acts of violence against the civilians, murdering and turning the dead against the living spread amongst the personnel. The biggest sin she had committed in the eyes of those in service, was the sacrificing of their friends, their brothers, and sisters, in the name of the greater good. General McKinley no longer felt duty-bound to protect the administration and could fill in the blanks.

"The Hope 2 has gone, just as you said," one of the freshly arrived marines announced.

"No survivors?" the general asked though he knew the answer.

"None," the other marine added.

"She will do it again. She's running out of time and ideas, she will sacrifice ships and people until there are only a handful left. The human race is a dwindling resource, and that bloody stupid cow is burning through it," the general complained. He had seen this coming, but still frustrated.

"A coup is a big move, I'm not sure we have the numbers," a naval officer whimpered.

"This isn't a coup! She took power. We will return it to the people. She will be punished for her crimes, and those of us who stood with her will take our medicine too. We need the SBS with us, then we can guarantee a clean handover with no bloodshed."

"They come under the admiral's control in the current organisational design. He's still loyal, very much so," the naval officer put in, he wasn't a fan of his new chief.

"He knows which side his bread is buttered," a marine chipped in.

"Go around him if you can. They've lost people like the rest of us because of her. They're excellent soldiers, they don't enjoy being ordered to machine gun civilians, they will do what is right when the time comes," the general said and stood up, signalling it was time for his guests to leave. "Keep me abreast of any developments. Otherwise, 06:30 tomorrow for the commissioned officers. Thank you."

The guests slowly shuffled out, a single lieutenant held back. She held a small satchel close and approached the general. "Take this, who knows what tomorrow may bring," she said and left with the others, leaving the general to close the door, acknowledging his guard as the door clicked shut.

He looked inside the bag, a Glock 17 pistol. He took it out and checked it, a single bullet was loaded in the chamber and the magazine was empty. If they were discovered or betrayed, who knew what the prime minister might do.

Chapter 37

The white Vauxhall Frontera was old, but it ran. The car had as much rust on display as it did paintwork. The tires were bald; the brakes required forward planning, and a wash was much needed. It was one of only two four-wheel-drive cars the community had that was in running condition and was definitely the most expendable. The added benefit was a large interior; if they were successful, they could maximise their return.

"You're daft, but good luck," Babs said and gave Amy a hug. Bo was on his bench watching on. He'd already said everything he needed to.

Bo had insisted they took a gun. Amy initially resisted, but she wasn't on her own. With Jack along for the ride, she wasn't just risking her life, but his. Jack gratefully took Bo's prized shotgun and a fistful of cartridges when it was offered. It wouldn't be enough to mount an assault, but it could cover a hasty retreat.

Jack settled in the front passenger seat as Amy climbed in behind the wheel. Several members of the camp waved them off as the car trundled off down the dirt track that led to the country lanes.

The car journey took nearly forty minutes. Without the dead to worry about, and if she was certain of the way, it would have been less than half that. But as always, the feeders were everywhere. Sometimes just a few, sometimes large mobs. It was better to avoid a fight than risk losing one. They had time, fuel, and a purpose, stopping to take out a few of the dead along the way was pointless, there were too many, and the living too few. There had been a war, and those stinking bastards won. Amy had acknowledged that their role was to survive, and not to look for a fight.

As they came closer to the camp, the groups of feeders increased. It was a good sign. At least the camp inmates wouldn't be massed within whatever remained of the fences.

"I'll take us off-piste. If the camp is empty, it'd be a shame to bring few hundred feeders with us," she said. Amy concentrated on finding the best route.

A lightly wooded area with several wide tracks going through it seemed like the way to go, driving through both peered into the light foliage and didn't see any dead. *Good.* At the other end, they saw it, the camp. It hadn't fared well.

Hundreds of decomposing skeletons littered the camp. A Warrior infantry fighting vehicle had made it to one of the outermost fences before it had flipped as it made contact with a watchtower. It sat on its side, hatches open but abandoned. The crushed bodies, fences, and tents behind it showed the hurry it was in before it met its fate. Two more similar trails flanked it, the other tracked vehicles more successful in their escape having punched out through the fences to freedom. The camp was now most definitely abandoned, by the living certainly and by all but a handful of the dead. With their belly's full of fresh meat, most had wandered off looking for the next feast. The creatures that remained were mostly those turned in the camp, or who had been crippled as the living had desperately defended themselves.

There were nearly three hundred metres between them and the first fence. The cleared field was mostly muddy, but weeds and grass had added green to the brown dirt. A few shallow craters from explosives offered little in cover or concealment to help them get closer to the camp. The large white car wouldn't be stealthy, anything in the camp would see it coming as soon as it broke the cover of the woodland.

"You stay here, I'll go in on my own," she said to him. Amy grabbed a large empty rucksack, her machete, and checked her knife was still strapped to her ankle.

"Amy, don't. We'll both go, watch each other's backs," replied Jack. He couldn't even believe she had suggested going in alone.

"We can't take the car. We might as well shout dinner is served as we drive up. If we both go in and there's trouble, we're both fucked. You stay with the car, if I get in the shit you can drive down and rescue me," Amy said, she had already decided.

Jack knew Amy, the only way he'd stop her going down to the camp alone was by knocking her out, and he's not sure that would stop her. "At least take the damn gun."

"I'll be better off without the weight. Anyway, there's a small arsenal down there, I'll be better armed than you in five minutes' time," he told her. Amy kissed Jack and exited the car as he shuffled across to the driver's seat.

It wasn't a walk she enjoyed as she made her way to the camp. One thing the survivors had learned is that if the wind was blowing in the right direction, as long as you didn't act like a human, the dead wouldn't give you a second glance. She staggered down the gentle slope, hunching her form. At a distance, she would definitely pass as a feeder. The breeze in her face confirmed that her scent of humanity wouldn't give her away to them. She'd smell the bastards long before they could smell her.

They would keep the good stuff in the centre of the camp, that was too risky. The checkpoints were her best bet. They kept a small stash of food, ammunition, and basic first aid kits. That would be enough. A bonus would be another discarded rifle in the blood-stained mud.

It made sense to make use of one of the improvised exits the Warriors had left. They were wide, direct, and reached all the way to the centre of the camp. As she walked across the first wire fence, she remembered her time in the camp. The civilians, the other police officers, and Diane. She never liked to think of Diane. She barely knew her but felt Diane deserved better than to be abandoned. She prayed she wouldn't come across her. She may lose it if she saw Diane ripped apart on the ground or staggering aimlessly through the camp. As she moved amongst the bodies on the ground she grew more wary. Anyone of these corpses could suddenly spring to life and attack her. She gripped the machete a little tighter.

Amy decided she'd only go as far as two rings in. That's all she dared. A lot of the tents had either burned out or partially collapsed. Many still stood intact. She neared the Warrior that was on its side. Such a waste of firepower, she thought. A small tank would certainly beef up the farm's defensive capability. But then she looked around, a small army hadn't helped these people. She was in awe of the sight of it. She walked slowly to the top side. The hatches were open, and the crew had escaped. She couldn't help but peer inside. 30mm shells had fallen out of place and other equipment hung awkwardly. The shells were large, but useless to her. She looked deeper inside and there it was, the first bounty of the day. A small medical pouch. She reached inside but could quite get her fingertips to it. She hesitated, then looked around. Nothing was close, she could do it. In a quick motion, she climbed through the hatch and grabbed the pouch. It was weightier than she had expected. That could only be a good sign. She shuffled backwards out when she saw something familiar. A butt of a rifle. She smiled. Climbing further in, she reached out and pulled it towards her. It was smaller than the other service rifles. Its carbine length was handier and lighter. She pulled out the magazine. *Balls*. It was empty. It was still a welcome addition, but they needed ammunition. They only had a few rounds at the farm, not enough if they were attacked by a sizeable force, another rifle wouldn't increase their odds of survival significantly.

A roar stopped her dead in her tracks.

Jack looked down from the car, trying to see what had made the terrifying noise in the camp. "Fuck me," he cursed. He saw the creature. This wasn't just a big bastard, it was fucking huge. It was an impossibility, surely. How had they not seen it? It was difficult to tell how big it was, but judging by how Amy appeared when she entered the camp, this thing looked nearly 10 feet tall. He wanted to drive down and get her, but she'd be furious. It hadn't seen her, she was smart and athletic. He was ready but would give her the time that she'd have demanded.

Amy tucked herself into the tank. Silently, she listened for what was lurking outside. Nothing. She looked around, hoping for a magazine or even a single bullet. Giving up, she slung the rifle over her shoulder next to the rucksack. Machete tight in hand, she looked out of the hatch. It was magnificent in its grotesque appearance. It was huge in every way. Some of its boils were the size of footballs, it's limbs like tree trunks. Its gut nearly reached down to its knees. It was maybe 100 meters away; it wasn't facing her as it slowly performed its own little patrol of the camp.

This changed nothing for Amy. She was determined to get more than just an empty rifle and a small first aid kit. The first checkpoint was close, and in the opposite direction to the creature. Carefully, she exited the armoured vehicle. She was all too aware not to concentrate too hard on the obvious threat. There were still regular feeders she needed to be aware of.

Jack watched as Amy crept the 20 metres to the checkpoint, her journey unnoticed by any of the dead. He was desperate for her to make her way back to the car, but he knew she wouldn't give up easily.

A dead soldier laid across the entrance to the checkpoint. They had ripped his body armour open to get at his flesh. Besides the scraps of uniform, the vest and a nearby helmet, it looked just like any of the other corpses. They had wasted barely a morsel of meat. His rifle was gone, Amy gingerly picked at the pouches attached to his webbing, but they'd already been looted or used. The checkpoint was littered with shell casings. They had put up a good, if futile, fight. Inside the small shelter a blood splattered magazine of 5.56mm ammunition and an undischarged taser were sitting on the ground. A good start. There were several boxes, mostly empty. Two torches and a sealed box of batteries would always be useful. Four unopened 24 hour ration packs put a smile on her face. She knew Bo would be keen on any boiled sweets held inside, and they would often be good for a bar of chocolate. A small luxury for the children at the farm. She loaded them inside her rucksack. The creature let out another roar, and she froze. It sounded close. Amy inserted the magazine into the carbine and loaded a round. It was big, but a magazine of ammo to the face would surely stop it.

She sneaked out and hid behind the checkpoint. The epic bastard was now 20 metres away. It stopped to listen and sniff the air, desperate to hear or smell the human foolish enough to enter its domain. She barely dared to breathe as her heart raced. The damn thing was hunting her. She darted to a group of tents ahead would give her cover to lose the thing. It reduced her visibility to only a few metres, any number of feeders could appear and attack. She was tempted to use the rifle, but that had to be the reserve choice, save it for the huge one if needed. The machete was in her hand as she spotted the first feeder. It thought it was its lucky day, but in fact it was its last as the blade slammed into the top of its head. Amy followed it to the ground and retrieved her weapon. Another roar. It was onto her, it just hadn't locked on to her yet.

Amy rounded the corner, and two creatures looked up. Their filthy faces would have smiled if they could. The machete again did its job before Amy's small knife entered the side of the other monster's head. She could hear it. She wiped the blood off her weapons and jumped into the nearest standing tent. Thankfully, it was empty. This thing was quick and persistent. A normal fat bastard wouldn't have followed her so expertly. Amy peered through the door of the tent and it was less than 10 metres away.

Jack felt helpless as he watched it getting closer to her. He was getting ready, he could be in the camp in 30 seconds and back out in another 20.

The beast started edging backwards in her direction. In a few moments she'd be trapped. Amy decided it was now or never before she leapt from the tent and pulled the trigger. A single bullet struck its throat with no effect. Amy yanked at the trigger, but nothing. She looked down at the rifle and the previous round was wedged in the extraction port. Had Amy been a trained soldier, she may have been able to clear the malfunction. She wasn't. Her aim was above average, but she knew nothing of maintaining a service rifle. As the creature edged towards her, she slung the weapon over her shoulder and produced the taser. The monster was close enough for her to deploy the prongs, making a good contact on its chest. The first discharge made it stop its advance. It was confused rather than hurt, but that confusion soon turned to anger. Amy gave it another jolt, and it didn't stop. She only had one option left, run.

It was faster than the other big ones; it wasn't the same as them. She was only just maintaining her slender lead. The conflict had attracted several regular feeders, and they moved to intercept her. She looked over her shoulder and could see to the centre of the camp. The stores were there and intact. Ammunition and food to last years. It was so close, but so far. The large feeder carried on its determined pursuit, making the ground up slowly, confident it would defeat its prey.

Jack slammed on the brakes as he charged through the camp 20 metres in front of Amy. He popped the door open as ran towards him. *Thank fuck.* She picked up the pace and dived in, Jack wasted no time in putting his foot down and getting the car out of the danger zone. The small group following didn't stop but had no hope of catching them. The giant feeder stopped and watched as the white car continued away at speed.

"That was new," Jack stated the obvious.

"Maybe that's what all the big ones grow into. Or another fucking version of these damned monsters." Amy slammed the door shut and removed the rucksack.

"Did you get anything good?"

"A busted rifle, a magazine, torches, batteries, and some ration packs. Not enough, but something I guess. It was all there, though. I could see it. Food, water, medical supplies, and ammo. They just left it there as if it was worthless, just like the people. Those fuckers ran and left them all," she ridiculed. Amy felt angry, with what those in charge had abandoned and that she had so little to show for the trip. She was already thinking about how they could go back and raid the camp more thoroughly. The risk was high, but so was the reward.

Chapter 38

Gerard had been served his meagre rations in the canteen and sat by himself, unnoticed by most. His talent of merging into the background had often helped him get the dirt on opponents when he enjoyed a quiet glass of Merlot in a bar or pub in Westminster. Whilst he enjoyed the finer things in life, he was such an ordinary looking human being he was barely recognisable and completely unremarkable. Life on the ship had changed little for Gerard. Despite his dress sense, others barely acknowledged him. Now his position had become more public in the past few days, he had worried that he might lose one of his key skills. It was soon obvious that nobody cared about him. He was just another suit. Four marines sat on the table in front of him. Each a bitter man, they had been at the sharp end of the recent conflicts and had little time for those in charge.

"It's not long, I know McKinley is close to making his move. Trust me," a young marine spoke a little too loudly, and Gerard locked on to the conversation. His eyes didn't move. He continued to eat with no change in behaviour, eager to hear more careless whispers.

"Making his move? He's locked up, I've even heard they have already executed him," an older marine said, he didn't believe a word of it.

"No, it's true. Guthrie has met with McKinley in his quarters. He told me their only problem is the lack of the special forces boys on their side. They're loyal to that berk Hollis, and he's loyal to her," a third marine got involved in the unnecessarily public conversation.

"It's still bullshit, there's no way anyone is stupid enough to mount a rebellion," the old marine replied. He was confident his experience meant more than these younger soldiers' enthusiasm for change.

"McKinley or her? Who would you follow, given a choice?" the young marine smiled as he pressed his elder.

"This is the navy, we're not given choices, we're given command structures and orders to obey."

"Who?" came the further pressing.

"McKinley, of course, but it doesn't matter. There will not be a coup," begrudgingly he answered, nearing anger at this kid getting him to play the silly game.

Gerard quietly listened. He didn't think McKinley had it in him to make such a move; he was nearly impressed. Even a hint of a coup d'état would be quite the development, one that would firm up his position as the prime minister's most trusted adviser. Calmly Gerard finished up his meal, and unnoticed returned his tray of dirty crockery before heading back the prime minister.

He felt like his head was going to explode with the information. He looked at everyone he passed with suspicion, how many were involved? Was he on the winning side? The prime minister was about to piss off the only man who may keep her in power. In a fit of anger, she may even relieve admiral Hollis of his duties. That didn't automatically mean the Special Boat Service soldiers would turn on her and join the usurpers, but it wouldn't help her cause. Maybe she hadn't bollocked him yet. That would make everything much more straightforward. He felt his pace quickening as he rushed to her quarters.

The sentry at her door wasn't expecting Gerard but saw his security pass and vaguely recognised him. "She's meeting with the admiral."

Maybe there was still time. "I have to see her now, it's of the utmost importance."

The sentry looked at him, unsure of whether he'd get in more trouble for letting him in or refusing access. He stepped to the side and Gerard swung the door open, startling those inside. The admiral seemed relaxed. He didn't look like a man who'd been sacked or screamed at. The PM seemed calm, but unhappy with the interruption.

"Prime minister, I need to talk with you immediately." Gerard couldn't bring himself to more than glance at the admiral.

"What is it?" she snapped.

Gerard moved towards her and led her to the back of the room. "McKinley is mounting a coup."

"He's what? He's locked up! He wouldn't dare!" she exclaimed. She refused to believe he'd be so stupid.

"There is widespread support for the general, he's making his move imminently," Gerard said, he needed her to believe him.

"I want him here in two minutes, send a dozen marines to secure him," she ordered. She could barely contain her anger.

"Prime minister, he has the support of the marines. As I understand it, we can rely only on the SBS to be loyal to your administration. And only with Hollis in charge," Gerard murmured. The hushed tones of Gerard as he mentioned the admirals' name made Hollis turn to see what was going on.

"Admiral, the reason I asked you to join me is that we've had word that a mutiny is afoot," she said and paused for a moment to read him, to see if he was part of the conspiracy. The look of shock on his face suggested he was innocent. "I believe there are few we can trust. I trust you, and I trust the special boat service. I need you to discreetly put the SBS on alert, I want a personal protection detail and McKinley brought to me at once to answer for his crimes."

Hollis was sure he was about to be unceremoniously fired and relished the loss of responsibilities. He had been looking forward to a simpler life away from command, but now seemed closer to the top than ever before. A greater sense of importance and pride swept over him. Maybe he did still lust after power. "I'll get right on it. I'll bring the bastard here myself."

The PM locked the door behind the admiral and produced a small revolver from her desk draw. She sat herself down behind the desk and gripped the pistol; ready to put all five bullets into anyone who thought they could take her position away from her.

Chapter 39

Whilst the soldiers were away, Peter had proved his value. Spencer had marked on the dirt and grass within the compound where he wanted more foxholes dug. It was a never-ending task, but the soldiers believed it was an important one. He thought there was an element of busy work attached to the task, especially to keep him out of the way. But he appreciated being kept busy. He'd been alone with his thoughts for too long, a task to occupy his mind was a welcome distraction. With the shovel and empty sandbags, Peter had been working for hours. It was exhausting work, especially for him. He had helped over the last few days digging several small defensive positions, so believed he knew what he was doing. Careful to ensure they were neither too deep nor too shallow. Looking at his handiwork, he knew the soldiers would mock him. He also knew anyone of them would happily dive into one should they come under attack.

When the sound of the helicopter reached him, Peter could barely stand. He thought to himself that if the feeders suddenly burst through the fence, he wouldn't have the strength to run or lift the pistol to defend himself. It did a single lap of the compound before it touched down on its spot.

The men hopped out, rifles ready, but were soon at ease.

"Been busy, Peter?" Gary asked. He instantly started admiring the new foxholes, "Good depth, right size. The sandbags look alright too. Nice work."

Peter smiled at the praise. Billy and Mike walked past him and nodded in approval.

"How's the fort been?" Spencer smiled at Peter, he was glad he hadn't just sat around and instead shown some initiative.

"Surrounded by the dead, as usual, otherwise fine," he replied. Peter's confidence grew.

"We're going to wash up in the barracks. You know, you should move yourself in. It makes little sense for you to sleep on the floor in a small office when we have over a dozen spare beds you could choose from," he said. Spencer knew Peter's concerns and didn't want to press him too hard.

"I don't enjoy sleeping on the ground floor with them about. I feel secure where I am," Peter stated. He shrunk back inside of himself, a little ashamed that he was still afraid.

"It's your call, Pete. Outstanding work on the foxholes," Spencer complimented. He left Peter as the crew unloaded the helicopter.

"Peter, little help?" Kyle called him over and Peter jogged to assist. They didn't need him, but it was nice to feel part of the team.

"How'd it look out there?" Peter hadn't dared to ask one of the SAS team.

"Dead everywhere. We saw some survivors, some friendly, others not so much. We didn't get our man though, so I think tomorrow we'll be doing more of the same," was the reply. Andy swept out the shell casings from the machine guns.

Peter felt a little disheartened. He'd be on his own again tomorrow.

"Petey, do you play poker?" Sebastian exited the cockpit, lighting his cigar.

"I used to play a bit online," Peter responded. PistolPete666 had won often at the virtual poker tables, but he'd never played a real live game of cards.

"Online? Of course you did," Sebastian said as he smirked and looked at his two door gunners. "We've got a game on tonight if you're interested?" Sebastian asked, he was always looking for a new mug to beat.

"I don't have any money," Peter shared. Again he withdrew into himself.

"Same as the rest of us then, don't worry. We'll work something out. Barracks at 9pm," Sebastian insisted, before he made his way to the barracks, leaving his crew and Peter to help clear the chopper.

Inside the barracks, the SAS team were already removing their gear and Mike was the first to disappear into the shower. Spencer was still in his full kit, examining maps and marking off the day's locations. He wanted to capture as much of their progress as he could before providing his superiors an update. They wouldn't be excited, but nobody expected them to disappear for a long weekend and return with their target. It was a needle in a haystack and one of many avenues those in charge were exploring. For 10 minutes his head didn't look up from the papers he'd spread out in front of him. His men were already showered and getting changed by the time he'd finished.

"Spencer, do you want me to report in?" Mike offered. He was more than capable of performing the update. The operator at the other end of the satellite phone didn't care who they spoke to.

"Cheers Mike. It's all marked down. I'll check the perimeter before I wash up."

Spencer left the barracks and observed Peter working with Andy and Kyle. It brought a smile to his face to see them just mucking about, but still doing the job. Walking the fence line, he looked into the eyes of several creatures. Why had they massed here? He couldn't think of a good reason. In the towns and cities, the noise of survivors would attract them and they'd develop into hordes as they followed their senses to food. But here? It was the middle of nowhere, yet half the local towns' inhabitants, who had turned, had wandered to this compound. He stopped and listened. All he could hear now were the groans and snarls of these monsters. He could see the large generators and walked closer to them. A low hum, that was barely audible. It couldn't have been that, surely? The feeders had impressive hearing and sense of smell, maybe they could sense its vibrations? It would help to explain the fall of all the rescue camps. The dead always turned up in large numbers, eventually. When it was chaos inside and the survivors revolted, the dead just had to wait for their chance. Spencer carried on his patrol. He'd finish, shower, eat and then watch the guys play cards. It wasn't fair for him to win their shit, so he'd just watch and relax.

Chapter 40

Only the moonlight illuminated the bedroom inside of the cottage, Natasha on top of William, slowly riding him. It wasn't an unusual occurrence, but neither seemed that into it. Natasha picked up speed, trying to get her obligation finished. William just stared at the ceiling, his mind elsewhere. Fed up, Natasha rolled off of William. "Why don't you just stay in your bloody lab?" she fumed.

William sat up, snapping out of his daze. "I'm sorry. I'm so very close, I know it."

"We have all the time in the world to be boring. Why the rush? We have live food here and we could even go for a hunt, we might stumble across a survivor and we could devour them together," she said. Natasha had the taste for the hunt again, taking down live prey rather than just picking at the souls chained up in the basement.

"We don't need to. With my cure, we'll have all the food we ever need, no risk, no starvation," William promised. He was very different from Natasha, he took no thrill from the hunt. The inefficiency and danger made the whole idea of hunting unappealing.

Natasha couldn't disagree more. Her recent venture out had reminded her the chase was nearly as important as the feast at the end. She knew she was a beast, a monster, and she enjoyed it. When she stumbled across those idiots in the village, she thought she wanted redemption. She didn't. She wanted to be the monster she had become, but that William has shackled with this gilded cage. "You can't expect me to stay the quiet little housewife forever. You have your work, I have your mother's old romance novels. I'm not going to just wait for you to summon me like I'm fucking on-call."

"You're welcome to leave. If you want to hunt so much, you go for it. I'm sure you remember what it's like to have an empty belly, to not be able to think about anything but your next feed? You like the thrill of the hunt? Did you like being shot? How about stabbed or beaten? You're a child, Natasha. When the dead are the only things walking this earth, you'll thank me for providing for us."

The worst thing was Natasha knew he was right. She stormed out of the room naked. She was furious and had a point to prove. She rushed downstairs to the kitchen and opened the door to the cellar. Turning the light on, a dozen scared faces turned away, not wanting to draw her attention. She didn't care. She picked a girl, a little plump thing in her early teens. She was complete and hadn't been harvested from yet. This one would really piss William off. Grabbing the girl the other captives gasped but were helpless to save her, she unshackled her and stood the girl in front of her.

Natasha looked her in the eyes for what felt like minutes but was only seconds. She was petrified and powerless. Just how Natasha liked her food. Slowly she moved her face closer to the girls, savouring every moment of anticipation. Her lips brushed against the girl's cheek gently, as if she was going to kiss her before pulling away. The girl trembled and wet herself. Natasha smiled then lunged at the girl biting her cheek ripping a small piece of flesh away.

The others screamed and cried out. The girl was frozen with fear as Natasha gripped her hard, ready to feed once more.

"Stop this now!" William shouted at the top of his lungs. He was already behind Natasha before she could turn and ripped her off of the girl, flinging Natasha to the ground. "What the fuck are you doing?" William screamed at Natasha. He looked down at the girl, her cheek was bleeding from where the flesh had been torn away. The stubborn bitch had purposefully bitten her cheek. If it had been her arm, he could have amputated and kept the girl going. The facial injury was a showstopper. *Unless...*

William grabbed Natasha and dragged her to a set of shackles at the far end of the cellar, away from its other guests. He chained her up and checked to make sure she was fully restrained.

"I didn't take you for that kinky sort Willy, maybe that's where I've been going wrong?" Natasha teased. She had a devious smile spread across her face. She had achieved what she wanted, she'd got to him.

"Calm yourself down, I'll be back in the morning," he said. William picked the girl up and took her up the stairs.

"She's underage you pedo!" she exclaimed. The smirk grew wider, then disappeared. "You can't leave me here you arsehole," she cursed. The door was already slamming shut as she screamed out her last words.

Quickly William carried the girl to his lab and strapped her to a gurney, making sure her limbs and head could not move. "It'll be okay, I promise. I can make you better," he tried to assure her. The girl saw no comfort in the words coming from this monster. She'd seen what he'd done to the others without a care in the world. Her eyes struggled to move away from the caged creatures in this nightmarish, mad scientist's laboratory. He wasn't her saviour.

William was determined to test his cure. *Could it save a recently infected human?* By now the microbe was working its way through her body, carried in her bloodstream. It was already starting to reproduce and feeding on her. The first people he had turned before society had fallen had taken days to become the unthinking beasts that now ruled the land. If he infected someone now, it could take as little as just a few hours for them to change. This girl was still herself. If he could apply the cure now before she lost any cognitive abilities, it would prove the effectiveness of the cure.

The wound looked sore, but Natasha hadn't taken too much flesh. She could easily have bitten a hole into the poor girl's face. Instead, it was just a minor wound. William cleaned the wound before he began injecting around it with his solution. The girl squirmed in pain. Each injection like a bee sting on her face. William applied a dressing to the wound and admired his handwork, but he wasn't finished.

After fifty small injections all over the girl's body, she had passed out with the pain. William stood back and stared at her, looking for any changes in her pigmentation or other signs that the infection had taken hold. Nothing. With the treatment having been applied, now only time would tell if it was effective.

Chapter 41

The prime minister had been restless since she had ordered the admiral to return with McKinley. The pistol remained in her grasp. She wasn't sure if the next person through the door of number 10 would be loyal or a treacherous usurper ready to shoot her dead. Either way, she was prepared to shoot first and ask questions later. Gerard stood a few feet away and looked more nervous than she did. He equally wasn't confident that the door wouldn't open with a hail of bullets. Best not to stand too close to their potential target.

"This is the state of the world? It's like a fucking banana republic. Nobody respects the rule of law, or the rightful government. They think they can snatch power because they have hurt feelings, because they don't like the tough decisions being made. If they think they have force, I'll show them bloody force. I'll show them I'm in charge. I'll show them and anyone else who thinks they can take my job!" she declared. She had already decided that they would execute McKinley. Extreme times call for extreme measures. He would have conspirators, the SBS would be tasked with extracting their names from him. They would become her personal army, ready to protect her and destroy her enemies. If they wanted a dictator, she'd give them one. Three knocks on the door heightened tensions in the room. Gerard took a further, subtle step away from the prime minister whilst she readied her small revolver. "Enter."

The door slowly swung open. A special forces soldier in black carrying an assault rifle stepped through first, followed by a bound McKinley and three more soldiers. McKinley had a small smear of blood under his nose and his eye was red, the start of a nice shiner. Roughly, they shoved him down to his knees. *Good, they had already started softening the bastard up.*

"Where is Hollis?" she barked, having expected to see her pet admiral proudly leading the traitor to her.

"Ma'am, the admiral is in sickbay. An altercation with the prisoner resulted in a minor injury," the first soldier stated.

A wicked smile spread across her face. She was pleased to hear of his loyalty and amused by the idea of these middle-aged men brawling. "Very good," she said and rose from her chair and stood over McKinley, "Do you know why you're here?"

He looked up at her emotionless and nodded, his eye already starting to swell.

"I'm interested in how you thought you would get away with this? Did I hurt your masculine pride so much by stripping you of your position, little me, a woman?"

"Well, I guess I thought you were a monster who had to be stopped, just like we'd put down one of those creatures rather than let it fester."

"Everything I did was to guarantee the survival of humanity. I took no pleasure in what had to be done, I will go down in history as a saviour, not a sinner."

"Myself, and many others know of your crimes, we won't let them be forgotten."

"Yes, your co-conspirators. How many of them have you infected with your silly ideas of a better tomorrow without sacrifice today?" she asked then raised her pistol and pressed it against his forehead.

"More than you can imagine, from cooks to senior officers. On this ship and others, your crimes are more than whispers, more than rumour. People know the truth, and you can't kill it. Do what you want with me, you'll be the one tied and bound by the end of the day."

She looked to the soldiers. "I want a list of names within the hour, and either the brig or mortuary full," she said. They each stared blankly without moving. "Take him away and get those bloody names!" she demanded. Still, they refused to move. She moved closer to the nearest soldier, inches away. "Do you understand! Do your damn job!" she screamed in his face as loud as she could. A small amused smile took to the soldier's face. It could have been that the thought of this politician thinking she could intimidate him with his years of service and training. Or it could have been the sight of McKinley slowly rising to his feet, his hands unbound and a 9mm pistol in his hand.

"Ma'am, you're relieved of your duties," McKinley stood behind her, his pistol pointed at her back.

Her heart skipped several beats as the situation dawned on her. Slowly she turned to see the general. "Do you think you will do better?"

"I'm not in charge, we already have a council organised. Like you, I must answer for my crimes and I will gladly do so. Hollis will answer for his too once his broken jaw allows him to speak."

She still had her pistol in her hand. The angry voice inside of her screamed at her to shoot everyone. The other voice, the fearful one, pleaded with her to give up and beg for mercy. Before either voice had successfully made its case, a soldier snatched the pistol from her, and showed it off to his colleagues. "This is cute, I think I'll give it to my daughter."

"It should never have come to this. The people looked to us for protection and at every step we decided who would live or die. Had we made different, better decisions we could have saved thousands more, but we protected the few, the VIPs, the rich and those who we decided were useful."

"Spare me the lecture general. If I'm to be arrested, all I ask is that you stop spouting your misplaced morality and take me to the brig so I might finally get some rest."

The general nodded, and as the soldiers took her out of the room, Gerard quietly followed unchallenged. The general touched his swollen eye and winced with the pain, Hollis had a decent left hook but a glass jaw. Left alone, he sat down and popped the magazine out of his pistol and ejected the single round in the chamber, placing them all on the table. The bottle of whiskey caught his eye, and he poured himself a small measure to help with the pain. He wasn't sure this course of action would have a better result than what the prime minister had been doing, but they wouldn't kill their own people. On that point alone, they couldn't be worse off. He knocked back the spirit and left the quarters. "There's a pistol on the desk, secure it then lock up before reporting back to your CO," the general commanded the bewildered sentry.

"What's happening sir?" the sentry asked, having heard parts of the altercation, but didn't understand.

"Something different, let's hope it's better."

<h1 style="text-align:center">Chapter 42</h1>

As the helicopter rose above Wellworth, the SAS team were already growing weary of their daily routine. Death was everywhere. The few survivors they interacted with were as friendly as the feeders. This scientist was probably dead, but they had to continue searching as long as those in charge ordered it. Every foray into the dead's domain reaffirmed the fact that unless he'd found a good, strong group, he wasn't alive to be found. Peter was again left on his own, waving them off from the ground as they flew further away.

Spencer had wanted to follow the lead they had received at Mackland's farm, but those in charge had their own preferred targets to investigate, and that's what he did. Today they would get close to Thornhurst, where the farmer had tipped them to a Johnson family living nearby. If not today, then perhaps tomorrow they might stumble across the right farm.

The helicopter was only in the air for five minutes before it began circling the chosen landing zone. The door gunners concentrated on any movement, ready to open fire at any threat. None was visible, and after the okay from Spencer, the helicopter began its descent.

"The satellites have recorded movement here that could be human in the last 24 hours," Spencer confirmed to his men.

"That's what they've said about every fucking shit hole they've sent us to," Gary rightly pointed out. "Sometimes it's a survivor, most the time it's one of them."

"We all have a job, yours is to shut up and do as you're told. As is mine," Spencer replied. He nudged his man just as the Lynx touched the ground and the men jumped out, taking up a defensive position before it soared back into the sky.

The farmhouse looked much like the others. Made of stone with a few more modern outbuildings, it was functional and only changed as it had needed to over the years. Animal carcasses littered the fields, but no roaming feeders. That was something. As they neared the courtyard, several downed feeders lay on the ground, each with a wound through the eye. Not from a firearm, but from a blade or something pointy. They were getting closer to the farmhouse, but before they could make themselves known a man exited the farmhouse waving his t-shirt in the air atop of his spear as if he was surrendering.

"Please don't shoot!" Kevin tightly gripped the spear.

The four man SAS team became more alert. It wouldn't have been the first ambush they'd suffered from a group of survivors feigning compliance.

"Stay there mate. Are you alone?" Spencer signalled his men to fan out to cover any potential attack.

"Yes sir, it's just me. I swear," he replied. He was hardly likely to tell the truth if he was the mastermind of an ambush.

Spencer didn't need to look at the picture of William, it was obvious this wasn't their man. "Secure him," he ordered Gary, who obliged and rushed to Kevin.

Gary threw the spear to the ground and forced Kevin to his knees, then his onto belly with his hands behind his back. A black cable tie secured him and he rested with his knee on Kevin's back. The other three men began clearing the farm. Minutes passed, and they all came out, happy the farm was deserted.

Spencer approached Kevin. "Is this your farm?"

"No sir, I'm just staying here for a few days," Kevin answered. Fear and hope, Kevin knew they may kill him, but they could take him with them. Either option seemed more desirable than being left alone to survive.

"Where are you from? You sound like a city kid, not some country bumpkin," Spencer asked. He was sizing up their captive, trying to decide what kind of survivor he was.

"London."

"We're looking for a man. He's very important and could help end all this shit. Have you seen any other survivors in this area?" Spencer asked, he never dropped eye contact.

"Just one, but she wasn't right. She was like one of those things. She killed my mate, bloody ate him, right in front of me. I barely got away."

Like all soldiers who had fought on the mainland, they had heard stories of the intelligent feeders. He'd seen the reports on the variants of the creatures. Even Peter had his own story of an intelligent one. Besides a slight issue with their complexion, they looked and acted like a normal human being. But they were cunning, which made them more dangerous. Spencer wasn't sure he believed they existed. He couldn't make his mind up if they were just stories made up to keep the infantry alert, or just genuine survivors who had suffered a breakdown. It wasn't a stretch to believe some poor bastard, trapped and alone, could lose their marbles and attack the living as if it were a creature. He understood the basic creatures, even the big buggers, and the more physically impressive feeders made sense. But smart ones? He really wasn't sure he believed the dossier or the eyewitness statements.

"A female?"

"Yeah, good looking. Natasha."

That name rang a bell with Spencer, but he couldn't place it and didn't put a lot of effort trying to recall details. "Where was she?"

"Thornhurst."

Getting closer, good. "Is she still there?"

"No. She saved me and Jules. She walked amongst them. She even helped us get out of that place. But she attacked Jules for no reason as soon as we were clear of that fucking village."

He was nervous and evasive, Spencer picked up on it and continued, "Where was she going?"

"Didn't say, didn't want us to go with her, that much was clear. She told us she was living with her boyfriend. Phil, Bill…" Kevin tried to recall the details, but all he could recall was the sight of her eating his friend.

"William?" Spencer offered. His interest was again peaked.

"Yeah, that sounds right. Will, William. Yeah, that was it."

Spencer felt some relief. Maybe they would be done with this mission soon. "Get that mad fucker on the blower, we need a pickup. We're heading back early," he seethed. He wanted to get back to Wellworth and report in. He'd plead with the head sheds to get every satellite they still had access to looking at anything within three miles of Thornhurst that even remotely looked like a house. He'd give the boys an early night, and they'd be out at the crack of sparrows, ready to get their man.

"Can I come with you?" Kevin piped up, embarrassed.

"No. We can't accommodate refugees," replied Spencer. He knew they could easily take the kid back to Wellworth, but they didn't know him. He couldn't risk the safety of his men when they might be so close to their objective.

"I'm all alone, I need your help," Kevin said. He felt a wave of desperation wash over him.

"Sorry, not our mission. You've made it this far, carry on as you have been," Spencer said and turned away from the kid, "Mike, test him. All good cut his restraints. If he fails, put one in his skull."

Mike nodded and followed Spencer's order. He took his small testing kit, taking the blood, and quickly adding it to the small ceramic tile before applying the white substance. Kevin was as nervous as when Natasha had attacked his friend. His fate wasn't in his own hands, and he was about to find out if his suffering could continue. "You're fine," Mike confirmed, bluntly advising Kevin he wasn't about to be shot before he cut the cable tie off. He reached into a pouch on his webbing and produced two protein bars, which he tossed to Kevin. It wasn't much, but it made Mike feel better about leaving the kid behind. The soldiers headed back to the landing zone, Mike monitored Kevin until they were a suitable distance away when he was happy to face forward.

Kevin watched as they moved further away as he scoffed down the protein bar, facing the reality he would probably die alone.

Chapter 43

It was a sunny day with a cool breeze that gently rode through the community. Since her return to the rescue camp, Amy was more determined than ever to increase their defences. Rising just after the sun, she had dug a trench which she planned would be the first in a series. Against a living threat, they could use them for cover. Against the dead, it would hopefully trap a few of the bastards. Those on watch looked at Amy with both admiration and pity. She was as brave and selfless as anyone in the camp, but she could not stop for even a moment. She was always looking to the next thing, never happy with what she had. There was little doubt after the trenches were complete, she'd want something else built or procured. They didn't know what she had seen at the abandoned camp, the riches that existed, the giant that could devour them all.

As the rest of survivors woke and began starting their day, Amy had already done a day's work. Jack had woken up alone. It wasn't unusual, but when he saw her digging the trench on the boundary of the settlement and the field he didn't question it. Instead, he grabbed a bottle of water and a bowl of oats and took it to her.

"You look like you need this," he said and handed her the refreshments, and she gratefully chugged down the water as they sat down beside each other on the side of the partially dug trench. "How many of these are you planning on digging?"

"Just a few, covering the main approaches. We need more than shallow stone walls. We're sitting ducks out here," she commented. She looked out to the surrounding area, aware a threat could approach from anywhere.

"We've done okay so far," Jack said, believing their community more a success than a work in progress.

"The jumper, the gigantic bastard, the smart ones. Jesus, what else is out there? We've all seen the herds, we've been lucky to lead a few away. We're not always going to be that fortunate."

"Eat and drink. I'll round up some idle hands to help us," he told her. Jack knew the trenches would be dug. Even if she had to spend 16 hours a day for a month doing it herself. A gentle hand on her back, a quick kiss, and he was heading back to the farmhouse.

Bo had been working late into the evening. The faulty assault rifle had found its way to him to repair, and he'd been successful but was eager to check his handiwork in the sunlight rather than that of the dim candles he'd used the previous evening. He cycled the action; it was clean and crisp, depressing the trigger the click helped affirm he'd at least put it back together mostly correctly. Jack approached and was waved over.

"Any luck with that thing?" Jack gestured to the rifle.

"Piece of piss. The damn thing was fucking filthy. It was just a jam, but it would probably have struggled to pass more than a couple of rounds before it jammed again." Bo rubbed the weapon down, taking a degree of pride in his work.

"So it's working?" Jack meekly asked.

"Of course it bloody is. Just needed a good field strip and clean. These modern service rifles, a pile of shit. Give me an Enfield any day of the week, even these kids today calling themselves soldiers could keep one of those running." Bo stated, insulted by the passing of time and progress in military small arms.

Jack had hoped it was beyond repair, that it would just be a lump of scrap metal. Good for little more than use as an improvised club. "Bo, you can't tell her it's fixed."

"What are you talking about son?" Bo asked. He already felt like he was surplus to requirements, fixing the rifle was the only useful thing he'd managed in a week and he was to pretend he hadn't.

"She'll want to go back. If that can fire, she'll go back to that camp and she'll die. There are too many of them there, it's too dangerous, and she's too damn stubborn."

He was right, Bo knew it. She was brave and intelligent, but she was a stubborn cow. A rifle with 30 rounds against hundreds of the dead and the mutations wasn't much use. Worse still, she wouldn't be alone. The community admired her greatly and would follow her anywhere, and if she felt the reward was great enough, she might just let them.

"We can't not tell her, she'd go fucking mental for starters," Bo replied. He knew her reaction wouldn't be productive.

"But Bo..." Jack pleaded.

"I understand, I do. Lord knows I do, but it ain't like that, is it? She's stubborn, but I don't think she's wrong that often. If I was 20, okay, 30 years younger I'd be storming that fucking place with my shooter to get my mitts on everything that's there."

"But Bo..." Jack began.

"Jack, it ain't worth the dick ache. She's right, we just don't want her to be. You follow her like a puppy and you never challenge her. Don't make it that when you finally do, you lie to the girl. Because I won't fucking protect you from her when she rips you prick off," Bo was serious.

"Can you give me a few days?" Jack asked. He was already thinking about how to outmanoeuvre Bo and Amy. He needed a little more time.

"I'll tell her it'll be fixed by teatime tomorrow," Bo relented, happier with the white lie rather than the outright one.

"You're a star Bo," Jack praised. He trotted off to rustle up some help with the trenches. The manual labour would keep her mind off returning to the camp and give him the time he needed. He refused to let her die there. It was time others carried some of the crippling weight on their shoulders.

Chapter 44

William had fallen asleep in an old chair that had remained from when his laboratory was just a holiday cottage. It was worn, but more comfortable than sleeping on the floor. He hadn't spared a thought for Natasha in the cellar as he'd covered himself in a warm blanket before he'd drifted off. The bitch deserved to be put back in her place. She didn't understand what he was busy achieving, she just wanted to play and fuck around. Every day she became more complacent, forgetting the suffering she had endured as food had become harder to come by. She needed a lesson. He'd keep her there for a day or two until the hunger overtook her, maybe then she'd remember how hard life was before she met him.

William stirred as the girl cried. She hadn't slept well at all, but she hadn't turned either. There was a battle being fought in her body between the microbe and the cure, and it was nearly over. William climbed from his chair, still feeling groggy, and stumbled to his patient. Her eyes widened as he approached, William barely acknowledged her fear and peeled the dressing from her face. It wasn't grey, the dried blood was red, and the flesh looked like a normal wound. William smiled, *it works.*

He was still unsure if she would be edible, but she was alive and human. As a scientist, he was proud that he had achieved a cure where the rest of the scientific community had failed miserably. As a monster, all he cared about was eating the fruits of his labour.

The three cages were covered with blankets, each of the occupants were unusually quiet. William hadn't noticed it overnight, but he had other things on his mind as he tried to save the girl. He pulled the blanket off of the boy's cage. He was slumped on the floor, alive, not infected but docile. The bloody bandage on his stump, a delightful red rather than grey. *All good.* The second cage held the female feeder, part two of his experiment. He pulled the blanket off and there she sat. Her pink flesh and vacant stare. *Damn it.* She too had been cured. She was now just a dumb, useless lump of living meat.

William knew it would be a long day ahead, testing samples and amending his formula. He was eager to get started, much like with FatBGone, the cure worked, but there was a problem. He couldn't overlook this issue. With FatBGone, he didn't think in even the worst-case scenario, they'd be condemning humanity to extinction at the hands of the dead. With the cure, if not perfect, he'd be condemning himself to that awful fate. And that wouldn't do.

*

Natasha was cold, tired and pissed off. The shackles were uncomfortable. She was still naked and her fellow prisoners stared at her, unable to trust she was truly secured. She hated William. He had treated her like one of the cattle. Keeping her down in the cellar with the food was humiliating. For a moment, she felt like the fat girl she used to be with the rest of the cellar judging her. She would take great delight in eating every last one of them. "You know that in six months you'll all be dead. In a few months you'll be limbless pieces of meat and you'll wish you were dead," she spat out with anger.

A sad and quiet male voice piped up. "We already wish we were dead, you fucking monster."

Natasha pulled angrily at her chains, but they were sturdy. She wasn't going anywhere until William allowed it.

Chapter 45

Peter woke in a bed in the small barracks after the latest late night poker session. His pockets were still full of the empty shell casings that the men used for chips, reminding him of a successful session. They all promised to convert the chips in to whatever riches the new world might eventually bring. None expected they would ever be worth more than fresh berries or a handful of spuds, but what was a game of cards without something to lose?

The soldiers were all getting into their kit or just returning from their daily circuits of the compound. This was how they started every day, grab their rifle and go for a run. Only once had they tried to get Peter to join them. It was clear he wasn't a runner, and they had liked him enough to not push the matter.

He had spent the last two nights in the barracks. He had started to see the barracks with all the firepower and trained professionals within it as a safer bet than being alone in an office if the feeders ever smashed through the fences. And the bed, no matter how basic, was better than the carpet tiles he had been sleeping on.

"Peter, get your glad rags on, we're taking you out on a date," Spencer boomed across the room.

Peter was still adjusting to being awake and didn't think he had heard Spencer correctly. "Sorry, what?"

"You're coming out with us today. Andy twisted his ankle on his run and we need you on his gimpy," Spencer spoke like it was the most normal request in the world to ask of this civilian.

Gimpy? Peter hadn't left Wellworth since he'd arrived. He thought he'd either die there or after the soldiers arrived, eventually be whisked off to safety. "I don't know."

"Peter, it's not up for debate. Don't worry, it's easy and we'll look after you. Kyle will run you through using the gun and will make sure you don't fall out of the helicopter," Spencer assured. He was confident Peter wouldn't let them down, if only Peter had shared that view.

"It's a piece of piss, look at Kyle and Andy. They're bloody useless and even they can do that job," Mike piped up.

"Am I allowed?" Peter asked. The naturally reserved law taker in him couldn't reconcile being put in control of a machine gun, surely someone higher up would tell him off.

"Allowed? I can give you a shiny badge that says soldier on it if you think that will make it legal," Spencer joked.

The rest of the men were exiting the barracks, ready to go as Peter scrambled to his feet and straightened himself up.

"You'll be fine, Pete. Don't worry, it's nearly impossible to fall out, just make sure the harness is good and tight. But not too tight, in case they have to ditch. You don't want to be tied to a helicopter that's about to go bang after a rough landing," Andy said. He gave him the thumbs up as he settled on a bed with a well-thumbed glossy lifestyle magazine.

Peter staggered out of the barracks, to be beckoned over to the helicopter by Kyle to run through his role. It took less than ten minutes for the teacher to be satisfied that his student had a basic enough understanding that he would be unlikely to kill himself or the others.

Spencer had lined his men up as he briefed them for the day's activities, "The head sheds want us to continue with their plan. It's bollocks. I know where I want to check. There are far more likely locations for our target than what we've been ordered to investigate. That kids intel fitted in with what we've found. However today, we're going to Nutwood, Lavender Hill, Burrow Heath and some other dead fucking end. I suspect we may have engine difficulties after Nutwood and may find ourselves touching down at several definitely not pre-planned sites north of Thornhurst." Spencer's delivery was completely deadpan.

The men smiled, they trusted Spencer. Boots and eyes on the ground were always more reliable than over educated men and woman hundreds of miles away, analysing satellite images. They had generated a list of hundreds of sites they wanted checking. Other teams no doubt working other areas and the job wouldn't be done until each blade of grass had been trodden on, or door kicked in at every target.

The helicopter engine started, and the rotor blades picked up speed. The men began jogging to the Lynx, ready for a day's work.

Chapter 46

Jack stared at Amy as she slept. Her lower lip often quivered when in a deep sleep, and Jack found it adorable. The trenches had come along nicely during the last two days, all those who had worked on them were suitably tired but satisfied with their efforts. There would be little chance Amy would rise early today. As quiet as a mouse, he got dressed and crept out of the small boxroom.

Leaving the comfort of the farmhouse, he acknowledged those on watch as he made his way to the Frontera. He'd made sure it was ready to go during the day and stashed a map he drawn from memory to the camp. It was basic but had a few key features he'd remembered from their previous visit. The sun was nearly up and the light was breaking over the horizon. He had his mallet by his side, and a knife strapped to his ankle. He knew what he was heading into, but if he didn't do this, she would. She didn't care about the risk; she saw the needs of the others above her own, and she'd die for anyone in the community. She wouldn't die today.

Jack slipped the car into gear and released the handbrake, allowing it to coast down the natural slope of land down the lane to the gate. It was only 50 metres away, but the less noise the better. He only started the engine after stopping the car to open, then close the gate after him. Looking back in his mirrors, he was relieved that Amy wasn't chasing him down half naked.

His map had proved nearly useless, but he got to the camp in not too bad a time. Stopping in the same spot they had used previously, he looked down at the camp. He searched for the biggest of the big bastards and couldn't see the giant. They hadn't seen it last time either. It could have left, that was plausible, it had pursued them for a while after they left. It's not as if there was any food for it in the camp anymore. Flesh stripped skeletons and other feeders were not food for any of the rotting bastards.

Jack didn't want to announce his arrival. Amy had been right to not use the car when there were two of them, but he was on his own. Much like when he left the farm, he could coast down the hill to get closer to the fence. If he found trouble he could get back and drive out. That was his hope, at least. He positioned the car close to an opening in the fence caused by a fleeing armoured vehicle, leading all the way back to the centre of the camp. He left the keys in the ignition and the door open. He opened the boot of the car and gently guided it open. Looking at the camp in front of him and his mallet in his hand, he suddenly felt woefully under-gunned. He couldn't go back now, so he went forward.

He hadn't been at this camp when society fell. He had been with a group of survivors who fended for themselves and had done a fairly decent job at it. In its destroyed and abandoned state, the scale of the camp was still impressive. He had heard how bad these places were and lost count at the amount of times he'd been told how lucky he was that he didn't end up in one. Looking around, it was hard to tell if it was as bad as everyone had said before they had abandoned it. Everything was stained with blood, soot or just good old-fashioned British mud. Carefully, he made his way through each of the fences until he'd reached the centre. His run had proved mostly clear, with only a handful of creatures visible, all at a comfortable distance.

The bounty was as Amy had described. Boxes of medical supplies, food, clothing, building supplies and ammunition. It had everything they would need for months, maybe even years. He wouldn't be able to take everything, so he would have to prioritise. Medical supplies and ammunition would be most important. Food was a close third spot for space. A few extra boxes of the ration packs would supplement what they had, they could grow or catch food, but they couldn't manufacture drugs or load their own ammunition.

The first run was the most tense. Every rustle of tent canvas in the wind, or crunch of shell casings underfoot, forced him to stop. He started with a can of 5.56mm cartridges. It would have been Amy's priority. He carried it back to the car, holding it with one hand and his mallet with the other, ready to defend himself when the first inevitable attack occurred. He popped the top and was disappointed that the 1000 rounds advertised as the contents weren't so. Instead, 15 filled magazines had been stored in place of the more plentiful loose ammunition. He scolded himself for not checking, but it was still more ammo than they'd ever had and he was far from the day. It was just a shame there were no more guns.

Several more trips yielded boxes of basic medical supplies and medicines, luxuries such as toilet rolls and the surprisingly important bottles of bleach. The Frontera was nearly at its capacity, but he wanted to get everything he could. He had already loaded one case of 24 hour ration packs, and wanted another, as well as more ammunition. His mallet was stained with the thick grey blood of the four feeders he'd encountered. They hadn't proved a problem and helped to build his confidence. Two more trips and he'd be gone. He'd be back at the farm in an hour with his bounty.

Its nose twitched, and its eyes opened. It was like the dumb, smart and strong ones combined. It was patient, had a hunter's intelligence, and was powerful. This giant creature was an expert at catching its prey and adapting. It had quickly learned that this abandoned camp was too tempting to any passing survivor who fancied a crack at its riches. The bait was there for everyone to see, the giant just waited and they came. It was a hunter, it could track or trap its meals. At some 10 feet in height and with a large, powerful build, it didn't just stand in plain view waiting to be spotted. It would lie on the ground for days at a time amongst the tents, listening and sniffing for the sound or scent of a foolish meal that ventured too close. Those meals had become far less frequent, but they still turned up. It knew its prey had arrived as soon as Jack had stepped into the camp, but it had to be patient. It had lost a meal because it had acted too soon just days ago, it wouldn't make the same mistake again.

Jack used the same path he'd taken at every run to the camp's centre. It was quick and offered him the best cover whilst not impeding his visibility. He recognised every corpse he walked past; the blood stained canvas of the torn tent, the mangled corpse under the crushed fence right as he reached the centre. If he wasn't so sure it was gone, he may have noticed the 10 foot tall creature standing fifty feet away watching him. It had seen his path, the car, and it slowly, quietly put itself between Jack and the car. As he was rifling through the boxes to find a ration case with a different menu selection, it crouched down, waiting for its own dinner to approach.

Jack had what he was after. Deciding to maximise his journey, he perched a can of ammo on top of the box. Together they were heavy, combined with his tired arms and heavy mallet as it took every ounce of strength. He couldn't push himself any faster for fear of missing a lurking monster.

Its nose once again picked him up first, then it could hear the pounding heart and heavy breath. As soon as it saw him, it would make its kill.

Jack carried on, his grip loosening on the box until the tin of ammo fell to the floor with a loud clatter. He froze. He'd fucked up, and he knew it. Picking up his mallet, he braced himself and he saw the first creature round a canvas tent, its eyes locked on to him. Another ambled towards him just yards away. He was done for the day; he abandoned the extra goods and ran.

The giant creature moved too early, eager to show its dominance over the lesser feeders who were trying to steal its kill and jumped into Jack's path. Neither was ready for the move, and Jack clipped the creature and took a tumble to the floor. He quickly climbed to his feet as it swung its enormous fist towards him, missing by inches. *The bastard was here all along.* Jack took an impotent swing with his mallet, only grazing its arm with no effect.

More feeders stumbled out of tents and from their resting places. The commotion only increased their curiosity. Jack looked ahead, and they blocked his path to the car, he'd have to run around them. The giant swung out again, smashing Jack's thigh with its rancid, overgrown black fingernails. The pain was instant, as was the realisation he'd just been condemned to death. He couldn't stop, not yet. He ran as fast as the pain would allow him, but several more feeders emerged at every turn as the giant didn't let up on its pursuit.

Jack made it to the outer fence but had no way of getting to his car. A nearby guard tower was his only option. He climbed the metal ladder to the top as the creatures gathered below, waiting for him to slip and fall to them. He didn't. His hand reached ahead to the wooden platform and something above grabbed him.

A soldier had made the same desperate move as him, injured he had climbed the tower, and eventually turned. It bit down hard into Jack's hand as it dragged him onto the platform. It was in terrible shape, its only meal the devoured carcass of another soldier in the tower. A brief wrestle and Jack flung it to the mob below. It distracted them for only a second until they realised it wasn't their target; it wasn't food.

The platform was carpeted in empty shell casings and dried blood. There was a rifle that was empty and a machine gun that was also out of ammo. He searched for something of use, anything. Pulling the remains of the dead soldier to one side, he found two grenades. His luck had changed and maybe he would get to see Amy just one more time.

The giant now took prime position at the base of the tower, making sure it was first in line. It was strong, but even it couldn't move the structure, no matter how hard it tried. Instead, it pulled off the ladder and used it to smash the tower. It was more terrifying than effective.

Jack carefully peered at the small but growing herd below and knew it was now or never. He pulled the pin and dropped the first grenade directly at the feet of the giant. He took cover in the tower and waited until he heard the explosion. It was louder than he had expected, but louder was good. He was sure the path was now clear for his escape. Looking down at the site of the explosion, he knew it was over. Maybe two feeders were dead, several more missing limbs or wounded but otherwise still as big a threat as before. But that giant bastard. Its legs were covered in its own grey blood, but otherwise it stood as if nothing had happened. There were no broken bones or destroyed tendons. The wounds were superficial; the grenade had done little more than piss it off.

Jack clutched the remaining grenade tightly and examined his wounds. It wasn't meant for them; he knew that now. His good fortune wasn't that he'd have the chance to fight his way out and see Amy again. It would be that he'd never have to turn into one of those evil pricks.

Chapter 47

The basement was dark and lacked any natural light. It was hard to tell how long she had been down there, it could have been hours or days. The hunger was her biggest indicator. She was in a room full of food but unable to feed herself. It only made it worse. That bastard, he didn't understand her; he didn't care. He only gave a shit about himself and his precious work. She knew she'd have to push the anger down, show him she was sorry and that she was wrong. She wasn't sorry. He'd keep her down there for a week if that's what it would take for her to see the error of her ways. It was best just to get it over and done with immediately so she could feed. Any revenge could wait. They had all the time in the world.

The captives were mostly silent. Their spirits crushed, they just waited for death and preferred to do so quietly. Some had tried to starve themselves to death and not eat the food provided, but something wouldn't let them give up completely. Before Natasha had arrived, William might leave them for days at a time without feeding on them or giving them their rations. When she had arrived, they were fed more regularly, but they were preyed upon more too.

The door at the top of the staircase unbolted, and William entered. Slowly, he walked down the steps until he was standing in front of Natasha.

"Well?" he asked her, expecting a tearful, remorseful response.

"I'm sorry darling, I was rash and I know I've been off recently. It's hard," she gave William the widest eyes she could, a tear rolling down her cheek. *Is that enough for you, arsehole?*

"I know, I'm sorry too. I've been distant, but it's important. Are you okay?" William was still angry with her, he didn't trust her, but she was the companion he had.

"I'm hungry," she spoke quietly, purposefully playing up how pathetic she was.

"Of course you are," William replied as he moved to undo the shackles.

He leaned in close to get them open, his neck brushing across her face as he fumbled with the lock. *He was testing her.* Natasha wouldn't take the bait. He wanted her to bite or attack him so he could leave her there to rot. No. She would wait. Finally, the shackles were open, and her hands were free.

"Thank you, William," she said and smiled sweetly.

"That's okay. I've run you a bath, freshen up, and I'll fix you a meal," he told her. The words made the other captives shudder in fear.

Natasha made her way to the bath and slid in. It was warm, but not hot enough to be enjoyable. She believed he'd done it on purpose, and that this would be how he was now. Mean and antagonistic rather than just uncaring. If he wanted her to react, she wouldn't give him the satisfaction. She'd play the good little housewife again for as long as she needed to.

She hadn't lingered in the tub and was dried and dressed when she entered the kitchen. A small bowl of meat was on the table with a note. It was hardly a meal, especially after her time trapped in the basement and starved. Again, she was certain he wanted her to react so he could put her in her place. Natasha sat at the table and smiled as she began eating the meat. The note was a simple memo telling her he would be in his lab the rest of the day. *Of course he fucking would be.*

With the small morsels of meat finished, Natasha looked around. Another day rereading the same books, watching the same movies, or maybe sitting in the same garden. She was beautiful, powerful and intelligent. She was an evolved species, the best of the old world and the new one. Sitting and waiting until she was needed or wanted. She was being wasted. She didn't want to sit on the sidelines, being on call for this nerd. This existence wasn't for her. If she killed William, the meat in the basement might last a few months and she could even add to it. Her trip to Thornhurst proved non-infected humans were still about. She touched her healed bullet wounds, given to her by Amy. This was the other side of the world, the danger and risk. It made it more fun, more exciting; but she still didn't want to die. She was strong, but not immortal. Food would run out eventually, and then that would be the worst possible death.

The time to reflect in the comfort of the cottage, with a small amount of food in her belly, had helped her to think straight. She would be free again one day. He'd create his cure, and then she could have her revenge and do whatever the fuck she wanted.

Chapter 48

When she had woken that morning, Amy didn't realise anything was wrong. She was normally up early and working before Jack, but today he wasn't beside her in their bed. Maybe he'd made an early start on the day's work, or maybe he was making her a romantic rice and baked bean breakfast in bed. She ached from the previous days' exertions but was enjoying the quiet and extra rest. It couldn't last forever, the day had to start and she couldn't lay in bed all day. She had to be seen to pull her weight.

Having clothed herself, she made her way downstairs, expecting to see Jack with his smile in the kitchen. She only saw Babs, who couldn't bring herself to look at Amy.

Heading outside, she could see the usual array of community members performing their chores. The work on the trenches continued, albeit at a less enthused rate. Anyone who looked at Amy quickly looked back away. Bo was in his seat, staring straight forward.

"Do I have a horrible rash on my face or did I piss everyone off?" Amy asked. She wasn't sure why she was being given the cold shoulder.

"Amy sweetheart, I will not beat around the bush. The daft twat has done something fucking stupid. I didn't know about it until a couple of these retards told me. He's gone back to the camp," Bo said. He hadn't suspected Jack would do something as stupid as to go it alone.

Amy's face dropped, "Why? When?"

"I'm guessing the kid wanted to impress his bird, that's why we do most of the stupid things we do."

"You should have come and got me," she scolded. Amy was in a panic, this was all her fault. "Is the rifle fixed?"

Bo already had it next to him and handed it to her with a magazine. "It works, fine. For a piece of junk."

Amy loaded the magazine and cycled the action. "I need to go."

"The Shogun is fuelled and ready to go. So are Wes and Abdul," he said. Bo hadn't sat idly, he'd arranged transport and help for Amy as he knew she would go after Jack no matter what.

"I don't need to risk any more lives," Amy replied. She was angry at what Jack had done and concerned for him.

"I'm not worried about you, that's the last fucking good motor we have, you can look after yourself," he told her. Bo was only half joking.

Amy didn't have time to argue and made her way to the four-wheel-drive car. Wes and Abdul were already waiting. Both men were in their forties, a banker and a solicitor. Intelligent, useful men before society fell, now their education and accomplishments counted for little. Like many others, they both eager to prove their worth.

Amy took the front passenger seat and off they went. The drive felt like it was taking an unnecessarily long time. Frequently she snapped at Wes and belittled his driving abilities. It was out of character. Neither man took her jabs seriously. They knew why she was acting the way she was. Despite how she perceived the journey, they'd made it in a decent twenty-five minutes.

When they arrived at the camp, the white Frontera was plain to see, parked close to the camp. It was almost as obvious as the thirty-odd feeders and the gigantic bastard under one tower. Amy exited the car and raised the carbine to her shoulder and stared through the optics. She couldn't see him. And then he stood up. *He's okay!* He was alive, they could get him out, they just needed a plan. Quickly he crouched back down in the tower, shortly after a minor explosion rocked his mob below. Amy stared intently through the sight at the tower. Jack stood back up and looked down at the feeders. Amy moved her focus to them and saw what Jack would have seen. It wasn't a stack of bodies, few had stayed down and those that did seemed to be flailing their limbs and snapping their angry mouths displayed they were far from harmless.

"Wes, you're going to drive us down to our other car. Abdul, you're going to drive that back to this spot. I'll cause an almighty distraction and draw them away from Jack. Wes, when he's clear, sweep him up," she ordered. The men nodded, happy to be useful, happier still to be doing it in the relative safety of a car.

The sound of the Shogun barely registered with the mob. They had a meal nearly within grasp. At the Frontera, Abdul leapt out and started the engine. It ran, and he drove off back to their starting position. The Shogun drove closer to Jack's tower and Amy leapt out. "Don't stop moving, unless one of us is jumping in," she said. The car sped away, leaving Amy vulnerable in the field one hundred yards from Jack.

He'd seen them arrive, and his heart had sunk. He couldn't let them risk their lives for him, he was already dead. When he saw Amy alone and on foot, he knew she was about to try something brave, and utterly stupid.

Amy raised the rifle, this time to do more than just look. She snatched at the trigger and started sending aimed shots at the creature's besieging Jack. She didn't have enough rounds for them all, that wasn't the point. She just needed them to see her as an easier meal than Jack and start chasing her. Several broke away and did just that, but not enough.

"Stay away! Stay away!" Jack screamed at the top of his lungs at Amy, but above the sound of the car engines, the murmuring of the dead and her own gunshots, it was futile. He tried waving his hands, signalling for her to go back, but she wasn't looking at him. She only had eyes for the feeders she was shooting at.

Fifty yards away and she'd used ten rounds and only got the attention of four of the stinking bastards. "Come and get me, you fucks!" she yelled. Her screams failed to attract any more. The giant glanced over at her, then back to Jack.

It was now or never. Jack looked at Amy one last time. Tears ran down his cheeks as he readied himself. He pulled the pin on the grenade, the fuse would take less than five seconds to detonate the explosive. His last five seconds. He had one more *fuck you* for these pricks. Holding the grenade to his chest with both hands, he jumped to the mob below. He didn't hit the ground before it exploded. The effect of the grenade exploding nearly two metres in the air had a greater effect on the monsters. Several fell to head wounds that would permanently remove them from the world. The giant was again mostly unharmed, nothing terminal at least. Jack died immediately, the explosion opening his rib cage, removing an arm and snapping his head backwards so violently it was nearly removed. He had made sure he wouldn't join the ranks of the dead.

Amy stopped and stared, unable to comprehend what she just witnessed, what Jack had just done. He was the little bit of normal she had in the world, and now he was gone. She couldn't take her eyes off of the sight of his remains being fought over by those horrific creatures.

All but one competed for a mouthful. The giant didn't have any interest in its former prey. It was spoiled and incomplete. It could pick up the body and take it from the others but it let them be distracted. It saw her. She would make a better treat.

Amy tried to gather herself. She wanted to run amongst them, screaming and lashing out at every single rotten beast. Caving their heads in with her own bare hands.

It walked through the other feeders, stepping on those fallen and knocking others out of its path. It quickened its pace as it strode towards her.

Amy snapped out of her trance and saw it beginning to close on her. Shouldering the rifle, she fired off several aimed shots towards its head. A clear strike in its forehead should have dropped it like a sack of spuds, but it barely acknowledged the hit. A head-shot on anything should be a kill. Four more rounds, one more hit, and no more luck. Instinct kicked in as it was less than thirty yards away and she ran. Its wide strides helped it effortlessly keep up and even move closer to her as she ran with all her might. She braved a glance back towards her pursuer and tripped. Her leg opening on a jagged piece of shrapnel at the corner of a small shell crater. Quickly she hobbled back to her feet and ran through the pain, the warm blood flowing from the wound on her ankle.

Abdul had seen the struggle playing out and had driven round to intercept her. The white car caught the corner of her eye as it closed in from her right-hand side. She had one chance to live. The car pulled up alongside her as the giant was within ten yards of them. The car slowed to match Amy's pace a few feet from her. Her arm outstretched and fumbled for the door handle, opening it with her fingertips. Abdul slowed the car ever so slightly, allowing Amy to open the door and throw herself inside.

Her legs still dangling out, Abdul put his foot down and put distance between them. Blood flicked across the field from her leg at every bump or shudder of the car until she could fully climb in.

The car disappeared with the Shogun, leaving the giant in the field, having again missed out on a meal. Its nostrils flared, and it crouched over, touching the blades of blood splattered grass. Bringing its fingertips to its face, it heavily sniffed the scent of the blood as if enjoying the first cigarette of the day. It didn't turn back to its favoured hunting grounds, they'd proved increasingly fruitless. Sniffing the blood and then the air once again, it slowly followed the direction of the cars.

Chapter 49

She hadn't spoken a single word in hours. The car journey back had been awkward, the silence deafening. Amy gazed out of the window the whole time, processing what had occurred, what Jack had done. Everyone had lost someone, it wasn't new. Death was this new world, and she felt shame of how sad she felt. She gave everything for the community and she still couldn't give herself permission to cry, to explode into tears. The two cars pulled into the farm and Bo was waiting. He looked at the occupants, only counting the three and not the fourth he was hoping for.

Jack hadn't returned, but the large beat-up white car had. Bo knew it wasn't good, and the look on Amy's face confirmed it. She ran to him and hugged him.

"It's alright sweetheart, it'll be alright," Bo spoke gently. He knew the words would do little to help, but he was never one for silence.

"Why Bo? Why did he do it?" she couldn't bring herself to look at him.

"He was a good kid, brave and selfless. Look at the car, look at all the loot he got. He didn't get that for himself, he got it for us, for everyone," Bo consoled her. He took Amy in his arm and walked to the near full car as it was being unloaded. "Food, meds, and bullets. The kid done good."

"It wasn't his job to do that, it was mine!" she shouted. She was angry with herself, she should have been there, she should have been the one who died.

"No Amy, your job ain't to do every bloody thing. We're lucky, it's not like those first few days with just old buggers like me. Look around, we have strong, young and capable people everywhere now. And just like you and that kid, they're all daft enough to want to risk the little they have to give back the rest of us," Bo said. Despite feeling less important in the camp, he was proud of everyone. They all pulled their weight, they all pitched in, and he trusted every single one of them.

"I'm going to need a day Bo," she said. Amy's head felt heavy, her arms and legs weighted her down. She just wanted to be alone.

"Sweetheart take two. Fuck it, take the week. You've earned it, we'll keep this rabble in line," Bo said as he squeezed Amy and smiled.

Amy stepped back, wiping away the single tear that had forced its way down her cheek. With her head down, she walked into the farmhouse, wishing everyone would stop staring, even though they weren't.

Bo got closer to the car. They had emptied its haul. A selection of goods; food, medicine and ammunition. The small group surrounding the bounty wanted to smile at what had been brought to them, but aware it had cost the life of one of their own.

"Save me one of the bog rolls, get everything else into the stores and the ammo in the armoury," Bo spoke softly, not wanting Amy to hear.

*

It had been walking longer than it had done since it found the camp. Its muscles didn't tire, its breath never became short. It just carried on, pausing only to listen for its prey, or sniff the air to regain its scent. It didn't care for the wrecked cars, the burned out properties or the rubble it had to step over. The occasional corpse stole its attention, but the flesh had long since been stripped. Just the disappointing bones remained.

Several feeders had followed it from the camp, where the giant one went, food was never far away. As it progressed through the country roads, past the small abandoned villages and past the farm shops, others joined it. A handful turned into 20, turned into 50. Soon a horde had grown and continued to grow, all following their uncaring leader. It knew it'd feed first and barely acknowledged its army, only showing irritation that their groans made it impossible to listen. Its nose wouldn't fail it. It could still smell her, no matter how faint it could follow. It might take a day or even two, but eventually it would find her and her friends.

Chapter 50

Amy had treated herself to a day to cry, but she wouldn't allow herself the luxury of mourning her love any longer. There was too much to do and too many people that depended on her. With Jack gone, they were one able body down, but patrols still needed to be made. The perimeter wouldn't watch itself, and the threat was as high as ever. Several members of the community had offered to help, to keep her company, but she had refused. She didn't want to be directly responsible for another life, not yet.

The usual loop felt quiet on her own. As she walked along the boundary she missed his voice, his laugh. A tear rolled down her cheek, but she wouldn't allow it and mopped it away quickly with her hand. This world was damned, millions were dead, or worse, and they had so little to hold on to. But they had something, more than they had any right to hope for. Jack had given his life for the community, for her. He shouldn't have died, but nothing would bring him back.

*

The horde was impressive. Nearly a hundred feeders followed the giant. Big ones, common ones, and strong ones made up its army. It struggled to keep the scent of its prey. If it had been capable, it would have been worried. Instead it pressed on, it had no idea how close it was. The narrow country roads led the creature to a crossroads. It stood for a moment and allowed its nostrils to flare. It sniffed to its left, then its right, before facing forward. A small stone wall lay between it and the long grass. It would have been able to step over it easily, barely an inconvenience, but the rest, all but the strong ones, would struggle. It knew it needed its army. Clenching its oversized fists, it struck at a section of the wall, knocking the first layer of stones clear. Swinging wildly, grunting with the effort, the strikes proved effect as a narrow opening appeared. Two more blows and the job was complete. It led the way through and the horde followed.

*

Amy had been patrolling for nearly two hours. She hadn't stopped once. Slowly and carefully she walked, trying her hardest to pay attention to her surroundings whilst haunted by her memories. Plagued by her most recent loss. Her thirst distracted her sufficiently to take a seat in the grass. Swigging from her water bottle she reached into her pouch producing a handful of raw pea pods. She looked at the outermost boundary ahead. Something caught her attention as she popped one of the fresh pods into her mouth with a crunch. *Probably a dog or lone feeder.* She squinted, but still struggled to confirm what it was. Another pea pod burst open in her teeth. It drifted, swaying. It was one of them. It was a way off, but in their territory, and she would have to deal with it and investigate where it got through. Another drink of water and the remaining pea pods consumed. She stood up. *Shit.*

It wasn't just one; it was over a hundred of them. And it was there. Huge and disgusting, towering over its army, it had to be the same one that killed Jack. *How had it found them? Why?* Amy held the handle of her machete tight in its sheath strapped to her leg. She wished for a rifle, the machete would be useless against so many. Even the rifle wouldn't be a match for their rotting force. She noticed the big ones; they looked far less imposing next to the giant. Several of the grey fiends were pushing ahead of the main group. They ran at an unreasonably quick pace compared to their compatriots. The powerful feeders, at least three of them. The only type missing were the intelligent ones, although she half expected to see Natasha riding the giants back, leading them to the kill.

They had either seen or smelled Amy; it didn't matter which. The damned things knew she was there. She paused for a moment. She thought she should lead them away from the settlement, from the community. But these weren't dumb feeders who stumbled across lunch, they had found them. Found her. The powerful ones were so fast they'd be on her in no time and she'd be unable to fight them off. Once they'd fought over her meagre corpse, they'd surely follow the scent to the rest of her people, with no warning they'd be decimated. She broke into a sprint back towards the farmhouse. She had to warn them.

She had been running for a few minutes, glancing back occasionally to see the first of her pursuers closing the gap. They didn't tire like her; they were muscle and teeth. The settlement was now in sight, but the creatures were too fast. She would not make it. Her lungs felt like they were on fire as she gave it everything she had. She couldn't stop now, she'd never be able to get going again. If she stopped to fight, she would be too exhausted, too out of breath to put up an immediate fight. She didn't have to get back to the farmhouse. She didn't have to defeat her pursuers. She just had to get close enough to her friends that when the grey bastards leapt on her, began ripping the flesh from her bones, the survivors would see. She would buy them enough time to get the rifles out, and the defenceless into the safety of the farmhouses thick stone walls. It might not be enough, but she could give them that chance.

Another glance back. The first of them were maybe a shade under 200 metres away. The farmhouse was nearly 500 metres ahead. It was so close, but she was too slow and they were too fast. Teeth gritted, she pushed on, pulling the machete out from its sheath, ready to get at least one feeble slash in when the first one struck.

400 metres from the farmhouse, it was only 50 metres from her. She couldn't have screamed out if she had wanted too, her lungs needed every drop of air to keep her going. She knew it was coming and it would hurt, but not for long. A minute's worth of pain would end her suffering.

Above her own desperate panting, she could hear its powerful stride. It was so close now. The faintest of touch on her back and she was ready to swing the large blade with as much force as she could still muster.

"Get down!" a male voice boomed.

Amy couldn't tell where it had come from, but she threw herself to the ground, tumbling across the grass, glimpsing the creature only feet from her. The delightful sound of multiple 5.56mm gunshots rang out, striking the first, powerful creature, sending it flying into the ground at pace just ahead of Amy. Grey blood staining the ground from several hits to the torso and the big one to the bridge of its nose.

The gunshots continued as Amy sat up with her machete. Three more of the powerful ones closed in on her as they were peppered with bullets. Two dropped, but the last continued, its wounds insufficient to do more than slow it down.

Panicked screams emanated from the settlement. Hurried, fumbled magazine changes were taking place between Amy and the first trench. The unskilled marksman had already performed beyond their ability in nailing three of the four creatures. Now their lack of training and experience betrayed them.

It had slowed to little more than a jog, still faster than Amy could hope to compete with. She climbed to her feet, the blade in hand. If it killed her now, at least the farm had been alerted. She stumbled, her body still desperately recovering as it lunged at her. Even Amy wasn't sure if she had dived out of its way or just fell. She did however manage to swing her machete at the beast, slicing its cheek open as it sailed past her.

It stopped, confused, its seeping wounds starting to take effect on its ability to function. Amy lashed out with the machete connecting with its Achilles tendon. The wound wasn't deep, but it had done enough damage for the leg to give way and the monster hit the ground. With two hands on the handle, she twice swung down on its neck with all her might. The two chops enough to separate its head from its body.

Cheers from the farmhouse at the victory against the dead. Amy climbed to her feet as Abdul rushed over to her, still trying to change the magazine in his rifle. Another man followed close behind, trying to do the same. "Are you okay?"

Amy concentrated on her breath, desperate to get the words out, to tell him. "They're coming."

Chapter 51

Chaos and panic hit the community. They could now see the approaching menace intent on devouring them. Amy still had yet to recover from her confrontation but was arranging their defence. Suddenly, the trenches she had insisted upon creating seemed worthless.

Amy had brought together the fit and the able, they had discussed what they should do in situations such as this, but everyone was still unsure now the threat was here. "Defenders form into your groups, one gun protected by five blades. The assault rifles, concentrate your fire on the big ones and the giant, but protect yourself from all threats. The shotguns, and the twenty-two, your teams are on the regular feeders. Everyone else, put down as many as you can!"

Abdul approached Amy with one of the assault rifles, handing it to her. "You're better with this than me."

Amy shook her head and pulled out her machete and smaller knife. "I'm just fine with these. Get with your team and into position."

The groups organised themselves to their zones. Each person had survived to this point. Most, if not all, had needed to fight to stay alive. But never like this. Never against something like the giant, organising its damned soldiers just as well as Amy had organised her own. The big bastards were tough, that gigantic creature looked near unstoppable.

Bo was arguing with two of the younger men in his small group, each eager to take the shotgun for their own use. "Piss off you little pricks, you can have it when I'm dead, and not a bloody moment sooner!"he blurted. His authority put the challengers in their place. Amy smiled at the old fool. His refusal to hide in the farmhouse was a testament to his bravery and stubbornness. Popular traits at the farm.

Amy moved her way to the first trench where several other melee armed defenders had already taken position. Each looked petrified, shaking as the monsters edged ever close. "It'll be okay, I can't promise we'll win, but we can give them a little bit of hell."

The common feeders were ever so slightly faster than the rest of the larger units, except for the giant that seemed to purposefully hold back. It was more than happy for its lesser companions to eat up the first wave of the defence. The big bastards were in the second wave with the remaining common grey beasts.

"Don't shoot until you think you can hit the cunts!" Bo screamed. He wasn't afraid, he was angry.

As the mob drew closer, Abdul let off the first round. Missing his intended target, it instead landed in the cheek of a following feeder, flooring it with a splatter of grey blood. Cheers rang out from the defenders. They had scored a kill. The beasts picked up their pace and more gunshots went off. They hit some attackers, a couple even fell to the ground. But they didn't stop. Those armed with just blades and bats in the first trench braced themselves as the first few reached them.

Knives slashed at the attackers. Axes swung with strength. Bats thumped down with purpose. The assault rifles started concentrating on the bigger feeders, the ones which would prove too tough to deal with using a mop and kitchen knife. The line of feeders thickened as they bunched up behind those fighting with the defenders. Amy was stuck in the middle, her machete and knife blade already covered in grey gore. "Pull back to the next trench!" she screamed and hoped everyone had heard her, but the noise of the fight was now overwhelming. She climbed out and ran to the next position. Several of the defenders followed. She looked back. A few had fallen, their mangled bodies now feeding the monsters. Several more were fighting off attackers, trying to make some space to escape. A man and woman fought valiantly but were on the verge of being overwhelmed as the dead concentrated on them, the nearest meat. Amy dashed back to help and pulled the man free as she swung her machete at the grabbing hands. They both reached back to pull out the woman who continued fighting, unable to turn her back on the monsters mobbing her. They surged forward, and she was lost in a swamp of angry grey. No screams, just the sound of flesh being ripped apart as the trench filled with the dead. They didn't have time to grieve for another fallen friend, they ran to the next defensive line.

The gun teams had scored sporadic kills, but as the hoard moved closer, panic set in. Bullets whizzed harmlessly over grey skulls or thudded into the ground with little more than a pop of dirt. Bo had been saving his cartridges, the shortened barrel of his sawed-off shotgun would be little use beyond 15 yards, and more dangerous to their own people. He could see the carnage, he saw that there were too many for them to handle. He couldn't wait for those in front to fall. "Come on you soppy pillocks, let's get involved," Bo said as he strode forward, shotgun held up, ready for the first target to present itself. His group followed, unwilling to let this crazy pensioner go it alone. They made it to within 20 yards of Amy's flank quickly, just as a group of the dead tried to break around them. Finally, Bo could start shooting. Both barrels blasted, peppering half a dozen feeders, knocking three to the floor. The two cartridges popped out of the breach and Bo calmly reloaded, before firing on his next target. "Eat shit you pricks!" Bo cursed. Those around him surged forward and engaged the nearest creature. The creatures they downed were instantly replaced by more eager to take their places.

Every survivor who had been involved with the brawl was already exhausted. The confrontation was minutes old, but the constant fight and unrelenting aggressors were already proving difficult. Enthusiasm waned as reality tore and bit its way through their numbers.

The big bastards made their terrifying cry, one after the other until each had bellowed as hard as it could. Now the giant was ready to make its move. Its mutated form towered over the others as it joined their ranks.

"Pull back!" Amy screamed. Those who could, followed. They drew closer to the house, bypassing a trench line and several prepared positions taking cover behind the original stone wall. Desperate to get a few extra seconds' rest before the next conflict. Both sides had lost half their number, but numbers were a strength the dead had over the living. Amy looked around at her troops. They were beaten, and they knew it. Those manning the firearms continued shooting, their small teams even smaller, their shots still not effective. *Where's Bo?* Amy double checked the survivors, but she couldn't see him with the main group.

Bo dragged an injured young man by his collar across the ground, moving backwards towards the old barn. Half a dozen feeders closely followed, tempted by the two meals slowly moving away. Bo couldn't make up enough of a lead to give himself space to give the vile bastards both barrels. The man was covered in blood and weakly swung a large carving knife at their followers. Dazed and confused, his swipes did little to dissuade the monsters they were worth bothering with. Bo slowed, his old legs had been pushed to their limits, he tried all he could, but they snatched at the legs of the bloodied man and pulled him free of Bo's grip. In seconds they had swamped the man, tearing at his flesh. "I'm sorry!" Bo said as he blasted the mass of grey flesh, but it was too late for his comrade. More creatures took interest in the old man and he started scurrying towards the barn, popping in two fresh cartridges.

The dead were at the small wall, the living hacked at limbs as the creatures tried to climb over it. The remaining large feeders smashed at the old stone wall, knocking chunks of debris flying towards the defenders. The twenty-two bolt-action rifle fell silent, as several creatures overwhelmed its operator. His fumbled reload with the small cartridges had given them the opportunity to climb the wall and attack his remaining team mate before pinning him to the ground. Only the lightweight rifle separated him from the gnashing chipped teeth as he laid on the ground, holding the beast back. Abdul opened fire with his assault rifle, striking the creature in the rib cage and knocking it clear of its intended victim. The man scrambled clear and attempted to load more rounds into the rifle when three creatures leapt towards him, dragging him to the ground and devouring him.

Amy felt weak, her legs wobbled. "Back, get back!" she yelled. They had nowhere to run. There were maybe a dozen defenders still in the fight. More than treble that of the dead remained, including several of the bigger units and the giant.

"I'm out!" Abdul screamed.

Amy could see they were down to one assault rifle and the melee weapons. They had been pushed back to the house, their backs against its thick stone wall. This was it.

Bo fired his last two shells at the monsters as he entered the barn. He remembered clearing away the bodies when they had found of the farm of the previous occupants. He was angry that he would meet the same fate, without perhaps the good fortune of being discovered and granted a burial. Three creatures remained and came at him. Bo was old, but he wasn't soft. He gripped the small shotgun like a baton and crashed it down on the first attacker's skull. The crunch was reassuringly loud as it dropped to the floor. "Come on you fucking prat, come on!" he screamed at the next feeder and landed a blow across its face. The eye socket was crushed, grey blood and flesh smeared across its face. A second, weaker crack in the same spot was enough to put it on the floor and out of action. Just one left. Bo's breath was heavy, his heart raced. His left arm tingled. "Lets have it, big boy!" Bo said as he clubbed the beast repeatedly on the top of its head as it bore down on him. It fell towards him, putting both of them on the floor, its damaged brain exposed and its thick grey blood leaking on to Bo. He couldn't muster the strength to push it off. He couldn't catch his breath back, his chest was tight, it felt like one of the big feeders was sitting on him. He clutched his chest as he grimaced in pain. "Babs!" he called. He felt fear, he wouldn't see his love again, he was dying alone. At least those damned creatures hadn't got him. He could only hope the others would succeed where he had failed.

The giant was closer, ready to pick up its prize. It filled those inside the farmhouse who could bear to look out of the windows with horror. Loved ones and friends torn apart. It was like the world was ending all over again. Others balled up and closed their eyes, hopeful it was all a bad dream. Desperate fists pounded at the front door, demanding entry, only to be pulled back by their colleagues to rejoin the fight. This was it, the last stand.

Amy could barely stand, her muscles ached, her heart raced. She should have fallen to the floor and given up, but the fight hadn't left her. Whilst there was the faintest of breath in her lungs, she'd fight them. Hacking and slashing, she took down two feeders and approached a big one. It was grotesque, its boils ready to burst. Amy reached up and slashed at the creature's lifeless eyes. The eyeballs burst with a milky liquid running down its face. Others joined in, finding the strength for one last brawl.

The giant was ready. Its nostrils flared, the smell of the living appeared to bring the faintest of smiles to its discoloured mouth. This close, they could all see how massive it was, and had the proportions to match. With its long, muscular arms, it reached across two feeders to grab Abdul by the throat. He lashed out with a piece of metal pipe, weakly striking its face. The blows barely tickled. The monster tightened its grip until Abdul's blood ran through its fingers. It wasted no more time and pulled the corpse to its mouth and took several large, greedy bites before ripping the body in two. Fresh human meat; despite the fight continuing around it, it savoured the mouthfuls.

The defenders had lost their last firearm, had been pushed back against the house with barely enough room to swing their weapons, but still they fought.

The explosion caught everyone off guard, none more so than the giant. It had been shoved forward by the blast, its right shoulder and arm missing, a good portion of its chest burst forward. It staggered backwards, unsure what was happening as its thick grey blood pissed out of the massive wound. Its legs gave way, and it dropped to its knees before falling onto its side.

The soldier was nearly 200 meters away on the back of a Land Rover. It was an impressive shot with the MBT LAW missile launcher. Liam put the launcher down and picked up his rifle. "Engage!" he commanded. Three other vehicles pulled forward, a Toyota Hilux had a GPMG mounted on the back and the operator put down heavy fire on the horde. Two more four-wheel-drive vehicles drove to the flank before half a dozen soldiers exited and began engaging, taking slow single aimed shots at their targets. They didn't panic, they had done this many times before.

The dead didn't stop their pursuit of those defenders with their backs against the stone walls. The monster's tunnel vision drove them towards food, at the expense of their own survival.

"Get down!" Amy belted out and ducked as the bullets started ripping into the dead and passing clean through, smashing into wall and survivor alike.

The soldiers expertly moved to the flank and closed on the mass of feeders. Felling every one of the stinking creatures they fired upon until all were incapacitated.

"Clear!" the first soldier screamed.

Liam's Landrover pulled forward, and he hopped off to join the other soldiers. "No fuck-ups lads, they were dead before you shot them and they were bloody dangerous, don't assume that's changed because you put a bullet in one."

"Yes mother!" one soldier sarcastically replied. They had taken part in dozens of these engagements, they had become experts at surviving confrontations with these things and the aftermath. Meticulously they moved forward, bayoneting or shooting any feeder they came close too before it had a chance to attack them.

Amy looked to her sides. Only six others had survived that she could see. The fight had been worse than she could have imagined. She looked at the dead, feeders and humans alike and couldn't reconcile this with winning the battle. They had won nothing. Everything they had built ripped through. The lives they had tried to forge for themselves, taken. The front door opened, and Babs came out waving a tea towel on the end of a fire poker.

The soldiers took notice of the movement at the house, and Liam signalled for two soldiers to cover the survivors.

Babs and Amy locked eyes, Amy shook her head as tears ran down her cheeks. Babs offered a forced smile. More of those in the house spilled out to aid their survivors.

Liam had made his way to the giant. "It's still blinking! I never noticed them blinking before!" he said. He shouldered his rifle and lined up the target's eyeball before putting three bursts of 5.56mm into it. "It's down," Liam confirmed. He approached the grief and shock stricken survivors. "Looks like you had a hell of a fight, I've not seen anything like this since the early days. How many of you are there?"

Amy looked at Liam, unable to speak she shrugged her shoulders.

Liam moved a little closer, speaking a little quieter, "Listen to me, just do what he says, he won't do anything rash if he isn't challenged. There aren't many of you left by the looks of it. Do what he says and you will be okay."

Another car slowly pulled in behind the soldiers' vehicles, a Bentley. The luxury car was out of place, it was immaculate, probably washed that morning. Charles stepped out from the back seat brandishing a pump-action shotgun, ready to bravely step into action now that the action was over and done with. Two soldiers flanked him, ready to die for their boss if they had to.

They walked Charles a careful, safe path to the survivors. "We're glad we've been able to assist you, I'm sorry that we didn't get here sooner. My men heard the gunshots, and I insisted we come to investigate." Charles said. He looked surprised at the giant feeders carcass. "Had my men not stepped in, I'm sure you can all agree the results would have been catastrophic," he began then paused as he saw the ripped apart freshly murdered survivors, and masses of grey corpses. "Well, more catastrophic. Freedom isn't free, and in this dead new world you have to prove you're worthy of survival. How will you pay for your rescue?"

There were gasps from the survivors. This man was as much a monster as any of the grey fiends. "We just lost our friends, our loved ones. Minutes have barely passed and you dare ask for a reward?" Babs talked for the community, Amy unable to muster any words.

"Sorry, sorry. You misunderstood. I'm not asking for a reward, I'm asking what you will give me for our service. It's not a reward, it's payment. You don't have a choice. My men will finish what these filthy creatures started, but at least they will be quicker and less cruel."

The survivors' relief turned back to fear. Amy and Babs looked at each other for guidance that neither could offer to the other. Liam turned his back. He'd seen this situation with Charles before, and it never got easier to witness. His next step would be to order one survivor to be executed, typically a man or older woman. Liam prayed Charles wouldn't order him to off the old girl and these people would cooperate. He'd never done it, but he had seen it done once and it had shocked them all.

"We have little. Our weapons are amongst those things. Our food stores are sparse or crops we're still growing," Babs pleaded, hoping he'd take pity.

"I understand, I do. One thing we always need is able bodies. We'll take that one and her," Charles signalled towards Amy and a 13-year-old girl.

"Just me, I'll go. She's only eleven. No good for whatever you need. Just me," Amy lied as she climbed unsteadily to her feet, still clutching her stained weapons.

Charles noticed her posture and slightly raised his firearm. "Be a dear and put those down," he ordered. He looked over at the young girl again and decided perhaps she was too young. There were few options amongst the rest of the survivors. No one else took his fancy.

"We'll take you. But we'll be back in a month and we'll want food. Whatever your people can muster from your vegetable patch or you can loot from the local Spar shop, I don't give a toss. If it's not enough, we'll take the girl and whatever else we desire. And then we'll be back again the following month," he threatened. Charles wasn't pleased, but it was obvious these people had nothing. At least this woman fitted the bill. She was filthy, covered in blood and gore, but underneath she was attractive and athletic. He would enjoy her after they hosed her down.

"It's okay, do what he says. I'll be back once everything is sorted," Amy tried to reassure Babs and the other remaining survivors. Babs gave her a hug before Liam led her away to the cars.

Chapter 52

The survivors stood in the ruins of their community in silence. Grey corpses, as far as the eye could see, intermingled with the mangled remains of their own fallen. Tents had been collapsed, vegetable patches trampled and solid walls smashed through. Those still breathing were the weaker members, the old, the young and the lame. Those few defenders who had survived the fight could not move through exhaustion and shock. Tears streamed down nearly every face. So much loss so quickly. When society fell they had survived, but now many couldn't see the point in carrying on. There would always be these feral beasts ready to attack. Their rescuers were worse than the monsters, they acted out of greed rather than instinct. At least with the feeders it didn't feel personal. The group of vultures had driven off over an hour ago, yet no one could muster the resolve to do anything but quietly grieve.

Babs had lost the love of her life, but they had enjoyed a long life together. On her own, she started dragging bodies into a heap. She struggled with even the smallest corpse, but she pressed on. Slowly, others joined her. They took great care to make sure the body they were moving was dead, and not just waiting for a chance to attack. They separated feeders from the fallen defenders. Little was left of their own people, the bloody remains were often with limbs spread out over a small distance. It was the most horrific of jobs, but it was important their own people were shown the respect to be buried, and not burned with their murderers. Everyone helped with the mammoth task, working together the heaps of bodies soon grew.

Excited screams of joy could be heard. "He's alive, he's alive!" a voice shouted from the old Barn. Babs looked up, hopeful. *Maybe the stubborn old mule had one last trick up his sleeve.*

Three people carried him towards the house, he was covered in grey blood and looked in a bad way, but he was alive. Babs could barely believe it, but Bo had always been a remarkable man. She rushed to her love and held his hand. "Bo, I thought I'd lost you!"

Bo could barely fix his focus on her. Unable to talk, he mumbled something unintelligible.

"Have they bitten him?" she asked. Babs looked at him, but it was hard to see if he'd suffered an injury.

One rescuer shook their head. "We couldn't see anything, but it was a mess back there. He had one of them on him. It looks like he had a hell of a fight."

Babs smiled at the thought of her Bo giving these evil things hell. "Get him into the house, we'll check for wounds and make him comfortable."

Bo was desperate to tell them, the words just failed to come. They carried him through to the house and onto the dining table. They undressed the old age pensioner, carefully looking for wounds, but none were present. Babs looked her husband in the eye and he found the strength to place his hand on his chest, patting it twice lightly.

"It's his heart. Bo, is it your heart?" she asked him. Babs was afraid once more. They had no way of treating him. Bo again moved, a light nod, but it was enough to confirm what they suspected. Babs gripped his hand. "You tough old goat, you beat those monsters, you can beat this silly heart nonsense. There is no man on this Earth stronger than my Bo."

"What do you want us to do, Babs?" one of the assembled survivors asked, they needed a leader and Babs seemed as good a choice as any.

"Clear the dead, bury our own, but not too close to any of the crops. Stack the monsters, maybe their disgusting stink will mask us for a few days from any others in the area. Salvage whatever weapons we can, everyone sleeps in the house now."

"What about Amy?" a concerned voice spoke out.

"We can worry about Amy once we've sorted ourselves out. That's what she would want, and that's what we're going to do. We can't fight an army, in our current state we're barely able to wipe our own bottoms. I'm going to stay with Bo for a little while," Babs replied. She had been a mother, grandmother and great grandmother; organising children was a more arduous task than this. The others in the room went out to carry on the recovery, leaving Babs smiling as she stared into Bo's eyes.

Chapter 53

The small convoy of vehicles headed back to the grand house. Amy was in the back of a Land Rover with Liam beside her and another soldier driving. She paid close attention to the route, trying to remember every detail for when she found a chance to escape.

"I'm sorry about this," Liam offered a weak, embarrassed apology. "It'll be easier if you just do what he wants."

"Don't be sorry, stop him. What does he have over you?" she commented. Only a few of the soldiers appeared to like the man in charge, even Amy could see that.

"He calls the shots. Without him, we'd all be lost and alone," Liam answered. He really didn't have a good reason why they had fallen in behind Charles, it had almost been accidental, but now they were stuck enforcing his tyranny.

"But what are you now, a team of thugs? Maybe if you helped people rather than hurt them, humanity might stand a chance." With trained and armed soldiers, the farm might not have been overrun. She wouldn't have lost her friends. Jack wouldn't have raided the rescue camp on his own.

"It's not that easy," Liam stated. He wasn't comfortable with the conversation, bringing his shame into focus.

"It is, he's just one man. You don't have to kill and kidnap for him.

If you carry on like this, what happens? Where's the future if you've killed everyone or imprisoned them?"

"There isn't a future, that's the point. We might have a few years, then we'll all be dead. At least Charles lets us go out on our terms," Liam said. Charles had made the soldiers feel worthless, drummed into them that life would be over soon and they may as well enjoy themselves. Not one soldier saw a future beyond two or three years.

"They're his terms. You're just too stupid to realise. Do you know what an armed force like yours could achieve? We had a community, a good one. With your protection, we would have lived many years, planting crops and becoming self-sufficient. Instead, you were out raping and murdering."

"I've never raped or murdered anyone," he denied. Liam hadn't, but if Charles had ordered him to, he would have killed everyone at the farm.

"You let it happen, you're just as bad," she accused. Amy didn't have the strength to continue talking.

Liam turned away. She was right, Kenneth was right. He knew at least two of his fellow soldiers took part in the assaults, none of the others approved. The world had ended, societal norms ceased to be. They told themselves that they kept the women safe and left the settlements they raided largely intact. They never left them defenceless or took everything they had. They could have acted far more brutally than they did, but they could have helped. They could have defended and trained the survivors, armed them, treated them, helped them.

The cars drove up the large driveway. The soldiers who defended the perimeter were eager to see what the latest patrol had produced and looked in the vehicles. The disappointment was nearly audible when a single female seemed to have been the extent of the haul.

As the cars pulled up at the side of the house. The selection of the vehicles amassed surprised Amy. Besides the large number of four-wheel-drive cars, two army trucks and a Warrior infantry fighting vehicle, there were sports cars. Toys amongst the tools. Charles wasn't a fierce leader, he was an idiot man child. He wanted to play with guns, fast cars, and shag a lot of women.

The door opened, and they helped Amy out of the car. Looking at the house, it was grand. In the upstairs windows, maybe a dozen female faces stared down at her. Some in their teens, others a few years older, but all shared the same blank look on their faces. Charles greeted her with a smile, "Welcome to my home, one of my men will take you up to the other women. You can shower and change into something nicer up there."

Amy didn't look at him, she was too busy studying her surroundings. For every soldier she had seen from the long driveway leading to the house, she could now see more, better hidden, ready to raise the alarm. There were too many of them. Escape past these trained soldiers would be difficult. Even if she wasn't physically and mentally drained, it would be next to impossible.

As they led her into the house, the opulence of the house again struck her. Beautiful artwork hung on walls, priceless statues and sculptures were in abundance. Even small things such as how clean everything was surprised Amy. This wasn't a house at the end of the world, it was a wealthy abode that hadn't changed one bit since people started eating each other.

Upstairs, she was greeted by a blonde woman in her late twenties. Like the others, she looked like they had taken all hope from her. "You'll find a bed at the end of the room with fresh clothes. There is a shower in the en-suite, he'll want you to use it straightaway."

"I'm Amy, are you okay?"

"Don't worry, he won't force himself on you for a few days. He'll want to make sure you're clear of infection first," she spoke drily, devoid of emotion, failing to answer Amy's basic question.

"Thank you," Amy replied. She was still examining her cage. A large room, no doubt it was once a grand guest bedroom, now it housed a dozen single beds and random, but exquisite, pieces of furniture. A small TV sat at the far end of the room, with several of the women transfixed by the DVD film playing.

Amy followed her orders. She didn't have the strength to fight, and if she had a day or two to recover, she'd use it.

Chapter 54

In nearly two days Amy hadn't been allowed to leave the room, instead imprisoned with the other women. Soldiers would routinely deliver meals or pick up women to take away for a few hours. When they returned they would quietly take themselves to shower, then sit in silence watching the TV. Amy would leave them alone, no need to make them relive the trauma. It's not as if she could take a statement, arrest the offenders and have them put behind bars for a very long time. She was feeling stronger, having been given the opportunity to rest. Her mind was filled with grief and concern for those who had died, and the others they had taken her from.

The other women were numb, Amy wasn't sure if this was through stress or if they were being drugged. Either way, she decided against taking her chances and only ate the sealed packets of food and drank water from the bathroom tap. Eager to keep her wits about her in case an opportunity, no matter how unlikely, presented itself. Her time was ticking down, she had shown no signs of infection, Charles would soon call for her.

Dinner arrived, a selection of tinned vegetables, stewed meats and packets of crisps and chocolate. Amy went to collect the trolley, keen to pocket a greater share of anything sealed.

Liam was the allocated delivery boy and was glad that Amy came to him. "You're right about Charles, about this whole fucking situation.

We didn't sign up to serve this country to then become what we are now. I once saved an Afghani kid who got caught in the crossfire when we were ambushed by the Taliban. How the hell did I get here?" he vented. The regret in Liam's voice was genuine.

Amy believed him. "The same way we all did. We survive, he led down a different path, the wrong one. But you can turn it around. Help us, please."

Liam reached into his pocket and produced a small folding knife, the blade less than three inches. "It's sharp, it will do what you need it to do."

"You want me to do it?" she asked. Amy was both surprised and annoyed by the idea.

"You'll be alone with him. You can do it before they realise, then we can protect you from them. We have the numbers," he said. Maybe Liam was being a coward, but he was right. Of the soldiers, only a few were truly in Charles' camp. Most hated him, but a handful would back him to keep the status quo. If that was removed, they wouldn't side with the rapists.

Amy slipped the knife into her pocket and wheeled the trolley away, taking what she needed before reaching the others. Even if they had seen her, she doubted they'd object. She sat on her bed and opened a packet of peanuts and deposited half of the pack in her mouth. As she crunched through the nuts, she slyly examined the knife. It was sharp, but it was small. She had slashed and stabbed so many of the feeders; she knew the damage even a small blade could do if it struck the right spot. The monsters needed the brain to be pierced, but Charles was a different kind of beast. He was far more susceptible to a fatal wound than one of the grey fleshed creatures she had often dispatched. He was big and strong, his frame would mean he would easily overpower her. She might only get a single opportunity to stop him.

The advantage she had was that he had no idea who she was or what she had been through. Underestimation could be a powerful weapon. In her former life as a police officer, many a taller, stronger drunkard looked at this smaller woman and didn't deem her a threat. As she expertly put them on the floor and placed the handcuffs on them, they regretted their poor judgement. Amy observed her fellow captives. If they, as she suspected, were drugged, she would need to imitate them, put him at complete ease. That might buy her the time to get the blade into him. She quickly finished her food and sat amongst the women in front of the TV as they slowly began collecting their meals and eating.

Maybe an hour of near silence had passed when the door burst open and a soldier stood in the doorway. "New girl. Make sure you're clean and wearing this in fifteen minutes," he commanded, holding out a small bag and waited for Amy to collect it.

She gradually rose and fixed her gaze a few feet away from the soldier. Her walk was slow and lazy, she felt she had recreated the demeanour perfectly of the other women. She reached towards the soldier, holding her hands out slightly to the side of the where the bag was presented to her. The soldier dumped the small bag into her hands. "Fifteen minutes. Be ready."

Amy drifted back to her bed and opened the bag. Skimpy underwear that was a size too small and a silk nightie which was a two sizes too big. Nothing with pockets, nothing much at all really. She remained emotionless as she obeyed the order to clean herself up and dress in the nightwear. She looked at the small knife, now thankful it wasn't any bigger, and then slid it between her buttocks. She wiggled to make sure it stayed in place. The underwear being too small held it firmly, the oversized nightie covered the small bulge perfectly. Carefully, she walked to the door, and the knife didn't budge. She stared at an imperfection in the door frame's paintwork and waited to be collected.

She wasn't sure she could murder this man, no matter how much of a monster he was. He needed to be stopped, and no one else was willing to try. It didn't give her the right to be judge, jury and executioner, but would she be any better if she let herself become another victim and let him carry on his disgusting cycle? If he tried to assault her, it would be self-defence. Amy felt comfortable with that justification. She had no choice but to go into this situation. If he attacked her, anything she did would be in the name of defending herself and not an execution.

The door opened, and a soldier looked her up and down with a wry smile and pulled her out of the bedroom. Liam watched from the end of the hallway. He hoped she would do what was needed, and if it all fell apart, not implicate him. He made sure to have his rifle ready and had jammed a few protein bars in his pockets in case they needed to shoot their way out and flee. They led Amy down the corridor and she passed Liam. She gave nothing away.

Chapter 55

The room was unlike any other in the grand house. Gone were the antiques, fine art and expensive furniture. The bed was from a high street store, the single set of drawers made of laminated chipboard, the carpet removed and unloved floorboards exposed. This room wasn't setup to impress, it was basic, but it served its sordid purpose.

Charles had his own routine before he had a girl brought to him. He undressed, neatly folded his clothes and placed them into the set of drawers. His pistol was removed and carefully placed under the bed, ready should he need it. Two sets of handcuffs were attached to the headboard. He had only needed to use them once, but he checked them to make sure they were ready to use and the key was close by. The last detail was the machete. It was stained with red, not grey blood, and it sat on top of the drawers. If a woman had any fight left in her when she entered, he would make sure she didn't have it for long. The large dirty blade would often be enough to scare the fight out of them. Combined with his powerful frame and unashamed aggression, he rarely found resistance a problem.

Naked, he sat at the end of the bed, the machete within reach, and waited for the new girl. He was looking forward to breaking her in. He enjoyed having an excuse to get a little rough. Before society fell, he'd had to pay off many a prostitute for taking things too far. He detested the victim for it, but he couldn't have his reputation or that of his family dragged through the mud by a whore.

After waiting perfectly still for several minutes, the door opened, and they pushed Amy through. The door locked behind her. He smiled, she scrubbed up nicely.

She tried her best to remain emotionless. He was naked. That was jarring enough, but the stench was barely tolerable. It smelled liked nearly every cleaning product created had been used recently to scrub this torrid room. She clocked the handcuffs, the machete and wondered just how far this animal takes his desires.

"Come on then, step a little closer. Let me get a good look at you," Charles said and motioned for Amy to come closer. She stepped forward and stopped a few feet short. "Yes, lovely. Now, you know everything that happens here is your choice. You can do what I want and say, or I can cut you into a dozen chunks and feed your parts to the first grey bastard I see. Do you understand?" he threatened and Amy nodded. "Good, now I want you to undress, slowly. We have all the time in the world and I want to see what you have to offer," he said. A dirty smile spread across his face in anticipation of the show.

Slowly? She was only wearing two items of clothing. Amy started by dropping a shoulder down of her nightie as she moved a step forward. She followed with the other shoulder and as it dropped she turned around, shielding her breasts from his view. Charles adjusted himself as he became aroused. She was another step closer as she turned back around to face him. The silk nightie glided off of her body to the floor, revealing her chest. Charles approved as Amy moved closer. Her hands clutched her own buttocks as she pushed out her breasts and retrieved the blade. If she dropped it, there was little doubt in her mind she'd add to the bloodstains on the large blade.

She held the small folding knife in her right hand behind her back, Charles was too busy staring at her tits to notice anything suspicious.

She unfolded the blade with her left hand, the blade now ready. Amy wasn't. He undoubtedly deserved what was coming to him, but she couldn't just kill him in cold blood. She eased off her panties to her audience's delight and took the step forward. She could smell his breath and see he was fully aroused. "Shall I start?"

Charles nodded enthusiastically.

Amy dropped to her knees. He spread his legs a little to give her better access. She cupped his testicles in her hand and squeezed them gently, and ever so carefully pulled them towards her. She didn't think, she hadn't planned for this. Within the blink of an eye, Charles was screaming in pain. His balls were still in her hand, now severed from his body. Her small blade had taken them clean off with a single fast slash.

Charles was in a panic and dragged himself backwards onto the bed towards the headboard. Amy threw the testicles at him, freaking him out further and allowing her to act before he could compose himself. She leapt across the room to pick up the stained machete; it was larger and heavier than the one she was used to.

"Kill her, kill her! The crazy bitch has stabbed me!" Charles pleaded for help. His excitement only made his blood pump faster out over the bed. He began reaching under the bed but struggled to reach the pistol.

Amy held the machete in her right hand and the small blade in her left. She was prepared to fight her way out, or at least take a few of them with her. From the hallway outside, she could hear shouting, followed by a gunshot. Then several more.

A moment of silence, then the door slowly opened, Amy hid behind it as the barrel of a rifle rounded the corner and edged into view.

Charles had got his handgun and pointed it towards Amy. He struggled to hold it up and keep it trained on her. The trigger pull was far heavier than it should have been and as he squeezed it he moved off of his target and slammed the round into the soldier entering the room. He dropped to the floor, clutching the wound to his throat as he struggled with the blood entering his lungs. Amy crouched on the ground as Charles fired two more times before the weight of the pistol became too much for him. The pistol dropped to the bed, "Kill her," Charles quietly ordered.

Two more soldiers burst into the room. The first, Amy slashed the machete towards him, missing by millimetres. The second soldier pushed Amy to the floor. "Stop, it's over!" Liam shouted at Amy. He checked on his colleague, who Amy had narrowly missed, but paid little attention to the final jolts from the soldier choking on his own blood.

"Charles had two steadfast supporters, this one and his mate outside. Anyone else was with us or on the fence. It's over," Liam assured her. He had blood dripping from his ear, a small piece missing, more ran down his arm from a wound to his shoulder. He picked up the nightie and threw it to Amy, who quickly slid it back on.

"Kill her, kill her." The words were barely audible.

The two soldiers approached wearily, staring at the bloody mess. "Jesus, you were supposed to kill him, not cut his dick off," Liam said. Both looked shocked at the extent of the wound and the amount of blood.

"It was his balls," Amy replied, still in shock herself.

"Balls, dick. I just wasn't expecting that. Are you okay?" he asked. Liam hadn't failed to notice she had blood over her, he assumed correctly it wasn't hers.

"Yes. Are you?" she asked him. Liam's wounds were obvious.

"I'll get checked out when he's fucked off down to hell. You've done a good thing, you have," he replied. Even Liam could see Amy was struggling, he could tell she was hard, but not cold-blooded.

"There was a time I'd have been able to arrest him, he'd have had a day in court and served a very long sentence. That was justice. This doesn't feel like justice."

"Maybe one day, we'll be back to law courts. At the moment, justice is whatever we can do to right a wrong," he said. Liam had a lot of wrongs to right, but was glad he could get back on the right path.

Amy shrugged, unsure of who was right. "When can I get back to my people?" Amy questioned. She'd done her job, her friends at the farm were vulnerable and needed her.

"The next day or two, we'll get you transport back," he answered. The adrenaline was wearing off and Liam winced as he touched his wounds.

Charles lips were moving, but no sound came out. Amy walked closer to him and watched his last seconds before his eyes glazed over as he drifted off into oblivion. She never wanted to kill a human again, no matter how dangerous or vile they were. If they were to survive as a race, those few who remained had to be better than the monsters who preyed upon them. She wasn't sure if what she had done was justice, or just another violent act in a violent world. She tossed the machete and knife at the foot of the bed, having no desire to carry the wretched things any longer.

"The women, they're going to come with me," she asserted. Amy wouldn't take no for an answer.

"Agreed. If you don't mind, some of us will want to join you too. We have food, weapons, and medical supplies. We can serve your community," he replied. Liam had thought about how unhealthy their situation had become. Being with people is what they needed, and they would be an asset.

"No rapists. Anyone who touched one of those girls is on their own," she told him. Amy was stern.

"You want a new society? How about you don't send out a bunch of armed and trained lads into the darkness to survive at any cost?"

Liam said. He knew only a few had touched the girls outside of those already dead. He blamed himself for not asserting himself and making it known it wasn't right. His silence green lit their behaviour when a few words at the right time could have prevented so much hurt.

"They attacked those girls," Amy accused. She wanted a society to rise again and people to be civilised, but it wasn't.

"And that was wrong, it was disgusting. They committed crimes, punish them, don't just leave them bitter and desperate, ready to fall for the shit the next Charles will lay on them," Liam pleaded. "I'll vouch for them, they will pay for their crimes. Just let it be for the good of your people rather than abandoning them again," he implored her. Liam was feeling the effects of his wounds.

"I'm not sure how much I trust you," Amy said.

"We'll earn your trust and redeem ourselves. We're British soldiers. That meant something to us, and it will again. So please, just think about it. I need to get this sorted before I pass out," Liam said. He touched his shoulder and stumbled back a little. "Head back to the women, I'll get some clean food, proper clothes and a weapon sent up. You let them know they're safe."

They left Amy in the room alone, two bodies and a lot of blood. One monster down, seven billion to go.

Chapter 56

His patched together trousers fitted better after cannibalising other pairs to extend the legs. They looked ridiculous, but Kenneth was much taller than anyone else in the village. They had a bountiful supply of clothes, but none for a giant like him. His fatigues had gone through a lot, and it showed. It had ripped in places, blood stains wouldn't shift. He wasn't a combat soldier anymore; he was a liked and useful member of the St. Joe's community. Wearing the uniform he loves so much, especially in its current state, didn't feel right. His new attire still raised a smile to those who saw him, and he liked it. In these dark times he was more than happy to be a source of light relief for his friends.

He had made several minor jobs his own, in addition to those more suited to a man of his hulking frame. Every morning he'd check on the chickens, collecting any eggs and bringing them to the store. He'd then pick up an air rifle and try to snag a squirrel or pigeon foolish enough to enter the compound. Any rat that may have desires on the little food they had would also meet a quick death. By mid-morning he'd check the air rifle in for a hatchet and do the rounds through the village, checking for any disturbances and dealing with any hungry intruders. He frequently aided Michael and Jake on supply runs, which grew increasingly fruitless, but as their home-grown supplies increased, it became less important. His stump had healed up nicely, and no longer gave him any pain. The doctor had done an excellent job with his recovery.

Life was as good as it could be. This small slice of, if not luxury, adequacy felt satisfying. He had many moments to think, shed a private tear when thinking of loved ones no doubt lost and even hoped for a better future. These damned monsters couldn't live forever. If they survived, in a few years it may be safe to venture further out, maybe other pockets of humanity could unite. Silly dreams perhaps, but he enjoyed them. Without hope of a better world, they may as well have given up when the outbreak occurred.

Kenneth had his air rifle and was stalking a wood pigeon that had landed amongst a small crop of lettuce leaves. It didn't care that he looked like a rodeo clown as the .177 pellet struck it in the chest. A small puff of feathers and a few desperate but pointless flaps of its wings before it fell still signalled a successful shot. He grinned, he'd never been one for hunting, but now took great pride in providing for the community.

"Nice shot Kenny, we'll make a soldier of you yet!" Jake complimented. He had been watching his friend for a few minutes. Kenneth beamed a smile and gave a mock salute that turned into a single digit greeting. "There are a fair few bunnies up on Jackson's field by the woods if you fancy it?"

"Ready when you are joker," Kenneth replied.

Jake jumped to his feet and eagerly ran to the stores before reappearing with his own air rifle, a large knife and a hatchet he handed to Kenneth.

The men walked towards Jackson's field; it was the closest one to the village, a mere ten-minute walk through the woods. Michael was planning on planting some corn crops there next May. The field had been ploughed and would have been planted up already if he could have made a working irrigation system in time. Mostly cleared, it now made the perfect place to claim a few rabbits for the pot. The men had become close, each unable to acknowledge their feelings to themselves, and definitely not to each other. Both were happy to put their feelings down to friendship and respect.

They stayed alert as they walked through the trees. At the edge of the woods they stopped and surveyed the field, crouching down. Attention was now switched from looking for feeders to looking for their own prey. Jake pointed to the side of the field 20 yards away. Two rabbits nibbled at stray tufts of grass, unaware of the danger.

"Think you can make the shot?" Jake whispered. He was confident in his own ability at this reasonably short range with the pellet gun.

"You watch your own target, kiddo. I'll take the left bunny," Kenneth said. Both men raised their air rifles, looking through the scopes, getting their rabbit in the crosshairs. Both whispered, "Three, two, one…"

Both men squeezed their triggers within milliseconds of each other, sending the tiny lead pellets towards their targets. The two rabbits tumbled over. A few other bunnies ran for cover as the men loaded in their next pellet and walked towards their kills.

"If we keep this up, you'll be able to patch you next pair of trousers with rabbit pelts. Fuck, we could make you an entire suit!" Jake laughed out loud at his own joke.

The rabbits had both received a clean, humane headshot, Jake scooped them up and placed them in his bag. Kenneth stopped and listened. The normally present smile dropped as he strained to hear.

"What's wrong, Kenny?" Jake asked. He was concerned by the sudden change in his friend's demeanour.

"Shush…" Kenneth began looking into the sky for the familiar sound. The feint engine noise was distinctive, he had heard it many times throughout his military career. The helicopter roared overhead, appearing as if out of thin air close to the treetops until it stopped and hovered above them. "Put the rifle down, get to your knees and raise your hands," Kenneth demanded of his friend.

Jake obeyed as he looked up at the helicopter as it descended.

"It'll be fine, just do nothing stupid," he said. Kenneth's experience of surviving soldiers had been sullied and didn't know what to expect.

The Lynx helicopter touched down in the middle of the field as the men knelt down, waiting to see what was going to happen.

Chapter 57

Since her incarceration, the pair had been distant emotionally. William had made use of Natasha physically, but he'd barely speak to her during the day. He spent more time than ever in his lab or rounding up specimens to test. Until the last few days, William had always kept the basic feeders away, having them close put his own supply of fresh meat at risk. He would stroll up to any that came too close to the farm and push a blade into their brain. It took no skill or bravery, the other feeders had no interest in him. They were equally useless to each other. Now, however, he was so close to success with his cure, and he needed subjects, having dispatched most of the closest ones. Heading to Thornhurst daily to risk injury or discovery, and most importantly time, was not desirable. It had taken him an hour to lure a single beast into his car and get it back to the lab. He needed a better plan, and the price of butchering one of his human cattle was well worth it. An investment. Dragging the bound man behind his car did the trick. The screams alerted those hungry monsters a meal was close, then the scraped flesh and gore led them to the field. The first dozen who followed the bloody trail all had a taste when finally allowed to enjoy their meal. They didn't care when the gate closed behind them; they had been treated to the freshest meat most had ever enjoyed. Once the corpse had been stripped of flesh, they were trapped. A few stragglers followed the trail of gore from Thornhurst but were too late for both the feast and the new accommodation. They roamed for a while, then eventually most stood still and waited. Easy targets for William to round up to take straight to the lab.

He was snagging only the second beast from the field. The lab now had seven subjects, and the girl he'd cured after Natasha's attack. Every tweak of the formula would use two feeders; one to administer the cure to, and the other to be fed the cured meat. This creature was an older male, maybe in its sixties. It had been turned a long time ago and was emaciated, it hadn't been a successful hunter. William had run out of cages, so instead now cable tied his subjects to whatever was secure enough to hold them. Its dinner had been prepared the previous day, the freshly cured feeder wasn't able to stand or do much at all. Whatever brain capacity it had left enabled it to breathe, blink, and not swallow its own tongue. It could not comprehend what was happening, it didn't mind when its hand was amputated and fed to the skinny old feeder.

Two fresh meals in as many days. The stinking grey bastard couldn't believe its luck. Fingers were torn clean off and swallowed whole. The remaining bones were licked clean before being discarded. It wanted more. William wasn't to be so generous. Now it was the tedious wait to find out if he had failed again. He wouldn't waste the downtime, he already had his next three solutions brewing, ready to amend them with the findings from his latest experiment. He began getting the fourth solution started, that would take all his attention for the next few hours.

The feeders in the field had peaked Natasha's curiosity. William had always been so careful to keep the mindless creatures at an arm's length, they were far too dangerous to the food supply. She wandered over to the beasts, careful to check that William wasn't watching. They were unremarkable. They were like all the other slowly rotting, moronic monsters. She walked back to the house and noticed it. Normally his lab, the old barn, was sealed shut. Curtains and blinds closed, doors locked, but not today. He had left a single window open, the curtain behind it pulled back. *Interesting.*

As she approached, she had doubts. *Was this a test?* He didn't trust her anymore; she knew the rules. *Was this just some loyalty test to prove she was still his obedient bitch?* Maybe his work had worn him down and fatigue had made him careless. She stopped and weighed up her options. If it was a test and she failed, he would surely kill her. *Or he could try.* She was powerful and smart, and she would be ready. She was going to look, and if she had to defend herself, she'd rip his damn throat out.

Carefully, she peered through the window. She wasn't impressed with the hotchpotch of equipment. Rather than a sophisticated laboratory, it more closely resembled an old science teacher's private storage unit. His tools were old and grubby. The Bunsen burners looked little better than she remembered from school. No wonder he hadn't wanted her to see the lab, it wasn't a desire for privacy; it was embarrassment. William was sitting at a repurposed dining table, covered in various beakers and test tubes. He was using one of the archaic microscopes, his back to her. She was wary of alerting him to her presence but assured that he was in his own little world. There were several beasts in the lab; in cages, strapped down or bound to radiators.

Something was off with them. They smelled almost, human. She strained to get a better look and saw the girl she had attacked days ago. She hadn't turned. *What the hell?* She should have become just another monster within hours, yet her flesh was pink and she whimpered. She was scared. She should have just been an unthinking slab of grey monster, but the little bitch kept all of her humanity. The others were thin and looked like death, but they were human. *He'd bloody done it, he had his damn cure!* She was impressed, but a fresh worry washed over her. If he had succeeded, why hadn't he told her, and why was he still working?

William rose to his feet and approached one of the cured feeders, Natasha stood back from the window. She'd seen enough. He had his cure, and he was lying to her. Whatever he was working on now, it wasn't for their benefit; it was for his. If he could cure the dead, he didn't need her anymore. He no longer interacted with her, he just used her for sex. She wouldn't put it past him to cure one of the better conditioned things and fuck that until he found something better. That's all she was to him now. A slab of meat to shag.

Natasha ran back to the house and slammed the door as she entered through the kitchen door. She wanted to destroy everything, burn it all to the ground, the lab, the house. Everything. And him, she wanted to reach in and pull his brain out through his eye sockets. Her only decision left to make was to run or end his existence. Her hands shook, and she wasn't sure if it was anger, fear or just hunger. She raided the fridge to make sure that hunger wasn't affecting her mind. A small tub of meat was quickly devoured. Her nerves calmed, her anger faded.

She wasn't going to leave. Whilst she enjoyed the easy life, she also still wanted the thrill of the hunt. On her own, she could have both. This life was as much hers as his now, and she would kill for it.

Chapter 58

They laid in bed facing away from each other. Natasha and William both hugged the edge of the mattress, keen not to get too close to the other. William had come to bed late, as he always did. He had barely spoken to her and fallen straight asleep whilst Natasha lay awake. With the cure now available, she was fantasising about her new life without William. She could hunt, play and everything in between, all the time knowing that when times got hard, she could just cure a mindless beast and eat it.

Before she made her move, she needed to know for sure the cure was available in a quantity to last her for the rest of her life. As tempting as it was to cut his throat whilst he slept, if it turned out he had little more than a few doses available. She couldn't possibly live the life she wanted. She was sure he was out cold and carefully grabbed his keys, before she sneaked out of the bedroom, the house and made her way to the lab.

The low groan of the captive feeders in the field, and those that had gathered nearby, aggravated Natasha. They rarely stopped, and the greater the number of feeders, the more annoying the din became.

Stepping into the dark lab, the smell struck her. A strong, artificial, nearly metallic odour filled the room. The next thing she noticed was that bloody groan of the feeders, one or two of them making their noise. But there was another sound, whimpering, not from a monster, but people. She looked for a light switch and saw the girl. She was asleep, the quiet, fearful noise wasn't coming from her. Natasha walked through the lab and looked at the captives, either in cages or bound and secured to something heavy or structural. Most were people, all with injuries and missing parts, but they were pink fleshed people. They smelled a little different to a normal human, but still appealing. The last two were feeders in cages, they stank like the rest of the dead. One had part of its jaw missing and was old. Natasha pondered what curing it would do, the injuries were devastating, with it restored to humanity, surely death would return quickly, with a little more permanence.

She knew what the creatures looked like up close; she wanted to see the cured ones. They made their pained, muffled and desperate whines. They could barely blink, they certainly couldn't stand. She noticed many had defecated and urinated, laying in their own messes. However grim the sight. He'd done it. They may be severely brain damaged, but they were human. None were plump or fresh, but beggars couldn't be choosers and when push came to shove, one of these in the belly would keep her going. The cured also seemed to all have fresh wounds, either limbs missing or chunks torn straight from them. Maybe the two monsters were the lucky recipients of the flesh, or William couldn't help himself.

The girl smelled better than the others. *You can't beat the real thing.* Natasha knew she would finish what she started, the girl would be her first meal.

The lab equipment was bountiful. Maybe someone with a more scientific mind would have been interested. Natasha was looking for the fruits of William's labour. Scrawled notes meant nothing to her, she was looking for the cure. She began opening the kitchen cupboards in the lab, but beyond more equipment and the odd piece of crockery, nothing. She popped open the tall cupboard to reveal the inside of a fridge. Her face lit up. Dozens of jars of pink liquid filled the shelves, several syringes were already drawn up and ready to go. Each labelled with a solution number. There was enough of the various mixtures to cure one million feeders. She smiled with relief. He had overplayed his hand and had disrespected her for the last time. She wasn't his slave, there to service him as he wanted. She was a powerful and intelligent predator. She didn't need William. His usefulness had ended soon after he'd saved her life, but she had repaid that debt many times over.

Natasha looked at the cured girl, and wondered, *time for a snack?*

<h1 style="text-align:center">Chapter 59</h1>

When William had woken in bed alone, he instantly believed the worst. She could have been fixing breakfast, cleaning or harmlessly reading a book. He knew that wasn't true. She was up to something; he knew it. His missing keys added further to his suspicion. He didn't rush as he dressed, starting the day as he would any other. Only once in his attire did he deviate from his routine. He went to the wardrobe to reveal a tall shotgun cabinet. Entering the code, he opened the door and removed the double-barrelled shotgun, his fathers, and picked up a handful of cartridges, stuffing them into his pocket before loading two into the gun.

He was wary as he sauntered down the stairs. The shotgun was ready to do its job. He checked the food hadn't been slaughtered. They were their usual miserable selves. After searching every room, there was no sign of Natasha. His anger grew as he imagined the damage she may have done to his work. The small-minded and impulsive girl was a liability, but she was like him. Trapped between two worlds, enjoying the gifts of both. Once he had the cure, she would see. She would realise he had secured their future and they could do with it whatever they wished. If she didn't murder him first.

The walk to the lab seemed longer than normal. He didn't want to see what she may have done. It worried him that if she had destroyed everything, he may just pull the trigger and kill her through pure fury. As he reached the door, he composed himself, but only felt greater tension. He had the shotgun lowered, but ready to pop up at a second's notice to give her both barrels if needed. He saw her lying on the floor. "You stupid bitch," he spat. She was on her side, covered in the girl's red blood. She had only consumed half of the girl's body before she had slumped to the floor. Grey vomit mixed with the blood. "You ate the girl? Why?"

Natasha stirred and looked up at William. "Because that's what we do. It's in our nature," she replied. Natasha looked in a terrible state and sounded worse. Her cheeks were a little rosier, her flesh more natural.

"You don't know what you've done, do you?" he asked. William couldn't believe that she had been so selfish, so idiotic.

"Relax, you can make as many as you want to replace her now. I don't feel great," Natasha responded. She wiped grey gunk from her mouth as she looked down at the mess she had been laying in.

"I can cure the feeders, that's right. It works. You can see that for yourself. If I was working for whatever government may still be cowering in a bunker, they would laud me a hero. I've developed the cure that could save the world," William praised himself. He walked closer to get a better look at Natasha. "But there is a problem. The cure stays in the system. It doesn't degrade. Much like with FatBGone, the cure never leaves the body." He smiled.

Natasha felt awful. She looked at her hands. Some colour restored. "No, no, it can't be?"

"Congratulations. You've cured yourself, you stupid woman. You've fucked everything up. You disgust me," he berated her. He was angry, he wanted to hurt her. She was useless to him now.

"Turn me back, please, I don't want to be this. Please!" she begged. Tears ran down her face. For the first time in a long time, she felt weak and vulnerable.

"It's too late. All I can do for you now is shoot you and burn your corpse. I can't risk you infecting the others," William said. He raised the shotgun, ready to pull the trigger.

"No!" Natasha yelled. She closed her eyes, not wishing to see the shot that would kill her.

The buttstock of the shotgun crashed into her face, the impact knocking her out cold. "You're just another specimen now," William scorned. He dragged her across the lab and bound her hands, tying her to the radiator next to another cured beast.

He didn't waste any time before he started testing her; they were the same breed of beast and she had been cured. However, was her reaction the same as the simple feeders or different? The first blood sample instantly confirmed the change by its colour, what should have been grey, was instead a more human red. If he had known her fate was to do something this stupid, he would have taken her as a full test subject. Such a waste.

Chapter 60

Peter wasn't sure he could keep himself from throwing up over the beautiful, deserted West Sussex countryside. It was only the presence of the soldiers that made him feel the need to man up. The helicopter moved so low and fast everything below was a blur. He had to fix his gaze on the horizon as he held on to the machine gun. The SAS team kept themselves to themselves, except for Spencer, who took everything in. Every building, village and abandoned tent.

"Two minutes," Seb bellowed through Spencer's headset, who relayed the message to his men with his thumb and index finger.

The soldiers started a last check on their weapons and kit. Peter didn't know what he should do, so just moved the GPMG's barrel left to right as if he was scanning for a target. The Lynx flew lower over a woodland; the skids grazing the tops of the tallest trees until it launched free and pulled up to an abrupt stop above a freshly ploughed field. Pausing for just a moment before beginning its descent.

"Two armed men in the LZ, engage?" Kyle asked. He was ready to obliterate them.

"Negative, cover and react as necessary," Spencer confirmed, hoping there wouldn't be bloodshed today.

As the helicopter touched down, the two men were already on their knees, rifles on the ground and hands in the air. Kyle had his machine gun trained on the pair as the SAS soldiers disembarked the Lynx and fanned out. Peter strained to see what was going on.

"Eyes forward, Pete, watch your fucking side!" Kyle ordered. He tried to remain calm, but he didn't much fancy getting shot in the back just because Peter was curious about what was going on.

"British Army, how many more?" Spencer asked as he pointed his rifle barrel at the large black man. A closer look revealed this giant was missing a hand. Their weapons laid out in front of them looked like toys rather than the tools of war.

"Us two here, a small settlement about ten minutes through the woods. We're harmless, we have nothing worth taking," Kenneth replied.

Mike picked up one rifle from the floor and looked at it, unimpressed. "It's a fucking airgun!" he said. He was confused and placed it back on the floor, eyeing up the men.

Spencer produced the increasingly dogeared picture. "We're looking for this man."

Kenneth looked at the photo. "I don't know him. He's not with us."

Spencer was neither surprised nor disappointed, he knew this would likely be fruitless. He wasn't about to waste any time dragging his men to the settlement to look around for five minutes, then head back. "Okay, what shape are you in?"

"We're okay, making do. Look, I was a soldier," Kenneth paused and corrected himself. "I am a soldier. Who is he?"

"Maybe he has the solution to this plague, maybe he's just another white coat with no answers but big opinions."

"I've scouted out most of this area, and miles around. I might be able to guide you," Kenneth replied. If he could help, he had to. He failed his men, but maybe he could make that right.

"We've got intel and the Lynx, we're fine, I'm sure your more useful here with your people. Where were you based?" Spencer asked. He tried to shut the conversation down, but then felt he should offer this fellow soldier a moment of respect.

"When this shit all went down, a research centre, Wellworth," Kenneth replied.

"Get the fuck out of here, that's where we're working from," Billy chipped in excitedly.

"It's lost, isn't it?" Kenneth queried, he was confused. Help had come. Maybe when he visited all those weeks ago, he should have tried harder, waited. He could have been soldiering all this time rather than enjoying retirement from the world.

"Not quite, besides the few thousand grey skinned neighbours, it was just Peter until we arrived there," Billy confirmed.

"Peter?" Kenneth had only known the frightened, unimpressive man for a few hours, *but surely it wasn't him?* "Was he okay?"

"Ask him yourself, he's on the right gimpy," Spencer said as he motioned to the helicopter and started walking towards it. "Come on then."

The pair walked around the front of the Lynx, Spencer acknowledged Seb as they passed the cockpit. Peter wasn't expecting them to walk into view and nearly let off a burst from the gun. His startled look brought a smile to Kenneth's face. *It was him, he'd made it!* "Peter, long time no see!"

Peter stared at Kenneth as if gazing upon a ghost. "You died?"

"Well, nearly. I got out after that bitch lost interest. I would be dead if these guys hadn't found me. Where's your friend, the police officer?"

"I don't know. We got separated when Natasha attacked us at Wellworth."

"And it, what happened to that thing, to her?" Kenneth asked as he rubbed his stump, thinking of that vile woman, his smile gone.

"I woke up in a field, with her laying on top of me."

"Dead?" Kenneth spat the word out with venom.

"I was pretty out of it, but I was soaked in her blood and she wasn't moving," Peter replied. He grew unsure of himself.

"It's good to see you, I'm glad you made it," Kenneth broke the tension and offered his hand to be shaken.

"You too," Peter obliged and smiled.

Kenneth turned to Spencer. "I can help you, I'm still a soldier. I know this area from the ground. Not some bloody satellite picture, not from the safety of a fucking helicopter. I've walked the terrain, I've watched and listened, I can help you."

Spencer eyed the giant up and down. Despite the missing hand, he was still a physical presence. He didn't know what would lie ahead, even if Kenneth was just another able body back at the base he could prove useful. "The best intel we've gathered on the ground points to an old farm owned by the Johnson family near Thornhurst. You think you can help, prove it."

Kenneth jogged towards Jake. "Johnson farm, near Thornhurst?"

"It's not been a proper farm for a few years, just a poncy holiday let. Or it was before they died."

Spencer gathered up his troops as Kenneth and Jake continued speaking. "The big guy is coming with us, he says he's a soldier, I believe him. No guns, not even his poxy air rifle. Okay?"

Kenneth rejoined the SAS team. "Is he friendly, this Johnson?"

"I don't see a reason he wouldn't be, but the end of the world does funny things to normally stable minds," Spencer replied.

"We should go on foot then. They're in the open, nothing but overgrown fields surrounding them. If we fly too close, they'll see us coming. If you're not sure, you'll want to walk in and keep the initiative right?" Kenneth asked. He wasn't about to walk into an ambush, Spencer was right, the end of the world does peculiar things to people.

Spencer nodded. "How far?"

"If your man can land us outside of Thornhurst, it's about 20 minutes at a quick pace," Kenneth told him. He had scooted around Thornhurst a few times with Jake and Michael.

"Perfect. Let's go," Spencer replied. He could see the end in sight. Either Johnson was dead or alive, but by the end of the day, they would know.

The men boarded the Lynx and Kenneth waved to Jake as he climbed into the chopper. He would be a soldier one more time, and it felt good. Suddenly he missed the uniform. His home alterations had drawn a few looks and sniggers from the soldiers, but none had been silly enough to risk the ire of the physically impressive man. It didn't matter to Kenneth; he knew what soldiers were like; he had fought in the uniform many times and it meant a lot to him.

"Look, I'm just going to say it, what the fuck is going on with your trousers?" Mike got the words out before bursting into laughter and joined by the others onboard as the helicopter took off.

Chapter 61

Natasha felt pain in a way she barely remembered. Her hands and feet were bound, and he had secured her to a radiator. The bodily fluids over the floor confirmed another subject had recently vacated the space. She was covered in her own vomit and the blood of her last victim. Her head pounded. Pain as a feeder felt different to that of a human. It may have been the confidence that her survivability gave her, even serious wounds would recover quickly, but pain didn't feel important. It hadn't worried her, as wounds were less likely to be fatal. Now, as a human once again, the pain was tainted by her humanity, by worry. Her head hurt, she could have a bleed on the brain. Her arms had sections of flesh cut away. Maybe the wounds will become infected and she'll succumb to septicaemia. So many worries, such a frail a body.

When she had first began changing into a monster, she would have given anything for a cure, to be human again. Now she prayed that she could be restored to her cannibal self. She wanted the power back, the confidence. She knew she couldn't survive in the outside world; she had seen it first-hand. She enjoyed walking safely amongst the feeders, passing as a human when encountering survivors. Now she was on the menu too. William was still testing the samples he had taken from her, paying her strips of flesh more attention in the last hour than he'd given to her in the last week.

"Will you let me go?" Natasha asked. Genuine fear caused her voice to tremble.

"Of course not, I've told you you're far too dangerous. When those things out there eat you, and they would, you'd cure them. They would then become victims to other feeders and suddenly you've gone and cured half of the South-East. No. You've done this to yourself and I won't have you jeopardise all my work and my life. I'll make it quick when the times comes. Until then, things will be… unpleasant," he simply said. A slither of a grin showed itself, he'd make her death painless, but the rest of her life until then wouldn't be so kind.

"What will your life be like without me to bully?" she asked. Natasha had always felt controlled, but she had given as good as she got.

"Come on dear, you haven't been a victim since you took that first pill. How many people have you killed? How much did you enjoy doing it? You're a far bigger monster than I am, I just did what I needed to do. You loved doing it," William accused her. He didn't even look at her as he carried on his work.

"It will be a lonely life here on your own." She told him.

"I found you, I'll find another. Who knows how many thousands of us are roaming the country? Maybe the next one will be a little more grateful, a little less excitable," he said and the grin grew a little wider.

Natasha looked away. At least if she was a walking cure, she wouldn't have to suffer the indignity of being served up as a meal for William. Suddenly he froze and listened intently.

"What is it?" Natasha asked, she couldn't hear anything.

"Shut up!" he snapped back. He listened as hard as he could, his heightened sense picked up the faint sound of a helicopter far away. It was unusual to hear any engine sound, and the loud helicopter was distinct, but obviously far away. Natasha tried to hear what William heard, but was obviously unable. "It was a helicopter. It's gone now."

*

The Lynx touched down briefly. The SAS soldiers hopped out and Kenneth followed. After the last boot hit the ground, the helicopter took off and flew away in the direction it came. The men covered each direction as the chopper disappeared.

"Come on then, big boy, which is the best route?" Mike asked, he didn't want to waste anytime. He had the map out in front of him and invited Kenneth over to instruct.

"These buildings we need to avoid, there's several cars blocking that road with maybe 30 of the filthy bastards trapped there. We head up through the next two fields, then cut across until we hit the road."

"How close have you been to this place?" Gary chipped in.

"As far as those 30 hungry twats," Kenneth stated, aware his blag to get back to doing some soldiering was unravelling.

"So why are you here then?" Billy enquired. He saw the crippled giant as a liability.

"I guess if it all goes to shit, I can get you out of it and not into more. I know this area. If I knew that farm, I could tell you if it was the white coat there or not," Kenneth defended.

"Come on ladies, lets get cracking," Spencer gave the order, and they moved out in double-quick time, Kenneth leading with Mike; Gary, Billy and Spencer formed up behind covering avenues of potential attack.

*

Natasha couldn't get comfortable. The injuries were minor but sore, the floor hard and cold. But it was the anxiety that was getting to her. She wished he would just shoot her now and put her out of her misery. Instead, he just examined her flesh under a microscope. She couldn't fathom what was so interesting that he had been examining the samples for nearly twenty minutes. He broke away and looked at the lab. He needed to make room for new feeders to test with, and the place was a mess. He'd have to remove the bodies, kill the subjects that were no longer useful, and thoroughly decontaminate the holding cages. Even a splatter of the dry, cured blood, if ingested, could cure its victim. He didn't look forward to spending the day scrubbing. He briefly contemplated making Natasha do it, but he couldn't trust her. If it took a day, it took a day. At least now his fresh food supplies at the house would last twice as long.

"I'm going to get the wheelbarrow and clean this tip up, don't be silly. You're human now, I can smell and hear you. Escape would only lead to a painful death." William threatened. He picked up the shotgun and left the lab. He walked towards the old tool shed. He had genuinely wanted to make a go of it with Natasha, but he felt relieved. It was no longer a question of trusting her. He didn't have to anymore. He reached the old shed. It was rotten and falling apart. The tools hanging were all stained with rust, having gone many years without being cared for. William pulled out the wheelbarrow and dragged it clear. It too had seen better days but would be more able to carry the emaciated bodies away for him to burn. He dropped in a shovel to dig out a fire pit and placed the shotgun alongside it for good measure.

*

"Jesus, here's another!" Billy quietly, but forcibly announced. It impressed him to have found yet another expertly dispatched feeder, a single wound in the side of the head. They had passed nearly 50 of these professionally executed monsters as they got closer to the house. They had barely seen a live creature, only now had they spotted them. They avoided where possible, otherwise used their own blades to kill. They all tried, but only Mike and Spencer could match the clean wounds on the bodies they had found. They got in close and struck hard. Billy and Gary both preferred to lash out at a further distance, weakening the power and accuracy of their blows. Kenneth hadn't been given a weapon and could do little more than hide behind Mike when a feeder was nearby.

"Farm is up ahead, 100 yards, I can see movement. A single male," Mike announced.

He was half-way between the shed and the lab when he smelled them. *Damn it!* The wind hadn't been strong and was blowing in the wrong direction, but they were close. William slowly picked up the shotgun and looked around, trying to see who was approaching. *A soldier, no, it's two soldiers.* He looked harder, and he knew he was in trouble. *Five heavily armed soldiers, shit.* There was little point in running. He was physically strong and agile, but even his extra speed he enjoyed was a long way off outrunning a bullet. He held his shotgun over his head and waved with a smile, putting on his best friendly act.

Spencer directed his men into position and signalled for Kenneth to follow him. They reached William. "Hello sir, I'm hoping you may be able to assist. We're British army, we're looking for a man, an important man vital to finding a cure for this mess."

William's blood froze. *How did they know about him, how did they find him?* "I can't say I've seen too many other people recently," he said. Spencer handed William the photo, a small smile at his own picture, at how fat he used to be, nearly betrayed him. "Fat people are even rarer," he added and handed the photo back to Spencer, who stared at him.

"Are you alone here?" Spencer questioned, but didn't stop staring.

"Yes. Just me, I'm afraid," William responded. There was very little truth that he was willing to tell these men.

Spencer looked over to the field with the group of feeders who had become agitated at the sight, smell and sound of food. "Would you like us to take care of them for you?"

"There's no need, really, I can handle them," William declined. He looked Kenneth up and down. The strangely dressed giant only had one hand and that interested him. This man was possibly a rare bite survivor.

"I don't doubt it for a moment," Spencer spoke again, his gaze was uncomfortable for William. "I think we might have seen your handiwork on the way over, you're good with a knife," he complimented. *Too good,* he thought.

"I've had plenty of time to practice," William replied. He knew they were suspicious, he just had to play it cool.

"Are you doing okay for food, medicines?" he questioned. Still Spencer stared, examining every wrinkle, blemish or scar on William's face.

"I have a small supply, always on the lookout for a little more, of course," William answered. These soldiers would no doubt have been a tastier meal than any secured in his cellar. Better fed, and in better shape. He knew the thought of eating them would be as close as he got. He'd be lucky to take a single bite before they floored him.

"Do you mind if we look around, we won't be long?" Less a request, more a statement from Spencer.

William's eyes looked straight at the barn, his lab. As soon as a soldier would step inside, he was a dead man. "The barn isn't safe, there's a family of those things in there. I've just kept them sealed in and they haven't been a bother."

"Don't worry about that, room clearance is one of our specialties, we'll sort them out for you. I wouldn't feel like I've done my job if we left you in peril," Spencer offered. He didn't trust this man. If he didn't want them in the barn, that's the only place Spencer wanted to be.

Shit. William looked at his shotgun in the wheelbarrow. It would be hard, but maybe he could get to it, if the soldier and the one-handed giant looked away for a moment.

"Gary, Mike! The barn, several hostiles, engage!" Spencer ordered as he looked away, William was tempted to move, but didn't.

Mike and Gary jogged into position and stood either side of the doorway, weapons ready. If the opponents were human, they may have tossed in a flash bang first, but with a typical feeder, better to calmly enter and begin shooting at your leisure. They tried the door, and much to their surprise it opened. They entered one after the other. The expected instant burst of gunfire didn't occur. Spencer shouldered his rifle to look down his scope at the barn to see any signs of what his men were doing.

Mike ran out of the barn, "It's him, it's him!"

This was William's only chance. He grabbed the shotgun from the wheelbarrow and tried to bring it up to fire. Only to be expertly rugby tackled by Kenneth. The tall Welshman hadn't taken his attention off the stranger. Like Spencer, he had sensed something was off.

Kenneth was strong, but William had an impressive amount of power, far more than Kenneth had expected. William rolled the pair over, his defensive instincts kicking in as he snarled at Kenneth. "He's one of them, it's a bloody feeder!"

His teeth snapped at his opponent involuntarily, anger filling his face. Spencer reacted on instinct and put a single 5.56mm round into William's chest, knocking him backwards off of Kenneth who scrambled free.

"What's going on?" Billy screamed from his position outside of the house, unable to grasp the full extent of the situation.

Mike had his rifle shouldered as he jogged towards Spencer, covering William. "Spenny, it's a fucking mess in there. Dead monsters and people. He was experimenting on them."

Gary stuck his head out from the barn. "There's a live one, a girl!"

Spencer approached William, rifle ready, passing Kenneth he asked, "You okay big man?" Kenneth nodded, wiping a few smaller drops of grey blood from his clothing. "You're William Johnson, right?" Spencer asked. He looked down at the man he'd just shot. The wound would have killed a human instantly. To one of these things, it was serious, but it would heal given time.

William looked up. "Yes. Before you kill me, you should know, I have a cure," William told him. He was completely at their mercy. The wound diminished his ability to move.

"Bullshit," Spencer let out. He held the rifle pointed at William's head. It was an empty threat, he had orders to bring him in.

"Get your men to look at those dead people, they were all feeders. Their chipped teeth healed over wounds. They were the thing that keeps you awake at night," William said. He had to make them believe him. He couldn't die today.

Gary exited the barn with the girl. She had several small wounds, but otherwise okay.

"Why did you kill them? Why not cure yourself?" Spencer asked. He couldn't see things from William's point of view. He couldn't understand why somebody wouldn't want to be cured. He didn't think for a moment that William couldn't understand why somebody would want to remain an unremarkable human.

"The cure doesn't work as it should. The test subjects were all severely brain damaged, they'd been infected too long," he explained. That was all the truth he was willing to tell them. He looked at Natasha, fearful of what she might tell her liberators. "Except that one. She was like me, she wasn't a simple monster…"

"But a complex intelligent one, like you?" Spencer finished William's sentence.

"Yes. She is evil though, she didn't just eat to survive like me. She enjoyed it."

Kenneth looked over and couldn't believe it. He slowly walked over and picked up the shotgun from where William had dropped it, looking at Spencer who gave him permission with a nod. He'd only known her for a few hours, but he'd never forget her face. Never forget what she had done. Calmly he walked towards the barn. Only when he got within a few feet of her did he raise the barrel at her.

Gary instantly pointed his rifle at Kenneth. "What are you doing?"

"She's evil, she's a monster," Kenneth said, ready to blast her.

"She's human, look at her wounds. That blood ain't grey, it's crimson like yours or mine," Gary countered. He had just seen what this poor girl had gone through.

"That's the bitch that took my hand. I don't care what she is now, human, feeder or a fucking patas monkey. She's a monster and will always be one!" he snapped and gripped the shotgun tight, balanced on his stump, his finger on the trigger.

Natasha smiled. "How I miss dark meat, so much richer."

Gary stepped back from her and lowered his rifle.

"I will not kill you. I'm going to let you go," Kenneth spat the words out.

Natasha stood still, smirking.

"I said go, run along now. Let's see how you enjoy being hunted," he said. His face was hard. He wasn't giving her an option.

The smile dropped from her face. She didn't move until Kenneth raised the shotgun once again, then she started a slow jog.

"Spencer?" Gary called. He didn't know if he should intervene.

"We're here for this one, I don't care about her. Let her go," Spencer ordered. He didn't have any time for her, he'd heard the stories from Peter and the kid Kevin. He'd lose no sleep at the prospect of her death.

"Run!" Kenneth screamed. She barely picked up the pace as he blasted off a single cartridge in her direction. Several of the small pieces of bird shot struck the back of her legs. Not enough to cause any real damage, but enough to ring the dinner bell and slow her down just a little more.

She made it to the road and the first feeder detected its meal and gave chase. She carried on running until she was out of view.

Spencer rallied his men. "Gary, Billy, check the house. Mike, get Seb on the blower and get a message back to HQ. We have our man and need support."

Chapter 62

The Johnson family farm was a hive of activity. Four separate helicopters had landed with two more gunships flying overhead, engaging targets that dared to so much as look in the wrong direction. Two Chinooks were being loaded with the released captives, lab equipment and William, hooded and bound. A dozen special forces soldiers overseeing the medical and scientific staff accompanied them as they performed their duties. Two Lynx helicopters were on the ground, Seb had his chopper close to the farmhouse and his people, Peter and Kyle, manned their machine guns. The other Lynx mirrored Seb's, ready to leave or spray bullets at a moment's notice. Its men joined Spencer's in covering the perimeter whilst the scientists took apart the lab. They were sure not to miss a thing, not so much as an empty beaker or half written note would be left behind.

The odd gunshot rang out as curious feeders emerged from nearby fields, seeing what all the fuss was about. Seb beckoned Spencer over to join him in the helicopter. "Two minutes and they'll be out of here. You've got thirty seconds after that before I join them!" Seb was only half joking. This wasn't his idea of a good landing zone, the amount of noise and the lack of visibility was less than ideal. His pistol was on his lap, ready to use on anything that got too close. Spencer nodded his understanding and left the noisy chopper to inform his men individually.

The Chinooks were fully loaded and their accompanying soldiers onboard. They lifted off quickly. This was the signal for the other Lynx helicopter and its men to start their withdrawal. As the Chinooks headed away, the two gunships joined them and escorted them off towards their own base of operations. Spencer and his men were climbing aboard the helicopter as their colleagues in the other Lynx flew off towards their own base.

Spencer was the last onboard, and he was barely in his seat as Seb quickly gained altitude and headed back to Wellworth. There was a genuine sense of hope amongst those onboard. They felt sure their mission was a fool's errand, that the scientist couldn't be found. Never in their wildest dreams could they imagine they'd succeed, that he had already developed a cure. Even if the motives behind its creation were far from pure. A cure was a cure.

The flight back to Wellworth was quick and uneventful. From the air, the numbers of feeders at the fences felt even greater than on the ground. Seb successfully touched down and Andy limped over to greet the returning men. "Good work boys, looks like Pete was your lucky charm!" Andy told them. He had been in communication with Seb and with command and was up to speed.

As the helicopter blades slowed, the men were already unloading their kit and heading back to the barracks. Kenneth jumped out and looked around at his old home. It was more overgrown, tattered looking, and of course the dead. There were so many more grey, angry faces at the fences. He thought last time it was bad, now it was much worse.

"What's it like being back?" Gary asked.

"Awful. I feel, guilty. So many died, and those that made it out, they took a bad path," he replied. The Welshman teared up, remembering his friends who had died, the major and the innocent white coats. He could have helped, instead he failed in his mission.

"There aren't good paths. There wasn't a right way of doing anything, it's not like we'd had experience of the world ending," Mike tried to reassure this big soldier. "We're soldiers, we do what we're told. It doesn't matter how awful we follow orders and do what we're told, no matter how horrific. You risked it all, it wasn't your fault the gamble didn't pay off."

"I think I'd like to go back to Nutwood," Kenneth revealed. He wanted to be back with his new people. He was determined he wouldn't fail them like he had failed Wellworth. He couldn't bear losing more friends, losing Jake.

"Spencer will get it sorted. Tonight you're staying here and celebrating with us," Gary said and put his arm around Kenneth and led him towards the barracks.

Spencer approached Peter. "I don't know what our orders will be now, but what do you want?"

Peter was taken aback, he had no idea what he wanted. He was enjoying being one of the boys and felt safe with current arrangement. "Can't I stay here?"

"I'll be honest Peter, you don't want to be here on your own and you don't want to be on one of the ships. If we stay, we'll probably be reinforced, and things won't be the same," he whispered. Spencer couldn't see a wonderful future for Peter if he got into the system. People like him didn't do well.

"We could see if we could find the farm where my friends were," he suggested. The only other place Peter had felt like home was the farm. His brief stay was memorable, and he'd had never left, if it hadn't been for Gareth.

"Sure. We're off the clock now. Tomorrow, we can start looking for your friends, until then you're one of us. If that doesn't work out, I'm sure the big lad will take you in," he assured him. Spencer had grown fond of Peter. He hung back as everyone headed into the barracks. Even Seb was in a rush to get inside. It was no secret that Mike had procured a bottle of Bushmills 21-year-old single malt, saving it for an unlikely celebration. A cure to this god awful plague seemed like it was a suitable reason to crack it open.

Alone, he took a moment to enjoy the prospect of a happier future. He was a hard man, but the relief he felt brought a lump to his throat. Even if the cure was good and could be replicated, there would be so much work to do. But he wouldn't ever have to play a part in a mass murder again. He'd never have to shoot an innocent woman in the back of the head on a boat again. Just because he was ordered to.

Chapter 63

The farm looked like hell but was much better than it had been five days ago. The tidy-up had been long and distressing, the mental strength of the survivors challenged, but not defeated. They had cleared the battleground of all but the giant feeder. The lost defenders granted a mass burial and a service for the survivors to show their grief and gratitude. Not much remained of the bodies, many were an incomplete collection of fleshy bones. It was next to impossible to identify one from another, but they treated each with the utmost respect. The bodies of the feeders moved to an unused field, stacked on top of each other. The desire was to burn them, but they were ill-equipped to deal with any attention such a large fire might draw.

Bo had been stable. He could sit up and speak, but he was still very weak. They suspected he wasn't long for this world and they had moved him to his and Babs' bedroom. Babs had only left his side sparingly, fearful every time he closed his eyes they may never reopen. Having assumed leadership, she made her presence known and any brief time spent away from her love was spent working. She may have been old, but she knew how to be useful.

"You don't have to stick around here. I promise I won't die on you," Bo was quiet, but still kept his cockney charm.

"You're too stubborn to die," Babs said and smiled back, hoping at least it was true.

"I've got a little more in me. You have a rest, otherwise you'll be joining me and we can't both be poorly," Bo grinned.

"Maybe just for a little while," Babs replied. She was exhausted, a sit down and doze in the house would have been perfect, but she wasn't the only one needing a rest. She left him alone but with the door open and wandered downstairs. Members of the community sat in silence, mentally and physically exhausted they took a break in the safety of the stone farmhouse. Babs started making refreshments, making sure everybody had a drink and something to eat. It was gratefully received, and she moved outside to see where she could help.

Several people stood around the giant, trying to come up with a plan to remove it.

"We could cut it up, drag the chunks over to the other bastards," a young woman offered.

"We'd need a bloody chainsaw to get through that thing. We could burn it here," a middle-aged man countered.

"Not so close to the house, it'd reek," the young woman said, she preferred her idea.

"Grab a tarp, one of the damaged ones. Use the cars to drag it onto the tarp, then drag the whole thing to the pile. As long as it's legs don't fall off, it should save the mess on our front doorstep," Babs stated, calm and confident.

There were nods of agreement, and people started putting the plan into action. Two elderly survivors were examining the destroyed crops, hoping they could salvage something. Babs approached. "How's it looking."

"Awful. The ground is swollen with their grey fluids. Even if it wasn't all flattened to buggery, I wouldn't eat anything grown here. We're going to have to start again in a clean area," he fumed. The elderly man was furious.

"Let's see what suitable seeds we have, and we can all start preparing the plot on the other side of the house. I'm sure with your green fingers we can get something growing," Babs was reassuring, even though she knew without the crops they wouldn't make it through the coming winter. Her words were taken onboard, and the couple went to examine their new vegetable patch.

They had come so close, worked so hard, and for what? They'd lost over half of their friends and family. Their idyllic home ruined, and they were right back where they started. Battered, beaten and robbed of hope. Babs rested against the wall for a moment and decided that was more than enough time spent feeling sorry for herself.

Babs heard the engines and assumed they had started to move the giant. It was only when she heard panicked shouts she took notice.

"They're back, they're back!" a young man ran forward carrying an empty, blood stained shotgun. They could do little more than show they'd fight.

Babs walked closer to the approaching vehicles. It was the soldiers, back to claim the little they had left. Blades and empty firearms took up positions, ready for a fight they could never win.

"Stop, stop!" Amy screamed as she jumped out of a large truck, a pump-action shotgun in her hands.

Babs breathed a deep sigh of relief as a tear rolled down her cheek. The sight of Amy was nearly as much a relief as when Bo had been found. "It's okay everyone, our Amy's back."

Amy rushed over to Babs and hugged her. "We've got soldiers, we have civilians and we have supplies. Lots of them."

"It'll be okay?" Babs wanted to explode as the weight had been lifted from her shoulders.

"It'll be okay," Amy confirmed. It was good to be back.

The soldiers exited their vehicles and looked on at their new home. It wasn't as plush as Charles' house, but it was honest and it was their future. The women who had been kept by Charles jumped out of the back of a truck and looked around. They didn't care the farm was basic, stank of the dead and had been a scene of a fierce battle. They were free.

Chapter 64

Natasha had been jogging for nearly 20 minutes. Crossing fields and running across dirt tracks, fleeing from her pursuers. She had been sick once already, but barely had time to compose herself. Now half a dozen feeders gave chase, able to keep up with their injured and tired prey. The blood trickling down her legs from the birdshot wounds spurring on the creatures to get their meal.

She had no idea where she was going to go, or what she was going to do. Her only thought was to get away from the monsters, she knew how cruel they could be. The lands she once roamed in complete safety now she was just like any survivor, desperate and scared. On the horizon, she saw something that gave her hope. A house. If she could get there and close lock herself inside, she could recover. Maybe there would be some food and a weapon. All she needed was a knife or hatchet, anything that she could defend herself with and take the monsters on individually.

Every step made her feel more human, feeble. She detested the feeling; she had been a magnificent creature, the top of the food chain. Strong, fast, intelligent and beautiful. Now she was just like every other sack of meat she'd ever hunted.

The house drew closer, now only 200 metres away. She dared to look back, eight of the creatures now ready to devour her.

She tried a little harder and moved a little faster. A terrifying cry rang out. She knew exactly what it was. Even when she was at the top of her game, an alpha feeder, these fat bastards didn't play nice. She saw it at the corner of her eye, slowly moving to intercept her. She was confident even in her current state she could out manoeuvre it.

Only 100 metres away. The mob was still behind her and the big one was too slow to get in front of her. Natasha looked at the house and prayed to herself the door would be open. Another two creatures appeared between her and the house. They were in poor condition, little more than the ripped mouldy rags on their bodies holding their bony frames together.

Still she ran. She could see the old stone house clearly now. It was small and had been well looked after. She easily overtook the big bastard before it could get near, likewise the two scrawny feeders were in no shape to get close enough to lunge at her.

Nearly there. A stumble over an unseen mound sent Natasha flying towards the floor. Her lungs were on fire, her legs began cramping up as she crawled to get back on her feet before stumbling again. The second attempt was successful, but now they were a few metres behind her. Inside she screamed, outside she struggled for breath.

She ran through the damaged low wooden gate into the small front garden of the formerly picturesque cottage. She reached the front door, and it was locked. Tears streamed down her face. She had been at the top, and her descent had been rapid, the only thing she had left, her existence, was about to be ripped from her. She had no time to reflect on her life. The good person she had been before she became the monster she wished she still was.

The first teeth clamped down on her flailing arms. The second, third and fourth sets of hungry mouths quickly followed, taking large chunks of her flesh as she screamed in pain. The big bastard grabbed her arm and pulled it free with little effort. It wasted no time in stripping the flesh off with its teeth.

The pain was gone and her sight and hearing had gone fuzzy. Random thoughts hit her brain that she could not make sense of, then nothing.

The creatures all had their fill of her corpse. They didn't know what she used to be, or what she had become. All they cared for was her flesh filling their stomachs. If their simple, instinctive minds had realised what they had just done, they may have been worried. They didn't know they had just been cured. They didn't know in a few hours' time they would be human again. As human as their deformed, injured and incomplete bodies would allow. All would be too far gone to have any mental capacity. If they didn't fall to the floor in a heap, they'd barely be able to move. Once turned, they would be easy pickings for other feeders, too greedy to pass up a free meal and involuntarily curing and condemning themselves to the same fate.

Natasha had suffered the same death she had inflicted upon many others. Nobody would mourn her passing. The creatures she had cured would cure many others, but it would never be enough to forgive her sins.

Chapter 65

They had transformed number 10 from the office of a lone dictator, to the meeting place of the council. The ship's briefing room was a larger and more appropriate space, compared to squeezing everyone in to the room that had been used by one person to order others. The first decision the council took was that they needed to own her legacy. Number 10 was the seat of power. It could barely fit in the six council members, their assistants and the table big enough to accommodate them all. The prime minister didn't care if her audience were crammed in like sardines, she was in charge so they were secondary. The members of the council were all equals, none outranked another or were deemed more important. It comprised a medical doctor, a scientist, two civilians, a representative of the navy and the general. He demanded his position be temporary to aid the transition, and that he too should face trial alongside the prime minister. Begrudgingly, his request was granted.

They had assumed power two days ago, and this was just the second meeting. The shift in power had been announced and a message broadcast to all the ships. The official story was that she had stepped down because of ill health. For the average civilian surviving onboard a rickety old ship, with minimal food and fresh water, news of a regime change didn't make a lot of difference. Today, the news would improve their lives.

"As you are aware, the onshore teams have recovered one of the original scientists who worked on FatBGone. William Johnson was himself a feeder, but an intelligent one. He developed a cure. I'm advised this wasn't an altruistic act he didn't want to save us all, he didn't want to starve once we were all dead," the scientist said. It excited the scientist to deliver the news. It was still fresh, and she had been receiving updates from her colleagues on the mainland every hour since the previous evening. "In short, it works. It works fantastically well. If we cure an old feeder, it will be little more than a quivering human body. It won't think, walk and breathing is touch and go. It has severe damage to many parts of the brain, they're human, but in a vegetative state. Fresher creatures may be a little more able, but loved ones too far gone won't ever return. That's the bad news. The good news is their flesh and blood is teeming with the cure. The cured feeders will become easy prey to others who will do what they do and devour them. They will then have the cure, and within hours, they will be ready to pass it on to whatever feeder feeds on them."

"Does it work as a vaccine then?" one civilian asked, eager to make the most of this miracle and get their people back on land.

"We're exploring that possibility. However, being bitten will no longer be a death sentence. With the cure quickly administered, little to no damage from the microbe will have taken place. This is the game changer we have been praying for," the scientist proudly beamed.

"Can it be weaponised?" the general asked. He liked the idea of the creatures taking care of each other.

"Actually, it requires very little of the solution to be effective. Adapting a tranquilliser dart should give you a little range and would be suitable to administer the cure, not that it would be instant. It takes several hours for the cure to take full hold. Not as impressive to look at as your machine guns or attack helicopters, but far more effective in the long run."

"How far away are we from utilising it?" the general asked. He already had ideas buzzing around his head of how they could start a true fight back and reclaim their world from the dead.

"It depends on how desperate we are?" the scientist asked. Until now, only the closest of the PM's advisors had known the true situation. The scientist didn't know that supplies of food were nearly down to zero. Why would she? It wasn't her area.

"Very," the general answered drily.

"We can begin producing the cure on the Reckoning, and the secure facility on the mainland. That would give us a healthy stock within two months," the scientist suggested. They hadn't read the room. She thought two months was impressive.

"We don't need a healthy stock. We need a few doses for some of those fiends and see how effective it is at travelling through them. We tried to take the Isle of Wight by force and lost time, resources and lots of good people. Give me half a dozen doses and we'll see how quickly we can make a dent in them," the general asserted, he felt the fight returning in him.

"We're expecting a sample of the solution here within the hour, along with Johnson. If all goes well, I believe I can give you what you need by the end of play tomorrow."

"Good. I can't speak for the others, but I promise I'll try to give your people the time to get this right. Now the other matter," he added. The general already had a few ideas to get the cure into the wild, so he was more than content with the timelines.

"The former prime minister?" the doctor piped up. The others around the table nodded. "We've performed as full a medical and psychological evaluation as it's possible to do out here. She's fine, blood pressure a little high, maybe, she's exhausted, but she is fit for trial. Admiral Hollis, bar his facial injury, is also in good health."

The older civilian council member was first to have his say, "We need to vote on the trial. Personally, I believe it's a mistake. Trust is at an all-time low, but a trial won't improve that. If we find them guilty, we confirm to every survivor out there that they are at the mercy of the authorities. It will be more chaotic than it was when the cities fell."

"We can't let her go, and if we hold her without trial, what will we say? What would we tell the people?" she asked. The younger female civilian, despite the fall of the world and how bad society had become, still believed in justice.

"She was cold-blooded, ordered the murder of hundreds and sent many more to their deaths. I suggest we execute her," she said. The suggestion may have seemed more likely to have come from the lips of the naval officer or the general, not the civilian.

"I agree that her actions reflect badly upon even the idea of a government. But so does an execution. We abolished the death penalty in the sixties, I don't think this council should be known for bringing it back. And what of the admiral?" the general asked. He knew a public execution wasn't the solution. He didn't care his fate was tied to that of the admiral and former prime minister, but their future couldn't impact that of the survivors.

"As far as the public knows, she's ill. It wouldn't be unexpected for her to fail to recover," the naval officer replied. He saw her execution as a far more private affair. "And as for the admiral, I don't think we need to worry that his death will be overly scrutinised."

There was silence at the table. Each member of the council weighing up the pros and cons of ordering these deaths.

"There is another option," the scientist offered. She seemed embarrassed. "We have a cure, it needs testing and we have little in the way of willing subjects amongst our healthy population. Nobody wants to survive the apocalypse to die from an allergic reaction to a new medication. I could administer it to them and we can see what happens and gain some understanding of whether it would be sufficient as a vaccine."

"Human testing? Is that any better than reintroducing the death penalty?" the general questioned.

"She's taken a lot, it's time she gave something back. Testing on the pair of them now could advance our understanding of the cure. It could save countless lives and begin the slow process or repaying their debts," she explained. As a woman of science, she'd never tested on a fellow human being, but it would be the fastest path to progress.

"I agree. Debts need to be repaid, and I was complicit in their crimes, so I should face the same punishment. That is what we agreed. However, I believe testing for a vaccine isn't ambitious enough, and doesn't solve the problem of what to actually do with us long term. You can administer the cure to us, then you have 24 hours for all of your tests. After that, we will be taken to the Isle of Wight, to where we lost so many of our own. Then we'll really see what this cure is capable of when those things get a taste. Two birds, one stone," he finished. The general knew it wouldn't be pleasant, but it would benefit the people they had betrayed.

None of the council members could look the general in the eye. They didn't want to admit they liked the idea of that bitch being ripped apart, suffering, whilst at the same time kicking off a chain reaction that may cure the entire island.

"General, you don't have to face their fate," the doctor said it, but perhaps didn't believe it.

"Nonsense. It was my condition of joining this council. If I can make right a few of my wrongs, you won't take that away from me," the general stated. He was tired of this life, his soul tainted by what he had been involved with. This would be a perfect redemption.

With that, the second brief meeting of the council was over. The new council had taken just two meetings to agree to murder, human experimentation, and to lie to the remaining human population. They believed it was for the good of the many. Much like an over promoted, newly installed prime minister had done not so long ago. The first time was always the hardest, but the trick was making sure there wouldn't be a second time.

Chapter 66

The new arrivals had been at the farm for a few days and had made themselves useful. The soldiers had helped repair the damage and prepare new defences. Their presence grew on the survivors, their firearms and willingness to train and arm others gave everyone a sense of protection. The new women stuck together, at first struggling to trust the men who used to keep them under lock and key or worse, but without Charles, things had changed. They had started to recover from their ordeal, now believing a better future was possible, more than they had been allowed to dream of for some time. They helped the older members of the community, many of whom still could not recover from the trauma of the attack. The new blood, supplies and weapons made everyone feel better.

One soldier, being a trained medic, could tend to Bo. He pointed out he hadn't needed to treat too many pensioners with heart conditions in Iraq but was happy to help. Bo didn't make the lad's life easy and was reminded constantly by Babs to behave.

Amy had resumed her role as leader, Liam finding himself her number two whilst Bo recovered. Between them both, they had the trust and acceptance of everyone in the community. They worked closely together and held a regular morning meeting to update members of the community and allow them to raise concerns. The day's meeting had just finished, they all even shared a joke, and a few laughs, the first time the mood had been light enough for that to occur. Amy pulled Liam to the side. "The women, they have agreed to allow all of your men to stay."

"Okay, good, but they're not my men," he said. Liam had naturally become their leader, not that he wanted that responsibility.

"Yes, they are now. There were two conditions. The first condition is that you are responsible for them. If one steps out of line in that way, you are to deal with them. Permanently," Amy declared. There was little room for confusion in her tone. Amy locked eyes with Liam and stared intensely at him.

"Okay," Liam agreed. He didn't have choice but to agree, and just hope it never came to that.

"The second is they don't want anyone else to know what happened. They haven't said a word and I doubt any of your men have been bragging about that god awful house. It needs to stay that way. This is a clean start for them and your men."

"Agreed."

"How many are left to burn?" she asked. With the unpleasant chat out of the way, it was back to the grim everyday business for Amy.

"We're down to the last dozen, and a leg of the massive one. We'll be done today, thank fuck, then we can fill the pit in." The soldiers had been burning the feeders' bodies one or two at a time in a large pit they had dug in their first few days. They had been careful not to create smoke or too grotesque a smell that an unfriendly passer-by might notice.

"Good. I know it's an awful job," she admitted. The soldiers hadn't grumbled or whined, and Amy respected that.

"They're all awful jobs. Doesn't bother me, I'm on light duties with the shoulder still recovering, I just point and order," Liam said and nearly laughed at the idea that there may have been a duty that wasn't horrific beyond belief. The soldiers would almost rather be chopping up bodies of the feeders and slowly burning them than scrubbing clean every spot their foul blood had tainted.

"I know, but that's one of the worst. I'll help later and bring a few of the other guys," Amy replied. They'd be in this for the long haul, Amy knew it would be best to head off resentment and bring everyone together early. The initial signs had been good, but there would always be work to do to keep the peace.

Liam gave a respectful salute and dismissed himself, leaving Amy alone. The farm was looking better, but the battleground out front couldn't be trusted to grow crops in. There was plenty of land at the farm, they'd just have to move further afield and maybe be more ambitious. The supplies the soldiers brought would get them through autumn, winter and if they played their cards right, spring. Rather than a glorified vegetable patch, they needed real crops on a larger scale. They just needed to figure out how.

She wandered the yard surrounding the house, making her presence known to those around her. She wasn't the first to hear the sound. She had noticed the soldiers starting to run around anxiously, grabbing their weapons and taking cover as they looked around. The engine was noisy, but she struggled to identify the direction from which it was coming. It was only when she looked back at the soldiers, she could see them preparing a GPMG, loading a fresh belt of ammunition, and pointing it south of the farm. The small spot in the sky, a helicopter, slowly growing in size as it travelled towards them. Amy took the shotgun from the sling on her back and clasped it. "Everyone, into the house, please!" She was firm but tried not to show any panic. *Why couldn't they just be left alone?*

The soldiers maintained their discipline as the helicopter slowed as it reached them. It was a British Lynx helicopter. It was close enough for them to make out it was armed with two door gunners manning the weaponry. It was hovering directly between the soldiers working at the fire pit and the farmyard. As it descended, the soldiers readied themselves for a firefight.

Amy shepherded the last of the civilian survivors into the house. Those not carrying a gun collected one from the store in the house. They wouldn't again be trapped and helpless.

Amy crouched behind a stone wall, only the top of her head visible as she stretched up to look over towards the helicopter. It touched down and there was a tense pause before two men hopped out. A tall black man, and a shorter, slightly chubby white one, both raising their hands up. *It was impossible, wasn't it?* Amy rose to her feet and shielded her eyes from the sun, hoping for a better look. A smile spread across her face and she put her shotgun down and began running to the helicopter. Suddenly she realised the soldiers may panic and shoot. She picked up speed and ran as hard as she could, "Don't shoot, don't shoot!"

Peter and Kenneth turned to see Amy running towards them. Liam had already begun walking towards the men, pleased to see Kenneth.

"What's that Amy, shoot them?" Liam said with a smile, but not foolish enough to raise his rifle barrel. "Kenny, you big bastard! It's good to see you."

"You still with your friend?" Kenneth asked, he wasn't sure he was pleased to see Liam.

"No, he's not around anymore. We're helping, we're here now with these guys," Liam said and dropped his smile.

"Good," Kenneth said and hoped it was true.

Amy joined them and hugged Peter. "I thought you were dead!" she exclaimed. She looked at Kenneth. "And I was bloody certain you were!"

Peter couldn't talk, as he struggled to hold back the tears. To see a friendly face, to be back at the farm after all this time, was nearly too much for him.

"Your boy did good, I got lucky," Kenneth beamed.

Spencer joined them and approached them. "What's the situation?"

"We're recovering from a substantial attack, these soldiers have joined us and are helping us get back on our feet," Amy said and straightened herself up as if talking to a general.

"Good. Peter is your problem now, I love the lad but my God, his sense of direction is awful. We've spent two days flying around trying to find our way back here. I'm sure if we hadn't found you today, Seb would have thrown him out at a 2000 feet," Spencer joked and gave Peter a playful nudge that knocked him back. "Do you require any help?"

"We're always happy for more able bodies to join us," Amy answered. She would be more than happy for more guns and a helicopter to join them.

"Sorry, we have a mission. Well, we're between missions, but I expect that won't last long. We can get in touch with command, they might assist going forward."

"Amy, there's a cure, it works!" Peter blurted the information out.

"A cure, how?" she questioned. Like most survivors, Amy had long since given up hope that there would ever be a cure, a chance of salvation.

"There's a lot to catch you up on. I'm sure Peter will oblige. There are better things coming. I need to get this one back to his village and then back to my men."

"We have an ill man, he had a heart attack. Can you help?" Amy asked. A catch-up could wait, Bo was Amy's priority now.

"We're not equipped at Wellworth, but there's a larger facility, they might help. Is he stable?" Spencer asked. He had been advised the new administration were far more humanitarian than the last, helping survivors on the mainland was a good place to start.

"Yes, for now, but he's not in a good way," she replied. Amy worried they might not help if the patient wasn't urgent.

"I'll get back and report in, I'll try to get at least a doctor out here in the next 24 hours. If I call it in this morning, they should be able to get something done for tomorrow," he said. He reached his hand out to Peter to shake. "It was a pleasure serving with you. You look after these guys. I'll get this one back home."

"I'm at a village called Nutwood, it's not too far from here. I'll try to come back in a few days, they're good people, I'm sure we can help each other," he said then patted Liam on the shoulder and smiled. "Try not to hurt too many people." he added. Kenneth was delighted to see another community, much like the one he had made his own. One that he was eager to return to.

Both Kenneth and Spencer jogged back to the helicopter, and it quickly took off, wasting no time as it headed away at speed.

"It's good to see you, Peter, really good," she said. Another returning ghost was always a pleasant surprise.

"I thought I was going to die alone for so long, I can't explain how it feels to be back here. I've got so much to tell you," he admitted. Amy put her arm around Peter and led the pair back towards the house.

Chapter 67

It was shortly after 6 am. The sun was barely up as the four passengers were loaded onboard the small rigid hull inflatable boat. They were accompanied by two armed special forces soldiers and another to guide the craft to its destination. An additional boat was crewed with six of the special forces soldiers, able to assist if there was trouble aboard the first vessel. Three of the passengers had been unwilling to board the boat, being forcibly placed in their seats and bound in place. One was calm. This had been the general's idea after all. It was time they gave back. The former prime minister had started angry and belligerent. Now she was just scared. The admiral didn't believe that what he'd been told was anything more than an idle threat. Only when he got to the small boat did he realise it was over and tried to mumble his objection through his wired jaw. William Johnson was just angry. He'd been at the top of the food chain, then taken from his home and his perfect future before being cured against his will by his own creation. He'd hoped to have been able to trade his knowledge for his life, but his meticulous notes and documented formulas along with the samples were all that was needed. His only value was as a test subject, and that usefulness was quickly outlived.

The three human test subjects had been given the cure, but not exposed to the microbe or anything tainted with it. Each had howled in pain as they were injected with the solution. They complained of a burning sensation throughout their bodies for hours afterwards. Their hands and feet would go numb and even a short period of loss of vision. Not ideal reactions, however, the cure remained in their bodies, wasn't passed in urine, faeces or any other bodily fluid. Only blood samples drawn from the subjects showed traces. They could work on the side effects to perfect the use of it as a vaccine, as a cure they had already proven it worked. Johnson's only reaction to the cure being administered was the colour returning to his skin, his blood returning to the more usual red colour and profusely vomiting grey bile for nearly five minutes. His gunshot wound had nearly healed before they cured him. As the cure took hold, the wound itself degraded as if the microbe had been holding the flesh together on its own. It was obvious without extensive medical treatment, he would die. There wasn't much in the way of an appetite in saving the life of this killer. He was human again, but he'd always be a monster. Better he too became part of the solution after being the problem.

The last 36 hours hadn't been enjoyable for any of them, shortly that trauma would pale into insignificance.

The boats pulled away and began their trip to the island. HMS Reckoning, along with most of the other naval vessels, had stayed close whilst they were waiting for their next move. The sea was calm, a small blessing for those onboard. The general breathed in the sea air and tried not to think about his fate. It would be bad, but at least it would be over quickly. His fellow passengers continued to plead, beg or scream angrily, hoping this would change their fortunes.

When the engines died down, everyone went silent as the boats drifted towards shore. The abandoned equipment and ravaged remains of dozens of soldiers littered the beach up to and beyond where sand met vegetation. None of the dead had made themselves known to the incoming vessels.

"This is your stop!" the soldier shouted as he placed the boat gently on to the beach.

"Come on, let's get this over and done with," the general announced as he stood up, the only one not tied in place. He assisted the soldiers removing the cable ties from his fellow passengers and jumped onto the wet sand at the front of the small boat. The others stayed put, "Come with me or they'll shoot you."

"Fine, I'd rather be shot than ripped apart you fucking simpleton," the former prime minister stubbornly refused to move.

"Margaret, they won't kill you, they'll blow out your kneecap and then throw you on the beach. You'll suffer that excruciating pain before you're devoured. Get out now and run. You might make it," he replied. The general was calm, despite the words his tone was kind.

"I'm not sure you've ever called me by my name," she whispered. Tears streamed down the former prime minister's face.

"You're not my boss anymore, I can't call you prime minister. Let's go," said the general. He remained calm and compassionate.

The soldiers threw Johnson off of the front of the boat, turning to give the admiral the same treatment. He crossed his head and made his way to the front and jumped on to the beach. As soon as his feet hit the sand, he ran as fast as he could down the narrow stretch of beach, just as likely to run into trouble as away from it. The general reached his hand out to the former prime minister and assisted her off the front of the boat. They walked towards the rough, stony terrain as they heard the first of the growls and moans beyond the grass and bushes. The two boats pulled away, edging back towards the channel.

"You won't leave me alone, will you?" she asked vulnerable. She wiped the tears from her face and straightened herself up as if she was an MP about to address a crowd.

"Of course not," the general assured her. He didn't want to die alone anymore than she did.

The admiral's muffled screams echoed down the beach. Two of the creatures had grabbed him and were beginning their feast. Johnson could barely stand, his chest wound seeping his thick red blood through the dressing. He stumbled in the opposite direction from the others, still harbouring hope of surviving.

"What do we do?" she asked. She reached her hand out to the general to hold.

"You can run, but I think we should just wait a few moments. I don't think it'll be long," he told her and squeezed her hand.

"I'm scared," she revealed. The former prime minister Margaret Norville tried to keep her dignity, accepting this was it.

"Me too," the general confessed. His heart raced.

The first creature emerged. A former marine, his uniform bloody and shredded. A large wound to its cheek showing its teeth whether or not it had its mouth open. The second emerged, a young boy, followed by half a dozen more. All of various ages and conditions. All hungry.

"They're coming," her voice trembled.

"Lets not look," the general said and turned them both around to face the sea. "It'll be okay."

The sound of dozens of footsteps and growls grew louder. They both gripped each other's hand a little tighter.

It took just seconds for them to be completely enveloped by the horde. Neither had a chance to scream. The feeders jostled for position, eager not to miss out on their meal.

Johnson didn't look back, he hobbled along before his legs gave out. He crawled a few more feet before he couldn't move any further. The dressing on his chest wound was drenched in his own blood. A single feeder had locked on to him and approached at pace. Johnson couldn't muster the energy to even throw a fist at the creature. It grabbed his arm and started chewing through the bicep, tearing at flesh and bone, twisting the limb desperately trying to remove it before the others came. His weak moan of pain just alerted more creatures to him. The first pulled his arm free, guaranteeing a meal for itself as a second and third feeder reached him and tore chunks of flesh from his body. He was helpless to stop them as they leisurely picked at him. In less than a minute he was dead, the last of the feeders hurrying over for their turn.

After several minutes, they had picked each of the bodies clean. The partial remains and scraps of clothing spread on the bloodied sand. Some feeders stayed, others walked back from where they came. Ready to start their own involuntary work of spreading the cure.

Chapter 68

It was a beautiful late summer's day; the farmhouse was bathed in sunshine, the garden in front of it in full bloom. The amateur gardeners had worked hard since the springtime to cultivate a garden that would offer beauty all year round for people to enjoy. The land had been deemed useless for crops after the big battle, but a rose looked just as beautiful grown in the tainted soil as anywhere else. Babs sat alone at the bench outside of the old stone building, where Bo used to enjoy a rest. Looking out at the thriving community, tents had given way to more permanent structures, small but secure from the terrors that the world may still throw at them. People were happy, the population had grown considerably, now nearly 100 people lived at the farm. The nearby fields were freshly ploughed, or housed crops nearly ready to be harvested. Peter emerged from his own small wooden dwelling.

"Pete, how are you on this fine morning?" Babs asked with a wide, proud smile.

"Feeling great, as always. I'm just going to check on the cornfield and spend some time with Michael and Jake," Peter replied and looked towards the fields, trying to catch sight of the men.

"I saw Kenneth first thing with that airgun on the lookout for rabbits. I've asked him to put a few aside for us. If you see him, remind him," Babs said, she still played mother to the dwellers of the farm.

Peter nodded politely. A year ago, he never thought he'd grow tired of fresh meat. Now he dreaded the rabbit in the pot. He always seemed to be the one who got a mouthful of small bones. "Great, rabbit," he replied sarcastically.

"Don't be so ungrateful! I saw Gina this morning, she had a smile nearly as big as yours," Babs scolded. She stared hard at Peter, looking for the coy reaction that she found so funny.

Peter could feel his face turning red. "I'm off to the cornfields, I'll see you later."

"Okay, Pete!" Babs enjoyed his embarrassment. It was sweet.

He made his way through the homes and shelters of the fellow survivors. Nothing was fancy, everything put function above form. Building supplies had been scavenged, and several survivors had the skills and the volunteers to help build the simple structures. Some had struck out alone and taken over existing buildings to call their homes. What they gained in comfort, they lost in security. Peter reached the edge of the cornfield and Michael was already there with Jake.

"Peter, sleep in, did you? If you want to be a farmer, you need to get up before the sun does!" Michael pretended to be annoyed, but wasn't, really.

"Sorry," Peter let out. He knew the scolding was fake, but still regretted his tardiness.

Michael smiled. "You're at our farm next week. We'll make sure you're up on time. You won't have your lady friend there, so maybe you won't stay up so late and be so tired."

Did everyone know about his love life? Peter mustered a forced smile.

"Looks like there is wireworm feeding on your maize," Jake brought it all back to business, he had plans that didn't involve staring at corn.

"Shit, how bad?" Peter had no idea what a wireworm was, but it didn't sound good.

"We can dig out the affected areas, hope the birds take care of what we can't. The crop is far enough along you should be okay. By the time they fuck the roots, we should be able to harvest the corn," Michael calmly replied.

"Lets get started then," Peter said, eager to get working.

"I've got plans Mikey, with Kenneth," Jake responded, already with one foot stepping away.

"Of course you do. At least bag a few pigeons or even a squirrel. That big Welsh bastard is the only one not bored with Rabbit every day," Michael went on. He too never thought he'd see the day he'd be so fussy when it came to fresh meat.

Jake smiled and jogged off. He'd grown quite used to this community, Nutwood and the farm had become close allies. Trading food, supplies, and skills, both sites benefited from the relationship. He made his way to the small stretch of woodland where he knew Kenneth would stalk his prey. He glimpsed the air rifle as the shot was taken and a bunny evaded uninjured into its burrow. "Kenny, I like rabbit as much as anyone, but maybe we should get a few squirrels? Babs makes an amazing squirrel curry."

"Rabbit curry would be just as good," Kenneth greeted Jake with a hug and a kiss.

Liam was lying prone on the ground, squeezed the trigger of his air rifle, and sent a pellet whizzing past a pigeon as it escaped into the sky. "Bloody hell boys, can't you keep it down? We're supposed to be hunting!"

"Sorry mate, how's it looking?" Jake peered at the small haul besides the men.

"Three rabbits, four pigeons, and a magpie. Can we eat magpies?" Liam proudly confirmed.

"You can, I wouldn't. I don't think they taste good," Jake claimed, his face confirmed his revulsion at the idea.

"I know what goes in your mouth, so they must be bad," Liam joked.

Kenneth gave Liam a light kick with his foot, a smile beaming from his face. "Easy mush."

Liam stood up and handed the rifle to Jake. "You're better with this than me."

"You heading off?" Jake, whilst eager to spend time with Kenneth, didn't want to get between him and his friends.

"Everyone's favourite government of equals are stepping up Operation Reclaim. We're expecting another batch of darts this morning to help some of those grey fiends find a worthwhile death. As soon as the chopper drops off the good stuff, we're out of here to a place called Dorking," Liam raised his voice accordingly as he walked away.

"Sounds nice," Kenneth lied.

"I said Dorking, not dicking," Liam laughed, only to be greeted by a middle finger salute from both men. "I'll catch you boys later," Liam shouted back as he headed back towards the farmhouse.

With the governing council now firmly established on the Isle of Wight with the popular support of the people. The feeders on the island had been nearly completely eradicated, so now they had been stepping up efforts to take back the rest of the United Kingdom. Liam and his men had been provided with several tranquilliser guns and would be sent to spread the cure in the surrounding areas. Hundreds of similar missions were taking place around the country. It was slow work and not without danger, but it was successful. When returning to the areas where they had deployed the cure, there were no feeders remaining. Plenty of freshly fed on corpses and occasionally the odd cured monster having died of natural causes. It being the last creature in the area, there was nothing left to feed on it.

Liam walked back to the farmhouse as the helicopter swooped in, a little too fast and a little low, the pilot enjoying himself. It touched down close to the shelters and homes of the survivors. A few faces who weren't already outside peered to see what the disturbance was. Four soldiers were already making their way to the Lynx helicopter, kitted up with service rifles, hatchets, a few tranquilliser guns and their own cure kits. Now standard issue to all soldiers, and widely spread to known communities, a cure kit had three pre-loaded hypodermic needles. Even those who had needed to use the cure on themselves still carried the kit to treat others. Liam, assisted by three squaddies, had even used a hypodermic on one creature when they had run out of darts for the gun. They had pinned it to the ground, injected it, then ran like hell.

"Liam, pull your thumb out of your arse, we're off in two," a soldier light-heartedly ordered his boss as he handed him his rifle and webbing set.

"Alright, alright. He'll wait, I just need to check out first," he said and continued his way to the farmhouse, awkwardly putting on the webbing kit whilst holding the L85A3 rifle. Babs maintained her place on the bench, smiling at him. "The ride's here for today's work, let the boss know we'll be back for teatime."

"Tell her yourself," Babs replied. She enjoyed playing with the soldiers, Bo would have enjoyed it too.

"Can you tell that crazy old bastard to not land so close to the bloody settlement? He's woken Jacqueline," Amy demanded as she emerged, angry and tired from the house holding a four-month-old crying baby girl, trying to calm her tears.

"Sorry, it's Seb. I'll tell him. Again. We'll be back before dark," he answered. Liam jogged towards the helicopter to catch up with his team.

"Stay safe," Amy shouted to her second in command.

Amy sat next to Babs. Baby Jacqueline had already calmed as she was rocked in her mother's arms.

"How is little Jackie?" Babs cooed. She couldn't help but smile at the little girl's peaceful face.

"Up half the night as usual, sorry if she kept you up too," Amy said and yawned, illustrating her rough night.

"Don't be silly, once I'm asleep I'm dead to the world," Babs reassured Amy.

"Tell me it gets easier, please," begged Amy. The single mother hadn't expected this life, hadn't planned for it, and didn't have the luxury of experience or the internet to guide her.

"It does. You'll look back one day and wonder how she was so small. You'll crave the days when you were her world, and all she wanted was a cuddle and to be close to you," Babs told her as she enjoyed the memory of motherhood.

"I know. Sometimes I think it was easier smashing grey skulls in with a cricket bat than being a mum," Amy confessed. She rested with Jacqueline, closing her eyes for a few seconds enjoying the quiet.

"You're doing an outstanding job. Jack would be so proud of you both," Babs assured her. She couldn't help but gently stroke the baby's sleepy rosy cheeks.

"How are you doing?" Amy switched the focus away from her. Babs missed Bo. He had made a good recovery, until one morning without warning, he sat on his bench as usual and his chest grew tighter. His breath grew short and he let go. When he was found a short while later, he had already passed.

"I still think of Bo. I do, but at least we got those extra few months, and he got to see that the world would carry on without him. He saw the cure, saw us, and knew we'd be okay. I'm grateful for that, I always will be. I think of my children and grandchildren nearly as much as Bo. They're out there somewhere, I know they are. Somewhere like here, looking after each other."

Amy didn't know what to say, so she said nothing. They sat in silence, looking out at the living new world, pleased with what they saw. People working together, helping each other. Different races and religions, young and old, laughing and joking like close friends. Humanity had been decimated, those that survived had experienced hell on Earth, but here they were. Making a better future together.

A small pill designed to make people feel like they could fit in, had destroyed the world. It was born out of a desire for instant results with minimal work. Desperation of the users and greed of its creators propagated it and slowly, quietly, it consumed the world. It had brought out the best and worst in people, but now the worst was over. The cure spread much more slowly than the infection had, but it did spread. Now every country in the world still capable of communicating had been given the cure. The formula shared and quickly replicated as grey flesh on every continent was gradually returned to pink, ready to be consumed and pass the cure on further.

It would take time, but there was no rush. Not now that people had a future to look forward to, together.

THE END

About the Author

I really hope you enjoyed "The Last Bite". It was always my plan to look at a little more of the world with the second book, albeit only really as far as the Isle of Wight. For me, Deadweight is a British zombie apocalypse story, and I really wanted to stick to that with the main story. The Deadweight universe will continue with a collection of short stories I'll be working on to form into a single book titled "Little Nibbles". There were many ideas I had for "The Last Bite", that I either wrote but cut entirely, or just didn't move beyond the planning stage. Here I'm looking to look to spread the grey fleshed menace further afield to other countries and continents, but still have a few more stories from blighty to tell. Before "Little Nibbles" I will release the novella "Thornhurst". Originally intended to be part of the short story collection, I decided its length would limit the amount of stories I could feature and in fact, it deserved its own release.

My next full-length novel will be "The Time Travel Agency", a touch of science fiction and a helping of cold war espionage. I'm really excited about moving away from zombies (as much as I love the undead) and hope you'll join me on a trip to the 1980s.

Writing a novel whilst working a full-time job can be pretty demanding. I mainly write in the evenings, spending the rest of my time either at work or with my family. I'm blessed with two wonderful daughters and an amazing wife, and I also have a great support network of friends and family who help keep me going. If you'd like to get in touch - to discuss my books or ask about my hatred of tinned sweetcorn look at the links below.

As always, if you enjoyed The Last Bite, please leave a review. As an independent author, positive reviews and mentions on social media really help to spread the word to new readers.

If you're interested in finding out what I'm up to next, you can follow me on social media using the links below.

You can connect with me on:
- https://www.paulforster.net
- https://twitter.com/paulmforster
- https://www.facebook.com/TheDeadWeightBooks

Subscribe to my newsletter:
- http://bit.ly/PForster